Lyta could see six figures staggering toward them in the darkness

Kane edged closer to her until they were back to back, surrounded.

"Any plans?" she whispered.

"Make it costly for them," Kane growled.

Lyta ground her molars, eyes flitting from one creature to the next.

The rifle she carried wasn't fully automatic, but at this range, against normal human opponents, it unleashed some serious damage.

Against normal human opponents.

She fired as fast as she could pull the trigger and watched as her target staggered in a dance of hammer blows.

When the thing finally toppled, she realized that Kane was no longer at her back. She heard the thud and crunch of fists on flesh, and turned toward a second creature. She tore another salvo of bullets into its face and upper chest, grimacing as this one struggled upstream of her gunfire even as chunks of its head were blasted away.

Other titles in this series:

James Axler
Outlanders®

NECROPOLIS

A GOLD EAGLE BOOK FROM
W🦅RLDWIDE®

TORONTO • NEW YORK • LONDON
AMSTERDAM • PARIS • SYDNEY • HAMBURG
STOCKHOLM • ATHENS • TOKYO • MILAN
MADRID • WARSAW • BUDAPEST • AUCKLAND

Recycling programs
for this product may
not exist in your area.

First edition May 2014

ISBN-13: 978-0-373-63882-6

NECROPOLIS

Copyright © 2014 by Worldwide Library

Special thanks to Douglas Wojtowicz for his contribution to this work.

Printed in U.S.A.

Even the bravest cannot fight beyond his strength.
—Homer,
The Iliad

The Road to Outlands—
From Secret Government Files to the Future

Almost two hundred years after the global holocaust, Kane, a former Magistrate of Cobaltville, often thought the world had been lucky to survive at all after a nuclear device detonated in the Russian embassy in Washington, D.C. The aftermath—forever known as skydark—reshaped continents and turned civilization into ashes.

Nearly depopulated, America became the Deathlands—poisoned by radiation, home to chaos and mutated life forms. Feudal rule reappeared in the form of baronies, while remote outposts clung to a brutish existence.

What eventually helped shape this wasteland were the redoubts, the secret preholocaust military installations with stores of weapons, and the home of gateways, the locational matter-transfer facilities. Some of the redoubts hid clues that had once fed wild theories of government cover-ups and alien visitations.

Rearmed from redoubt stockpiles, the barons consolidated their power and reclaimed technology for the villes. Their power, supported by some invisible authority, extended beyond their fortified walls to what was now called the Outlands. It was here that the rootstock of humanity survived, living with hellzones and chemical storms, hounded by Magistrates.

In the villes, rigid laws were enforced—to atone for the sins of the past and prepare the way for a better future. That was the barons' public credo and their right-to-rule.

Kane, along with friend and fellow Magistrate Grant, had upheld that claim until a fateful Outlands expedition. A displaced piece of technology…a question to a keeper of the archives…a vague clue about alien masters—and their world shifted radically. Suddenly, Brigid Baptiste, the archivist, faced summary execution, and Grant a quick termination. For Kane there was forgiveness if he pledged his unquestioning allegiance to Baron Cobalt and his unknown masters and abandoned his friends.

But that allegiance would make him support a mysterious and alien power and deny loyalty and friends. Then what else was there?

Kane had been brought up solely to serve the ville. Brigid's only link with her family was her mother's red-gold hair, green eyes and supple form. Grant's clues to his lineage were his ebony skin and powerful physique. But Domi, she of the white hair, was an Outlander pressed into sexual servitude in Cobaltville. She at least knew her roots and was a reminder to the exiles that the outcasts belonged in the human family.

Parents, friends, community—the very rootedness of humanity was denied. With no continuity, there was no forward momentum to the future. And that was the crux—when Kane began to wonder if there was a future.

For Kane, it wouldn't do. So the only way was out—way, way out.

After their escape, they found shelter at the forgotten Cerberus redoubt headed by Lakesh, a scientist, Cobaltville's head archivist, and secret opponent of the barons.

With their past turned into a lie, their future threatened, only one thing was left to give meaning to the outcasts. The hunger for freedom, the will to resist the hostile influences. And perhaps, by opposing, end them.

Chapter 1

The yoke hung around Lyta's neck as she staggered along in the line. Her shoulders were raw and bloody from the weight of the steel collar and the attached chains, which kept her in the queue with the rest of the "tribute." The collar's edge sawed into her skin, and each shift of weight as she stepped was a brand-new spike of pain. She kept her composure, the tears having long since dried out, shed for her lost family.

Lyta was nineteen, and just a week ago she'd been tall and athletic, with long blond-frosted curls styled by a friend utilizing peroxide. Now, six days later, she had lost fifteen pounds through sweat, lack of food, even blood loss. Her scalp was covered with slowly healing scars, nicks made when her hair was shorn off by a soldier of the Panthers of Mashona. He'd scraped her from hairline to nape of neck with a sharpened knife, and years of growth and hours of coloring ended up in the dirt, along with slivers of her scalp.

Thankfully, Lyta had been in shock at the time. The Panthers had swooped down on her town, one of many located on the edge of Zambia, close to the dangers posed by various bandit groups. She'd watched as her father was shot through the face, and then the marauders, having slaughtered all the armed opposition, got to the task of preying on the survivors.

Lyta remembered her face jammed into the dirt,

cheek abrading against rocks and pebbles in the soil, her eye so filled with grit she couldn't close it. Thus she was unable to look away as the militiamen grabbed her mother and threw her to the ground.

Lyta saw everything that happened, all the way to her mother's death, and after it. Even demise was no excuse for the cruel, bloodthirsty thugs to stop having their way with the woman's remains.

Lyta didn't think of her own fate. She couldn't remember anything, or maybe she just wouldn't remember. Her brain had shut down, and she focused on the agony around her neck, weighing on her shoulders, her collarbone. Maybe someday the memories would surface, but she hoped that they wouldn't. She only had the memories of being shorn, being stripped, being chained.

The Panthers of Mashona didn't say why they were herding humans, but Lyta doubted it was for slavery. After the miles they'd gone, the weight she'd lost, she'd be useless for physical labor.

The sun was half of a molten disc in the sky. Sunset had arrived and painted the African skies a rainbow of purple, orange, red and yellow, deep blue at the far end of that spectrum behind her back, Lyta surmised. This part of the countryside was miles and days distant from her home, but here, there seemed to be more pollution, even though they marched away from Zambia, deeper into Mashonan territory.

"All right! Stop!" the whip master shouted.

The queue stumbled to a halt, and bodies bumped against each other.

"Sit!" the whip master ordered.

And there, the group, having been at it for six days, plopped to the ground heavily. Better to get it done and over with in one fell swoop than stretch out the torture of shifting collars and bouncing chains as they gently tried to lower themselves. Links of steel bounced between Lyta's shoulder blades, and she wondered how much longer her backbone could take such abuse.

Water, filthy and tepid, but water nevertheless, was handed out in ladles. Lyta slurped at the muddy slurry, swallowing and feeling the grit of sand wash down her esophagus. She drank as much as she could in a single gulp; then, as her lips parted, the cup of life-giving moisture was gone.

Lyta's stomach churned, but she was glad for a lack of food and a minimum of water. That way she wouldn't have to worry, as days before, about having to relieve herself on the walk.

Above her was the vast expanse of the universe. They'd traveled so far from relative civilization that instead of a black night, they were beneath a swirl of stars. The spine of the Milky Way looked like a scattering of diamonds across black felt.

Lyta wanted to sleep, but as she stared into the infinite night above her, her mind drifted to the world she'd occupied only a week ago.

It had been a world where she'd read every night, even after being with her fiancé, Usain. It had been a place where she'd had a future in telecommunications. For decades, Zambia and Harare had shared a wealth of radios stored in the depths of some underground facilities along the Zambezi River. The two nation-states used the hydroelectric power of the dams to keep their cities modern. The urgency to keep the two entities in the technological manner that they'd become accustomed to had been the impetus to discard the last remnants of pre-twentieth-century prejudices about women's places in society and the broadening of the education system.

Trying to keep a relative island of paradise, or even just normalcy, in the middle of a region as tumultuous as theirs was a full-time job for the military forces of Zambia and Harare. Most of Lyta's electronics training came from a two-year stint in the army, learning her support role and apprenticing to more highly trained experts, all the while being taught the theories necessary to give her a basic grounding. With the actual science rolling around between her ears, as well as math and physics, she had the tools available to improve on the present technology.

That was something that Zambia needed desperately. Zambia and Harare weren't in a race against each other. Mashona, on the other hand, was a large region with little in the way of central government, defined now more by the Panthers militia than anything else, and even then, the bandit army was still in contention with smaller gangs and individual madmen who sought domination. Because Zambia and Harare cooperated but didn't try to become a whole nation, they were able to support each other while the forces of chaos were fragmented, pitted against their neighbors.

Maybe that's what we're here for. We're going to be the ingredients for the glue that makes the Panthers of Mashona into the only game in town.

Lyta looked to the stars, her mind turning that theory over and over.

So who would want nearly dead people? she asked herself. *How could I, as I stand now, be of any worth to a force that would provide this militia with the undisputed position of power in this region?*

She gave her lower lip a bite. Things moved around

her, but the damned steel collar left her with only one position to look—straight up. Lyta had long since gotten used to the sound of boots crunching on the stalks of long grasses, the snap of twigs and the grinding of dirt as guards paced up and down the line, making certain that their cargo of the walking damned stayed in place.

Odd that the guards are not interested in taking a little ass while we're lined up like this.

The Mashonan soldiers didn't want to assert themselves over this queue of the doomed. They didn't need to feel the kind of cruel control that rape provided. They *had* control. They had the power. There wasn't a shred of weakness in the gunmen who lorded their might over this hungry, thirsty, battered mob. They didn't feel like they needed to be violent, to crush them.

Maybe it's the collars.

Lyta took a deep breath.

"We're human sacrifices." The man behind her spoke softly, a whisper that was so light, if it needed to travel another inch, it would have been swept away by the night breeze. "The old gods awaken. And they hunger."

Lyta peered at the speaker out of the corner of her eye. She couldn't make out any physical details. None of the people shared names with each other, as they hadn't been allowed to by their guards. The only details she could distinguish were the back of the man's head in front of her, the breadth of his shoulders and the signs of scars woven across his flesh.

No one else had a face.

The man before her could have been Usain. He was of the right height, but those knives had taken the hair off everyone, and whips and swagger sticks had left wounds on shoulders and backs, changing the familiar terrain so that even Lyta couldn't tell who he was.

And the yokes prevented speech easily even without the menace of the whip.

Lyta was alone. Everyone was alone in this line. There was no more sense of community. The chains and collars took away every chance of intimacy and communication.

And again, we return to the theme of communication. The guards discourage it, prevent it, grind it into the ground. They don't need it, and they want no one else to have it.

"The gods want us to remember that we humans are alone." The man's whispers returned.

It sounded as if he were reading from an ancient book, occasionally stopping to paraphrase to his listener for clarity. Lyta strained to get a look at him. His voice was old, raspy, weathered.

But no, she couldn't without turning her head.

Lyta ground her molars against her tongue and twisted her head just an inch. Just an inch, and she felt the collar cut into her neck like a hot knife, shredding the skin of her throat and upper chest as she forced herself to get a good look at the man she assumed was speaking.

It was a young boy, no older than fourteen. Too old to be taken to the rape camps for education as a child soldier, too young to have the experience and skills necessary to be put into forced labor.

And he was asleep. Beyond him, there was a woman, and another woman beyond that.

There was no one who matched the voice that had tickled her ear, threading legends from ancient times. Lyta straightened her gaze up to the sky.

The agony of just that slight movement, holding her

head to see who was talking, had all been in vain. And it stole the last dregs of strength she had for the day.

She closed her eyes, wishing that her sleep would be eternal.

Now is not the time for any to sleep. Death will die, and the Queen awakens, stirring from her millennial slumber.

Lyta opened her eyes again.

And as she did, she looked up into a pair of catlike eyes, slitted in the middle, amber wreathing the narrow flames, and a flat face framed by a cobra-hood of muscle flexing in sheets from top of head to shoulders.

Before Lyta could open her mouth to scream, scaled fingers covered her lips, and a hiss issued from his.

Chapter 2

As always when the Cerberus warriors said goodbye to those whom they'd assisted, the parting moments were filled with a quiet sadness and embraces that seemed to last a moment too long. Of course, Brigid Baptiste might have had a biased view of those hugs, especially since she realized that she was an attractive and desirable woman. She'd noticed that among the other women they'd traveled with, too: Domi and Sinclair were offered extended and enthusiastic embraces by the Zambian soldiers. Meanwhile, Kane and Grant kept their farewells to hearty handshakes.

"Ah, dear Brigid, your presence here in our little outpost has been an experience," Lomon said. "I wish it were all delightful..."

"I understand," Brigid responded. "You and your men have been excellent hosts. We'll miss you."

Lomon nodded. His eyes glazed for a moment as he thought of the past couple of days and the losses incurred. They had come under the assault of a pair of groups; each had taken turns at controlling the strange clone hybrids called the Kongamato. The Kongamato, named after an African cryptid, were brutish, powerful winged creatures that were equal parts bat and gorilla. They had killed a great number of Zambian troops, first the outpost defenders at the power station attached to the redoubt, and then a company of soldiers who had been on their way to relieve the besieged trio of survivors.

"Don't worry," Brigid spoke up, breaking the elder Zambian soldier from his recollection of the horrors he'd endured. "We'll find the ones responsible."

Lomon rested a hand on her shoulder. "I wish I could send an army with you, girl."

Brigid smiled, looking toward her companions, former Cobaltville Magistrates Kane and Grant. "We've taken care of armies before. I doubt that Durga has that much of a force left. The Millennium Consortium members were wiped out, and Gamal and the Panthers of Mashona turned out to be using him as a distraction."

Brigid wanted to feel regret over the deaths of the members of the Millennium Consortium betrayed and murdered by Makoba, but there had been more than sufficient bad blood between the millennialists and Cerberus over the past couple of years that all she could manage was disappointment at the consortium's vetting process for new members. Even then, she wasn't too surprised at the millennialists picking the wrong person for the job. Austin Fargo and Erica van Sloan both boasted affiliations with the assembly of technocrats who sought to create their own new world order.

This time, the Millennium Consortium had thrown in their lot with Durga, the fallen prince of the Nagah, as both parties searched Africa for Annunaki wonders and ancient technology. In the process, the combined force had stumbled on a subterranean facility attached to the Victoria Falls redoubt that had a breed of mutants inside it to serve as their new shock troops.

Durga had maintained control of the monstrosities, but only for a brief period of time, until an African named Makoba had betrayed both the Nagah prince and the Millennium Consortium by stealing the control "crown." Makoba was the brother of a local warlord, Gamal, who himself had already discovered the technology to control the Kongamato and had usurped control of them. With a major contingent of Panthers of Mashona soldiers and the means of growing an entire army of winged horrors, Gamal had been poised to conquer the continent of Africa.

Unfortunately for the deadly warlord, Gamal had run straight into the heroes of Cerberus redoubt. Grant and Brigid had disarmed Gamal of his control system, and Kane had set off a self-destruct after the Kongamato horde was summoned back to their birthplace. The self-destruct brought down the cloning facility and the winged monsters with a blast nearly as powerful as a nuclear weapon.

The threat of an army of cloned winged horrors was ended, as well as the more conventional threat of Gamal's forces, thanks to planning, positioning and surprise on the part of the Cerberus operatives. With grenades and precision rifle fire, they'd scattered the bandit army, then watched as an ally wrested control of the creatures to send them to their doom in the self-destruction of the cloning facility.

That ally walked outside the group, standing at the edge of the Victoria Falls hydroelectric power station. Thurpa was freshly healed from major injuries inflicted by the ancient artifact that had brought Kane running to Africa. Thurpa himself was an artifact, a member of the Indian Nagah, a race created by the benign Annunaki Enki to watch over the subcontinent of India.

He'd come, one of the fallen prince Durga's last followers, as an emissary for the crippled regent. Thurpa had been a true believer, having a low opinion of the

Westerners who made up the bulk of the consortium gunmen who'd joined in this African trek.

And then the millennialist Makoba usurped Durga's control of the Kongamato, and Thurpa was wounded, on the run, about to be killed by his prince's perfect living weapon. What had saved him was the intervention of Kane and his allies.

Thurpa had gone from contempt for mammals—as he called normal humans despite his half-mammalian DNA—to a new appreciation for people. Kane and the others had protected him, had trusted him more than they trusted one of their own human companions, had nursed him back to health. Then when it came time to engage in final combat with the Kongamato, Thurpa had only barely survived Makoba's betrayal of the millennialists to Gamal. Had it not been for the warlord summoning all the winged horrors to aid him against Grant and Brigid and the other Cerberus Away Team, Makoba would have killed the last of the Zambians.

With only a rifle, Makoba had taken one of the injured men hostage, only to be ambushed by Thurpa and beaten to death with a length of steel rebar. It was then that Thurpa and Lomon had combined their wits to take the stolen control headset and work with the Cerberus heroes to send the beasts to their doom.

After that, Thurpa had denied the newly healed and awakened Durga's demand to rejoin him. The fallen prince had teleported away, using an Annunaki relic, abandoning Thurpa in a strange land among strangers.

Brigid and Lomon walked toward the Nagah man. He was wearing a pair of Zambian uniform pants that replaced his standard clothing. Thurpa's upper body was covered with iridescent scales, predominately bronze in hue, but there were other glimmers of color along them, as well as black striped designs. His chest was plated in heavy panels of the same scales, only larger. Those same scales were present on the soles of his feet, as thick and durable as any boot. Had he worn a shirt, he might even have seemed fully human, except for his head and the hood of sheeted muscle that flexed between his shoulders and the sides of his head. His scaled face was fine featured, flat nosed, with yellow-amber jewels for eyes; the pupils were slits that adjusted to brightness by widening or turning to mere slivers.

"You are welcome to stay among us, Thurpa," Lomon offered for what was the eighteenth time in the past day, by Brigid's eidetic recollection. There may have been instances when she hadn't been present to hear such a request.

Thurpa looked to the elder officer. "I'm honored. And I'd love to return, but there's a lot of damage I feel I have to undo."

"Helping the injured and rescuing Jonas went a long way," Lomon said.

Thurpa smiled weakly. "It doesn't feel like far enough."

"We're honored to have you with us," Brigid said. She offered her hand.

The young Nagah accepted the hand. His palm and finger plates were smooth, supple and slightly warm, a sign of his mammalian metabolism. He still seemed uncomfortable around people, and Brigid could empathize. Her intellect had isolated her when dealing with others in years gone by. Only since she'd thrown herself into the world as one of the exiles from Cobaltville, adventuring around the world, had she lost her self-consciousness. Even so, there were times when she felt like an alien in the room; others did not possess her perfect recall.

Extrapolating that outsider's discomfort with an inhuman exterior appearance must have been a crushing bit of alienation.

What made it all the more painful was Thurpa had aligned himself with Durga, a traitor and murderer, responsible for the deaths of many of his people and intense suffering. Returning home would be just as alienating. People would remember.

And they would shun him at the very least. At worst, his life would be in constant peril.

Maybe the Cerberus redoubt would be a good place for Thurpa, and, ultimately, Brigid would invite him to become a part of their ragtag family of misfits, exiles and refugees. But for now they needed him and his knowledge here in Africa, especially as CAT Beta had returned to Cerberus in order to protect the redoubt and respond to other emergencies if necessary.

Brigid worried for the young man. Life with her, Kane and Grant was not an easy one, not with all the enemies they'd made. And Thurpa had made himself just as much a target since he'd turned his back on Durga, the very sociopath they were off to chase.

The other newcomer to their little assemblage was Nathan Longa, a young man from the city-state of Harare, in a territory that used to be the nation of Zimbabwe.

"Thank you again for the use of the pickup truck," Brigid said to Lomon.

"Think of it as repayment for helping us hold the line against the Mashona Panthers," Lomon replied. "And be thankful that there were enough spare parts from damaged vehicles to keep it running."

Brigid nodded. "And that it was one which I had read the specs on, including an exploded view."

Thurpa chuckled. "You and the others exploded enough trucks as it was."

Grant, six foot four with rippling arms, hefted the first of the last pair of jerricans into the bed of the pickup. He then used both hands to pick up the other. Forty pounds wasn't much of an effort for the big former Magistrate, but it was still impressive to see his shoulders bulge and flex as he put the cans on board.

Kane opened the nozzle on each and took a whiff before closing and writing on the sides, separating fuel from water. There wasn't going to be a guarantee of access to fresh and potable water on their journey. The maps and layout of the countryside differed vastly from the current high-altitude satellite photos of the region. The Earthshaker bombs used in the megacull had not been kind to the continent.

"It's not a Sandcat, but it runs," Kane pronounced. "Ready to saddle up, cowgirl?"

Brigid chuckled. "Don't make me regret showing you those old Westerns."

Kane smiled back, then offered a hand to Nathan and Thurpa and helped them into the bed of the truck with him.

"You ride with Grant," Kane said. "I'll enjoy the breeze in my hair."

Thurpa looked dubious as he rested an arm on the sidewall. "We're out in the open, aren't we?"

"It beats walking," Nathan said. "Besides, Kane will pick up any danger. That's his thing."

Thurpa nodded. Lomon and the Zambians had given him sufficient equipment to deal with most threats. He'd gotten a Heckler & Koch G3 rifle with a stock that col-

lapsed, nearly halving the length of the weapon for easier carry and storage, and a Colt .45 automatic, which
shared magazines with Nathan Longa's own pistol.
After the conflict with the Kongamato, Lomon knew
that Thurpa would need power and mobility. As it was,
Thurpa had almost died in hand-to-hand conflict with
one of the creatures, saved only by being out of reach
and blinding it with his natural cobra venom. The G3
and the .45 would go a long way toward making Thurpa
the equal of most challenges.

Especially if he were beside the explorers from Cerberus and the wielder of the Nehushtan.

The trouble with that thought, Brigid mused, is that
we've got plenty of enemies who shrug off bullets as if
they were grains of rice. Even Durga qualified as bulletproof for a moment.

Brigid slid into the cab beside Grant, who took the
wheel.

"Heavy thoughts?" Grant asked.

Brigid blinked, then looked at her friend. "Heavy
thoughts. Yes. We're going into uncharted territory
in Africa, hunting a man who nearly killed us as he's
searching for the means of returning to godhood. Kane
says that he's hooked up with a queen who was dangerous enough that the Annunaki imprisoned her, rather
than kick her off the planet or kill her, and who has
enough power to psychically reach out and even pluck
people from their bodies. Add to that we've got two
young men to take care of, because as much training
as they've had, they haven't seen a tenth of the shit we
have."

Grant frowned. "You make it seem as if we're bad-
ass just because we've fought gods, dinosaurs and living mountains."

"We had the luck of surviving and outwitting them," Brigid said. "Remember, a lot of our friends have ended up dead."

Grant nodded.

"We'll do our best to protect them. We always do," Grant said.

Thurpa rapped his knuckle on the window on the back of the pickup's cab. "You do know Nathan and I can hear you, right?"

"Not doing a lot of good for our confidence on this mission," Nathan added.

"Hey, we protected Lomon," Grant countered.

"And defeated an army of winged monsters," Brigid spoke up.

"We were there," Nathan said.

Thurpa nodded. "Not totally impressed with the protecting Lomon's men part. In fact…"

Grant smiled at Thurpa. "You did some protecting yourself, son. Both of you. That's why we want to keep you with us."

"Any particular reason why Kane just doesn't take the stick himself? He utilized it pretty well when we were in the cloning facility," Nathan inquired.

"Because I'm not used to running around with a walking stick," Kane replied. He slapped his hand on top of the pickup truck's cab. "Let's go."

"Sure thing, grouch," Grant returned. He started the engine, and the Cerberus explorers drove away, waving to the Zambian contingent they'd come to befriend.

Brigid returned to her doubts as they drove toward their future reunion with the Nagah prince Durga and whatever horrors he planned to awaken.

Already Nathan had spoken of an assassin who had slain his father, a mysterious, seemingly amorphous entity with translucent skin that shimmered in the firelight.

The killer with no apparent visible features seemed as if it might have been a trick of the mind or the shadows. But Brigid Baptiste knew a thing or two about human perception, as well as the intricacies of memory, especially since hers was completely photographic. Her time as an archivist had only been enhanced by the ability to recall every detail she'd ever seen, and Kane often wondered aloud if she were a "doomie"—a Doomsayer mutant who had some manner of psychic ability. Brigid doubted that she had transcendent mental abilities, but she presumed that her brain chemistry was somehow different, as her recollection skills and natural curiosity served only to increase the ever-growing database between her ears.

That Nathan Longa didn't have the same kind of intellectual function as she was not an indication of the untrustworthiness of Nathan's description of the assassin who'd slain his father, the previous protector of Nehushtan. Also, the moment had been one of intense fear and shock, meaning that Nathan's senses would have been enhanced by adrenaline, his eyes sharper, probably dilated further to gather even more light, so shadowy hints wouldn't have been so indiscriminate as he'd assumed. Plus, Brigid had gone with Nathan over the incident a couple of times, and she had asked questions about more than visual descriptors. She'd asked about the sounds, the smells, the feel of the room.

The smell of the murderer was something that made Brigid feel that the description as gelatinous had more validity. The thing smelled, according to Nathan, of salt and copper, two major components of blood. A translucent outline with no physical features, backlit by firelight, could easily have been a nontraditional physical entity. Supporting this observation was that it had disappeared in the brief instant that Nathan had looked away from the killer to see his father on the ground.

There were no windows that a full-grown man the bulk of the slayer could escape through, but there was a window open about three inches high. There was the sticky, slurping sound of fluid as the being moved, and Brigid could imagine an entity with no skeletal structure could easily have compressed itself down to three inches to squeeze out the window. She knew that octopi could fit through any opening large enough to accommodate their beaks, the only hard part of their anatomy, and that small rodents *with* skeletons could flex their bones to fit through openings only half the diameters of their bodies.

That was the cement for Brigid's assumption of the assassin being a nontraditional physical entity, an expression she'd coined on the spot. Kane had asked her why she didn't just call it a "blob," but Brigid was not certain if it was an entirely fluid-based organism, a mollusk-like humanoid or just one with an extremely flexible skeleton as per a mouse.

Brigid coupled the appearance of that creature with Kane's account of the void entity he had battled while he'd been comatose, left within a prison constructed in his own psyche. He'd also described her—it had taken on a more feminine appearance and addressed itself as "the queen"—as originally an amorphous, almost fluid-formed entity constructed of void. The limited shape-shifting on her part had a similar "feel" to Brigid's presumptions about the killer who'd slain Nathan's father.

The similarity between Kane's psychic opponent

and the elder Longa's assassin was too coincidental for Brigid's tastes. She'd studied more than enough mythology and parallel stories to realize that if something was vaguely related in the views of two separate people, there might be even stronger ties once exposed to the light of day.

Thurpa had added to the chain of coincidences. There was a strangely hued woman, Neekra, who seemed to come from nowhere, then disappear, and who could peer into Thurpa's thoughts. She was at once dangerously alluring and viscerally disturbing, and she seemed cast in rust- or cinnamon-hued flesh that flowed easily.

Mind reading. The ability to appear and disappear like the wind. A voluptuous, curvy woman whom Durga had offhandedly referred to as his "queen." Mind reading would not be too far off from the skill of telepathy and the construction of mental illusions, such as had been the case with Kane's daylong, coma-like imprisonment.

Kane had described the queen's interaction with Durga as more seductive than tortuous, as it had been with Kane himself. Thurpa had noted the obvious romantic relations between this very healthy, odd-hued woman and Durga. Right now, Brigid wasn't entirely certain of who this Neekra was, but she knew full well that she and the queen were as related as the amorphous assassin and Kane's psychic tormentor were.

Neekra was this woman's self-appellation, and Brigid immediately returned to the dream wherein Kane had become aware of the artifact Nehushtan and the tales of a Puritan adventurer in the heart of Africa. Neekra matched up with not one but two names: Negari and Nakari—a hidden city and its queen, an immortal, vampirelike queen.

Nathan's father had died of massive blood loss, and yet there had been very little blood spilled in the Longa home. The smell of blood was quite salty and coppery, Brigid knew from too much experience. Perhaps the reason no blood had been spilled was because it had been ingested, swallowed by the murderer.

Brigid's mood turned black. A vampire queen and a hidden city.

Before skydark, Africa had been known as the Dark Continent. Now Brigid was certain they were going to find out exactly how dark. And that darkness could swallow them all whole.

Literally, Brigid feared.

Chapter 3

Kane's mood was not good as he and Grant crept through the forest, closing in on the caravan that had crossed their path. Normally, he wouldn't have been too interested in another group traveling through the jungle, and they had hidden their pickup truck, parked well off the formation's route so as not to draw unwanted attention.

The group was armed to the teeth, and they had settled down for the evening not far from where Kane and his companions had set up their camp for the night. Traveling all day by truck was *still* tiring; there weren't many roads, and the suspension could only take so much out of the bumps and jolts, especially for those who rode in the bed of the truck.

It was just good strategy for Kane and his allies to scope out a new group before coming out and greeting them, and seeing the column's armed guards was more than a little unnerving. What made things even more tense was that they wore the uniforms of the Panthers of Mashona, the very militia they had battled back at Victoria Falls. While it was unlikely that Gamal could have communicated with this column, Kane was keen on keeping a low profile.

Well, he *had been* keen on that low profile.

Then he saw the row of naked Africans lying on the

ground, connected to each other by chains and heavily burdened with steel yokes.

"We're not going to leave well enough alone," Grant murmured, counting on the Commtact to amplify the words in Kane's ear.

"Slave traders. Damned straight we're not leaving this alone," Kane answered.

Grant nodded. Kane turned to regard his friend, and the massive former Magistrate's brow wrinkled, knit with a mixture of concern and anger. His drooping gunfighter's mustache only served to deepen the man's frown into a grim mask.

Grant had no sense of solidarity with the blacks of Africa. Sure, his skin was dark like theirs, and they shared general facial features, but, culturally, Grant was a product of a world where race and familial history removed ties to anything other than fellow Magistrates. But here, Grant felt for the poor victims, lying immobilized by steel collars on their necks and shoulders, evidenced by the cracked, dried rivulets of blood on their torsos and the raw redness of scraped-off skin near the edges of those inhumane yokes. Kane heard the tendons in his fists pop as he flexed his big hands, and anger swiftly bled away as his eyes flitted from guard to guard.

Like Kane, he was sizing up the armed resistance, thinking of ways to kill the Panthers and to free their prisoners.

"We're going to have to be very slow and patient," Grant mused.

"Careful, yeah," Kane agreed. "Even a silenced Copperhead would draw attention. It's going to have to be knives and garrotes."

Grant nodded. Neither Magistrate enjoyed murdering unaware opponents, but such ruthless tactics were going to be a necessity. If just one of the men standing guard over the prisoners suspected that someone was attempting a rescue, the Panthers would open fire, killing the group rather than giving up their treasured human cargo. "My bow, too."

Kane turned, regarding the big man. "You brought that?"

"A collapsible version," Grant replied.

Grant's lover, Shizuka, the leader of the samurai force known as the Tigers of Heaven, had been teaching Grant to use the bow and the sword. It was a shadow of a skill that Grant had retained from when his tesseract—a physical "time shadow"—had been hurled back to the time of ancient Sumeria. Back then, Grant's tesseract had been mostly amnesiac and just enough "off time" to have superior reflexes and durability, as well as his natural strength. His captor, a son of Enlil named Humbaba, had named Grant Enkidu, the man-bull, because of that physical power. In that era, Malesh, a rogue Annunaki, had been first Grant's target, then his lover and co-warrior in a rebellion against Humbaba's rule of the region.

Malesh was the inspiration for the mythic hero Gilgamesh, and she taught Enkidu the use of the bow as a replacement for Grant's firearms knowledge. When Kane, Brigid, Domi and Shizuka had managed to arrive in the time stream where Grant's tesseract had been deposited, the shadow had developed enough that its spirit gained reality in a spare body of the Annunaki court, returning Grant to his mortal form. All seven warriors had engaged the leonine, eleven-foot-tall Humbaba in direct conflict, finally killing the scion of Enlil after throwing everything at him, including flights of arrows, magazines of bullets and the slashing of deadly blades.

Grant had left his tesseract Enkidu back in antiquity, husband to a warrior goddess, and he'd returned home with the love of his life, Shizuka. Grant found great comfort with her.

"Bow's pure silent, as opposed to a silenced gun," Grant said. "And it packs a lot of power, especially with my strength and its construction."

Kane didn't doubt that. "Let's get back to the others."

The two Cerberus Magistrates slithered back through the forest. They moved slowly, cautiously, from where they'd closed on the slavers' position. The two men took care to watch out for any sign that someone had come across their trail, and they felt secure once they didn't pick up any. It helped that the two of them utilized the multiband optics in their shadow suits to look for spoor or tracks. Someone might have been good enough to evade high-tech optics capable of focusing on single broken stalks and twigs and disruptions in the dirt, or the talents of a skilled tracker, but when both combined, there was little sneaking up on them.

Then it would take an hour for the assembled travelers to make up a plan on how to assault the slave caravan.

The plan was simple: kill quietly or the failure would be measured in helpless prisoners executed.

Thurpa's approach to the prisoners on the chain was at a midpoint on the line. There was only one member of the Cerberus group who could handle opponents at range with utter silence, and that was Grant. However, if there was one thing that the Nagah outcast knew he was capable of, it was a silent kill, by virtue of his half-cobra nature and the gifts that Enki had endowed every Nagah with—transformed or native born.

His fangs were folded against the roof of his mouth, and his legs were bent beneath him as he stood at the edge of the clearing, thigh muscles tightly coiled. He was to wait until one of the guards was close enough for him to strike, and Thurpa knew that his calculations had to be exact. One misstep, a few inches short or even a simple stumble could result in an armed killer turning his automatic weapon against Thurpa, his allies or the very people they were there to rescue.

Thurpa hadn't cared much for the Panthers of Mashona when he and Durga first encountered them alongside the Millennium Consortium. They were brutish men, the type of beings who exemplified Durga's description of mankind as nothing more than a pack of barbaric apes. It was their disregard for their enemies and victims that reinforced Thurpa's initial prejudices. He'd seen what the Panthers had done to their captives already.

It had been that negative impression, and the consortium's equal disregard for the militia's cruelty, that had primed Thurpa to become so disgusted with "mammals" that he'd used a grenade against a small family of meerkats who had made too much noise. The last thing Thurpa had wanted to do was seem weak in front of the hairy-knuckled, thick-browed thugs who took the defeated and helpless and used them as glory holes, men or women, if they weren't already pressed into hard labor.

Thurpa hadn't wanted to think what would happen to him if they saw him as a pushover. He had little interest in becoming a rape rag. If there was one thing that Durga didn't appear to tolerate among those fighting for the purity of the Nagah race, it was that the cobra men didn't engage in that kind of sexual violence, against their own or against others.

That was before Thurpa had met humans with a conscience. People who protected their injured, who cared for others despite differences. That was before Brigid Baptiste had related Durga's sexual cruelty toward Hannah, his princess, and the evidence of what he had done to other women who hadn't been his perfect little toys.

You've been following a rapist, a kin-murderer, a despot, damn you, Thurpa told himself. That only strengthened the young man's resolve to take the gunman guarding these prisoners out quickly and certainly.

The Panthers are so strong, so cocksure against the helpless, Thurpa thought. You haven't faced a son of Enki, though. We were born with fangs to ensure that you do not poison the other beloved of our Father.

The Panther gunman drew closer. Kane and Grant had timed out the patrols of these men perfectly. Everyone seemed to be stepping into position as the two men had predicted. Even so, there was no guarantee that his timing would be right, and Thurpa's heartbeat increased.

Just in case he had to take out more than one opponent silently, Thurpa also had his knife in hand. He had venom and long fangs, but a broken fang or an empty venom sac would make it impossible for him to bite two opponents. He wondered at the ability of Brigid Baptiste and Nathan Longa when it came to close-quarters murder, but he didn't want to think about it too much.

Thinking about how hard it could be for others to take down a murderer with a swift, ruthless strike made him think about how cruel his act would be.

Brigid Baptiste was not a murderer, nor was she a trained assassin, but she hung around with some of the best masters of sharpened steel in the world. She *knew* how to use the knife in its sheath as more than a tool or utensil. Kane, Domi and Shizuka had taken turns at teaching her the art of the fighting knife, not any intensive set of exercises, but they'd shown her moves, explained to her the discipline and made her go through every step.

They hadn't gone easy on Brigid simply because she had a photographic memory; they'd expected her to copy their maneuvers. They had her go at it with blunt, rounded cornered blades for intense sparring matches. Muscle memory was different from the data that came in through her eyes and ears, and they worked her in the gym until her arms and sides ached, her flame-gold hair was matted to her scalp and her breaths came in long, ragged gasps.

In the end, no, Brigid was not going to take on another knife fighter as a master duelist, but she would be able to show a good accounting of herself if she was separated from her pistol.

That *if* had come enough times in Brigid's adventures around the globe for her to know that losing her firearm would be a *when*. Any distaste for an assassin's strike had been washed away with Kane's depiction of how the caravan of prisoners had been treated. Naked and manacled about the neck and ankles, as she could see now, thanks to the light amplification optics in her shadow suit, the captives were in miserable physical condition. They were gaunt, exhausted, with blood dripping down their torsos.

To a child, they were naked and ragged, and each had to sleep staring straight up into the night sky because the metal yokes about their necks would cut or tear skin if they moved their heads one inch. Brigid's heart ached for the poor victims of the militia members, and she was able to make out the insignias on the patches of the soldiers.

They were the Panthers of Mashona, the same group who'd laid siege to the Victoria Falls power station, who'd allied themselves with the mad Nagah prince, Durga, and the Millennium Consortium. They were known killers, murderers, raiders who had no concern for human life except for what they could get out of them.

Brigid examined the line of prisoners. Women, men, those in their early teens, none of them seeming as if they were good for forced labor, especially after the march that had turned their necks and backs raw with the weight and abrasion of their slave collars. These people were going to be shells of human beings if they had to go much farther.

Her thoughts went back to the killer who had all but drained the last drop of blood from Nathan Longa's father. The murderer would have made use of biomass, draining either blood or other moisture and plasma within the human anatomy. Sure, the prisoners spilled some blood, but they still retained more than enough to feed—

Feed what? Brigid asked herself, but she fought off the urge to visualize the horror or horrors that awaited them. She had her knife pulled from its sheath, the keen edge held in an ice pick grip, and the Panther guard ambled closer on his prescribed patrol route along the chained line of prisoners.

Concentrate on the horror before you, Brigid told herself. We'll deal with an entity or entities who'd devour two dozen human beings when we get to it.

She locked her green eyes on the gunman, who

showed no concern for the suffering of other human beings. Slipping a knife between his ribs or into his kidney wouldn't be a pleasure, but it'd be one step closer to the safe emancipation of twenty-four human beings.

Brigid promised herself not to take visceral satisfaction in gutting the bastard.

Grant assembled the recurved bow he'd brought with him. He screwed the two arms into the central riser, the grip that an archer held, complete with an arrow rest where the shaft would stay during the draw. The riser was made of rigid, high-density carbon fiber around an aluminum core. The arms themselves were composed of sandwiched layers of carbon fiber and wood, making the limbs of the bow denser, harder to flex, and thus building up greater potential energy when the string was drawn back.

Grant also had the *yugake* glove that Shizuka had made for him. Grant was a student of *kyudo,* the samurai art of archery, and the *yugake* was specifically designed for the kind of hold an adherent of the style used, one in which the other fingers trapped the drawn string against the thumb. The *yugake* had ridges on the thumb designed for securing the drawstring, especially under the pressure of an eighty-eight-pound draw weight. That translated, with the 750-grain broad-head arrows he had, into 58.5 foot-pounds of energy when the recurved snapped straight and hurled the shaft at 188 feet per second.

The kinetic energy downrange might not have seemed like much in comparison to a bullet that moved much faster, but the dynamics of an arrow, especially with razor-sharp leading edges, translated into better aerodynamic passage through flesh and a larger wound cavity. And the fact that the wound channel was filled with the shaft of the arrow added to the disruption of physical function.

With this bow, Grant had dealt with a rogue deinonychus on Thunder Isle, a wounded creature weighing in at 250 pounds of lean muscle and reptilian hide. Grant first had assumed that he'd missed his shot, as there was no arrow jutting from the rib cage of the time-trawled predator, but the animal dropped to the ground immediately. Grant's arrow had punched through the deinonychus's rib cage, breaking one rib and turning both lungs into slurries of destroyed brachial tissue, and burst out the other side, embedding into a tree just behind it.

The impact had had such force that Grant had broken the shaft retrieving the arrow, and its hunting tip jammed into the cedar trunk. That kind of trauma was more than sufficient to end the life of a desperate, limping, but still deadly, dinosaur with a single shot. Grant knew that few humans would be able to stand against him. He pulled back on the bow, arms raised in the traditional *kyudo* draw, his shoulder muscles flexed and tensed.

His would be the shot that initiated this conflict with the Panthers of Mashona. Through the light amplification sensors on his shadow suit's faceplate, he could see the others, perched and ready to begin the butcher's work for this night. Grant, with the reach of his bow, and his speed and grace, was given the task of taking down two more men subsequent to his first target. Kane had another target, as well, but Thurpa, Brigid and Nathan were limited to only one ambush apiece.

Kane was a veteran of a dozen blade battles, and he had both the swiftness and certainty with which to bring down a militia maniac in a minimum of effort and time, freeing him for a second opponent. Even so, Grant braced himself to fire a fourth arrow in this dark plan.

Grant cleared his thoughts, entering the samurai state of *zanshin,* relaxed alertness, his thoughts in a smothered calmness. He was focused on nothing but aware of all around him. It was part of the art of *kyudo* and as much a mental state as a series of physical movements. He was mentally standing on the razor's edge, uncommitted to any single action, to leave himself ready for anything.

The guards were in position, Grant stretched the drawstring back, packing the two-ounce arrow with kinetic energy. The stiff, reinforced limbs struggled to return to their natural state, fighting against Grant's manipulation of them. He opened his thumb, and the string was freed to slip over the ridges on his glove. Now, at close to 190 feet per second, Grant's first arrow sliced silently through the night.

The arrow struck the Panther caravan guard at the knot of muscle and bone where his neck met his shoulders. Razor-sharp steel cracked the man's spinal column, splitting a vertebrae before the broad head slashed through the trunk of nerves that connected his body to his brain. The arrow would have gone farther, but vertebral bones were designed as thick armor to protect the spinal cord, and the shaft had already expended much of its energy shattering one half of the ring of bone.

It didn't matter. The instantly quadriplegic man turned rag-doll limp and spilled to the ground, struck so hard and quickly he didn't even have a lungful of air to cry out before he was facedown in the dirt. Grant pivoted, drew another arrow from his quiver, nocked it and turned toward his next opponent. In the shadows beyond, he spotted four people emerge from their hiding spots along the tree line and lunge toward four other guards. In a heartbeat, Grant pulled back, aimed and fired his second arrow of the night.

Grant's shot met its target in the breastbone, broad head cleaving through rubbery cartilage and squelching off ribs before it shredded two ugly holes in the Mashonan's aorta. The Panther militiaman's only sound was a grunt of expelled breath as the impact of fifty foot-pounds of energy slammed into his chest. This arrow wasn't stopped by the heavy bone of the man's spinal column, and it burst out from under his left shoulder blade and continued on into the shadows.

Had the arrow stopped, the two yawning wounds in the man's main pipeline of lifeblood would have been somewhat staunched, except where the four blades of the arrowhead had widened the wound beyond the diameter of the shaft. With the fletching gone through the blood vessel, causing more tissue disruption of already sliced tissue, the man's chest instantly filled with high-pressure blood gushing through an entrance and exit wound. That arterial pressure pushed hard on the man's lungs, making him unable to inhale as he knelt, eyes bulging from his horrific internal wounds.

Kane, whom Grant recognized from his location and his build, dropped the Panther he'd ambushed, and dashed with all the speed and power of the wolf he was often described as, overtaking the next of the Mashona slave masters, leaping at the last moment. Kane clamped his hand over the man's face, and all his weight pushed the man backward to the ground. There was the ugly grind of steel on bone as Kane thrust nine inches of blade through the gunman's sternum, slicing his heart in half.

Grant turned toward the last of his targets, drawing and nocking even as he was aware of Kane's victory.

The third of the militiamen had heard the rustle of silent, brutal combat, and he'd pulled his rifle from where it hung on its sling, swinging it into position. Grant took this into consideration for where he aimed, and he let fly.

Grant hit the would-be killer on the bridge of his nose. The arrow punched through the relatively fragile bones around the nasal cavity. That target was specific; Grant's Magistrate training had kicked in and reminded him that an enemy with his finger on the trigger would be unstoppable with anything but a "fatal triangle" hit. The triangle formed by the eyes and the nose were not only the weakest part of the human skull, but they were also directly in front of the huge cluster of nerves and brain functions that narrowed down into the spinal cord.

The broad-head arrow destroyed that, and the third gunman was shut off instantly. His finger would never reach the trigger of his rifle; no shot would blast into the night, bringing down the rest of the slave caravan, rifles blazing. He could see Thurpa attending to a prisoner lying on the ground and Kane watching them.

"Mission accom—"

The crackle of a rifle discharging into the night sky cut Grant short.

He turned and saw that Brigid and Nathan were both atop a militiaman. Though Nathan's target was no longer struggling, he'd still managed to fire his gun.

Yards away, the caravan quickly stirred at the burst of gunfire.

"Kane…"

"The prisoners have a chance. But we have to make it better for them," Kane answered over the Commtact. "Get loud and get bloody!"

Chapter 4

Kane wrenched his knife from the heart of the second Panther gunman, then took a step back, looking toward Grant, who was using that weird samurai archery to dispatch yet another of the Mashonan thugs with a single shot. Kane saw the muzzle-flash and heard a Panther's rifle. Bullets sliced into the night sky to where they wouldn't hit anyone until they fell back to earth. Nathan had his arms wrapped around the legs of a guard, and Brigid Baptiste was on the gunman's chest. She had her knife deep in the goon's face, having ended his existence.

The cacophony that the rifle produced was damage enough.

Fortunately, all eight of the gunmen assigned to the prisoners were down, snuffed out before they could shoot at any of the chained victims. That meant anyone armed and willing to harm the helpless prisoners would be coming from the caravan camp themselves.

"Kane…" Grant spoke over the Commtact.

Kane spoke up; the need for stealth was gone with the echo of gunshots in the night. "The prisoners have a chance. But we have to make it better for them. Get loud and get bloody!"

With that order, Kane reached down to his belt and unhooked a fragmentation grenade. He plucked the pin from it and hurled it toward the enemy camp as guards roused from relaxation to alertness. Some of them were fast, rushing halfway up the trail between their quarters and the prisoner area. It was these men who ran right into the flying gren, hurled by Kane with all the speed and accuracy he could muster.

The miniature bomb struck the lead militiaman in the center of his chest. The impact knocked the wind from the gunman and caused him to stop cold. One of his fellows plowed through him, tripping them both and throwing them to the ground bracketing the high explosive, just in time for them to catch a wave of extreme overpressure and flying metal shrapnel.

The surge of force slammed into the downed pair and the three men with them. The blast wave burst blood vessels in their bodies, killing them swiftly. It was a quick, merciful end for the men who'd been marching unarmed, naked prisoners across miles of the wilderness of Africa.

The exploding grenade slammed the door on that approach from the column of militiamen. They now knew that someone was covering that route, and very few people were ever armed with only one grenade. At the very least, that would mean more hand bombs or firearms covering the trail between the two locations. And these militiamen weren't stupid. The group that Kane could see beyond the explosion skidded to a sudden halt as they realized that if they cut through the bottleneck, they'd be cut down.

As if to punctuate Kane's unspoken point, Grant loosed an arrow, sending the high-velocity missile into one of the groups who'd stopped. The arrow sliced through a rifleman in the center of the group. The fletching disappeared into his chest before the rest of his body got the message that it had been perforated through center of mass. The man dropped an instant later, blood bursting from his lips, much to the shock of his fellow soldiers.

Because Kane and Grant were wearing the night-black shadow suits, they were invisible to their opposition, and neither had used a weapon that gave a muzzle-flash. Grenades and arrows were good at keeping their users relatively unseen in darkness.

Kane knew, though, that the Panthers hadn't become such a feared enemy without learning common tricks such as flanking maneuvers. They would come at their former prisoners and the rescue party from another angle, and when that happened, Kane intended to meet them with every ounce of violence he could muster.

Nathan Longa decided to leave Nehushtan balanced against a tree trunk. He didn't want to inadvertently unleash a bolt of power, and he wasn't certain how stealthy he could be with the ancient staff. Sure, the artifact had granted him superior speed and strength in the past, but he didn't want to produce more of a spectacle than necessary. If things came to a worst-case situation, he was only a few feet away from the propped-up staff and the battle rifle he'd shed for stealth.

Then he made a mistake as he lunged at a Mashonan gunman and clamped a hand around his mouth, stifling him swiftly. As he brought the knife around and toward the man's heart from the front, his blade slammed into the Panther's rifle. The thrust was a powerful one, meant to pierce his target's breastbone and spear the heart behind it, but the frame of the gunman's weapon deflected the force of the blow, disarming both men as they toppled to the ground.

Then came the wrestling match: Nathan pitting his might against the disarmed gunman's. The militiaman reached for his own knife, but Nathan chopped the edge of his hand hard against his enemy's inner elbow, striking the cluster of muscles and nerves, which left the guard's fingers numb and unable to hold on to any tool. Nathan suddenly saw stars, and the center of his face and left eye ached from where the militiaman headbutted him. Nathan lashed out, eliciting a grunt from his foe, finger sinking into wet, ugly tissues. Whatever cry the man would have released was superseded by unintelligible choking as the man's eyeball burst, paralyzing his throat with terror and agony.

Nathan heard footsteps, a solitary figure racing toward him and the Mashonan soldier, and he expected to catch a back full of lead. When no bullets came, he glanced up and saw the lithe silhouette of Brigid Baptiste rushing to his aid, knife in hand. Nathan's distraction caused an awful turn of events. The Panther punched Nathan hard in the chest, bowling him back just enough that the thug could crawl toward his rifle.

Nathan threw himself atop the gunman, grabbing his legs, even as Brigid Baptiste came down. The militiaman had a handful of his rifle, and he swung it upward; the stock of the weapon struck Brigid in the ribs. Her shadow suit redistributed the impact, but it slowed her, delaying her knife strike long enough for him to wriggle his finger into the trigger guard.

Nathan tugged the man's legs hard, jolting the muzzle of the gun away from Brigid's body. Despite the shadow suit, at this range, with the heavy slugs in the rifle, the Cerberus archivist would have been blown to pieces by a contact gunshot.

Nathan saved the woman's life, but gunshots ripped into the night sky.

"Dammit," Nathan swore. He heard the scrape of

knife on bone, Brigid ripping her blade free and plunging it down again.

By the third time, Nathan was on all fours, grabbing at her wrist. The militiaman was dead already, but Brigid's frustration was such that she nearly broke Nathan's grasp.

"I'm sorry," Nathan whispered.

Brigid shook her head. "I couldn't keep his arm pinned. It was my—"

She was cut off by the boom of an explosion in the distance.

Kane was throwing grenades, which meant the enemy camp was up and active.

"I can make up for my fumble," Nathan muttered.

He turned back to his tree and retrieved the artifact staff and the rifle he'd left behind. Brigid returned to her original hiding place to get her heavier weapons, as well.

Kane's Commtact reached Nathan's radio earpiece. "Nate, I'm going to need you at the bottleneck here. We've got the enemy force delayed, but you'll work as the bar. You've got your grens, right?"

"Yes," Nathan answered. "It's because I screwed up?"

"No prisoners died. You kept the guard from harming them. You succeeded," Kane countered. "I need a big, powerful rifle. Thurpa, you back up Nathan."

Nathan nodded; then he noticed Thurpa jogging alongside him, holding his mouth. The captive Africans were already conversing among themselves as they reached the path between the two encampments.

"What's wrong with your mouth?" Nathan asked.

"I pulled a muscle," Thurpa returned. "The guy

twisted once I bit him, and that flexed my fangs the way that they shouldn't have."

"Oh," Nathan replied.

"This shit is not going as easily as we thought," Thurpa muttered. "I ended up talking to one girl who seemed awake, but she was scared out of her wits."

"She didn't scream," Nathan noted.

"No. I put my hand over her mouth, but gently. I told her we were rescuing them, but right now we need them to stay down and out of our way," Thurpa responded.

The two men set up at bracketing sides of the path entering the prisoners' clearing.

"Stuck on defense again," Thurpa murmured.

"We do what we can, Thur," Nathan answered.

The young cobra man nodded.

"Look at it this way—at least you'll have grateful new friends," Nathan added.

Thurpa managed a smile.

The two young men lapsed into silence, their eyes and ears peeled for signs of enemy movement down the path.

Brigid Baptiste linked up with Kane and Grant as they cut through the woods that separated the Panthers' encampment and their line of prisoners. She had her suppressed Copperhead in hand now, firmly gripping it and keeping its stock against her shoulder, finger off the trigger and against the frame so as not to accidentally loose a shot and perhaps hit her companions. Though all three were in the darkened shadows of the copse of trees, they could see clearly, thanks to their shadow suit hoods, and were able to pick up the movement of Mashona troopers away from the path.

She glanced at Kane, and he held up his fist for a hold position. Brigid knew that Kane had a plan to intercept the force that was rapidly trying to flank Thurpa and Nathan. Whatever he had in mind, it was going to be simple but devastating.

Simple but devastating could have been the mantra of the Cerberus warriors as they often had to "wing it." Even when working around their more familiar areas, such as the Tartarus Pits, flexibility was of the essence. As such, improvisation and tactics gained from observation of the terrain and evaluation of the enemy troops were applied.

So far, it had carried the day for them across dozens of adventures. Brigid anticipated that the Panthers of Mashona were a trained, disciplined force, despite the horrors they wrought. They had been well organized back at the power station assault, but the Mashonan militia hadn't counted on fast-firing, quick-reloading grenade launchers and sniper rifles to flank them, surround them and hammer them with two dozen explosions and precision gunfire to slice through their ranks. The guards of this caravan moved on a schedule that gave the Cerberus explorers perfect placing to ambush them. There was a route—a slender game trail through the trees—that the Panthers were aware of and savvy enough to leave lightly attended.

Unfortunately for the Panthers, Kane's woodcraft and stealth had allowed him to penetrate the forest between the two camps and stumble on the trail. He'd seen the sentry at that position, unobtrusive and mirroring the one on the other side, the one he'd ambushed immediately.

Brigid noticed movement on the game trail ahead, and she braced herself, waiting for Kane to give the hand signal to open fire. Grant drew back on his bow and took aim. Kane nodded, and the big archer loosed

his arrow, putting it through the ear of the lead gunman on the trail. For a man who was a relatively new
student to archery, Grant was proving to be quite lethal; Brigid marked that up to natural marksmanship
training and his phenomenal strength. At six foot four,
he was larger than most of his fellow Magistrates, and
was much faster and smarter than he appeared.

Brigid had formerly had a low opinion of the Magistrate Division, seeing them as faceless ciphers, right
down to the deletion of their "given" names and the
fact they existed as surnames in service to the hybrid
barons. Then she'd worked with Kane and Grant and
discovered that they had a sense of duty, quick wit and
humor, and were far more observant and resourceful
than she'd imagined.

She remembered the Thunder Isle incident, before
Grant had become lost in time. He'd used his *kyudo*
lessons back then to deadly effect, alongside his lover
and teacher, the samurai Shizuka. Now Grant was comfortable enough with the bow to bring it on their mission, meaning that he'd all but mastered the ancient
combat art.

Kane gestured toward Brigid, and she swung her
Copperhead up and targeted the heads of the next few
gunmen, tapping off short bursts from the submachine
gun. The bullets made soft popping sounds, like the
flutter of a large bird's wings, but when her bullets
struck flesh and bone, the result was no less bloody
and damaging. Unfortunately, the loss of three of their
number sent the rest of the Panthers to cover on the far
side of the game trail, seeking the protection of tree
trunks and the concealment of foliage.

Kane motioned, and both Grant and Brigid hit the
dirt, ducking below the inevitable stream of enemy gun-

fire in response to their ambush. Whatever Kane had planned became apparent when she saw him make two throwing motions. Two more grenades sailed through the night, going past the game trail and landing behind the line of Panthers. They exploded in quick succession, and Kane rose to his knees, watching stunned and wounded militia bandits stagger into the open.

Kane popped his Sin Eater and opened fire on the dazed survivors, chugging short bursts from the compact folding machine pistol. He tore through them, using the high-density slugs of his gun as a chainsaw, ripping open chests and bellies in a grisly display of vulgar firepower. Grant had set his bow aside and cut loose with his own Copperhead. Brigid joined in the grim and brutal slaughter.

She didn't enjoy this butcher's work, but she knew that there were dozens of helpless people on the other end of the game trail who needed protection. If she didn't help to destroy this spearhead flanking maneuver by the Panthers of Mashona, they would burst in on the unarmed, naked prisoners and either retake or coldly slaughter them.

She was protecting lives, and that made the murder of these men all the more easy to bear. She'd sleep at night because she'd seen the condition of those poor humans, wrecked by a forced march, scoured bloody and raw by manacles and yokes about their neck. This wasn't murder. This was the end of torturers.

Brigid caught movement from the corner of her eye. Kane motioned for her to stop shooting. She paused to reload the Copperhead, feeding it a new magazine.

They didn't speak. The snarl of bullets through suppressed firearms was enough of a risk to compromise their position in the dark. The enemy knew that there were gunmen in the tree line, and they could quickly adapt to the situation. Brigid didn't know how many of these soldiers there were. Kane had mentioned about thirty, maybe more. She wanted to do the mental math, but all that would accomplish would be counting how many more lives had ended this night.

The only true determination of victory was the retreat of their enemy and the cessation of gunfire.

Kane motioned to Brigid, gave the finger signal for grenades, then quickly pointed in the direction he wanted her to throw them. No need to risk being heard, even subvocalizing into their Commtacts, especially when they were under fire. Brigid sized up the targets for her grenades and braced herself to let loose.

"Now," Kane whispered over the radio.

Brigid pulled the first pin, threw, then quickly armed the second miniature bomb. Both flew straight and far. She could see that they were fanning out their explosive counterattack along a wider front. Kane had kept an eye out for firing positions from among the Panthers beyond the tree line, and now they hammered the militia hard. Six explosions ripped through their ranks, and men screamed, torn asunder by shrapnel and concussive force.

The thunderclaps of the detonations stretched out in two distinct staccato roars. Whatever would be left of this group would not be keen on making another attack.

Back from the original path between the two clearings, they heard the rattle of heavy rifles.

Kane nodded for her to go check on the scene, to support the others. Now it was time for the Cerberus expedition to strike back, to force the Panthers into retreat. Thanks to cover and concealment, they'd presented a nearly impenetrable front against the enemy.

Now it was time to press the advantage and make them retreat and give up the struggle.

Brigid gave a whistle, the signal for Nathan and Thurpa to know she was behind them. The last thing she needed was to be blasted at point-blank by either of the young men thinking that she was trying to ambush them. She saw Nathan wave her over, and she rushed to his side.

"They heard you fighting inside the thicket, so they thought they could cut this way again. We dropped three of them," Nathan told her.

Thurpa's rifle thundered, big bullets slapping the night air and cracking it before he shot down another of the Mashonan gunners. "Make it four."

Brigid nodded.

"Do we pull back or hold?" Nathan asked.

"Hold," Brigid said. She unscrewed the suppressor from the muzzle of her Copperhead. At this point, they were going to be on the attack, so they'd need to make noise. Silencers in the trees helped to keep them hidden against return fire, but now they needed to sow fear and scatter the militia's surviving defenders.

In the distance, Kane and Grant cut loose with their automatic weapons, the unmistakable throaty booms of the Sin Eaters and the high-pitched cracks of their Copperheads. They were sweeping against the Panthers in that direction, guns blazing.

"Now," Brigid said, and Nathan and Thurpa picked up on the cue for violence. Their rifles and her submachine gun cut through the darkness. They fired at shadows, pouring out a wall of bullets. Bodies fell, struck by rounds, but the blasting was to break the will of the enemy. The militia abandoned their camp, racing off into the forest, half of their number dead and likely more wounded.

It was a decisive strike, and one that would force the gunmen to reorganize and recuperate.

That would give them time to free the prisoners.

"Grant and I are going to stick by the camp," Kane said. "You three unchain those people. We won't have much time."

"Acknowledged," Brigid responded. Thurpa and Nathan heard him over their hand radios, which were tuned to the Commtacts' frequency.

The three people turned back toward the line of prisoners, seeking out keys among the dead guards to undo the painful, heavy manacles.

The Panthers undoubtedly would either stage a counterattack or call for help from another group. Either way, Brigid was determined to free the prisoners and get them out of the clearing within an hour. Half that would be optional.

Anything to free these victims was necessary. Otherwise, she was a cold-blooded assassin for nothing.

Chapter 5

Lyta grimaced as the yoke came off her neck. The harsh corners of the steel collar took tiny slivers of flesh with it, peeling away whatever upper epidermis was left where the metal had chafed against her skin. The other prisoners were already up, moving drunkenly but with a semblance of speed and energy. The men immediately picked up firearms from the dead guards, and one of the three people dressed in jet-black skinsuits pulled off a hood.

Brigid Baptiste revealed herself as a woman, a *white* woman with hair that looked like streams of curled copper spilling over her shoulders. She was so tall, Lyta had originally thought her to be a skinny man, like the African with the staff or the humanoid who looked as if he was half cobra.

"Most of us speak English, if you do," Lyta spoke up to the woman.

Brigid smiled. "Thanks. We've found that out working with your countrymen. We need to get to the other camp and get more stuff for you. Food, water, weapons and ammunition. Clothing would be good, too."

"That's a good plan," Lyta replied. "Who are you people?"

"He is from India," Brigid said, pointing to the cobra man. "His name is Thurpa. The other man is from Harare. His name is Nathan Longa."

Lyta glanced toward the man she'd indicated. "Longa…I had an uncle named Longa."

Nathan frowned. "What was his given name?"

"Nelson," Lyta replied.

Nathan squeezed his eyes shut for a moment. "I'm his son."

Lyta didn't take long to put the subtext of Nathan's painful reaction into context. "How did he die?"

Nathan looked around, hating to take time from preparing for evacuation from the area, but he spoke after only a moment. "He was murdered. By *something* that might be working with the Panthers."

Lyta nodded, repeating what he'd said. "*Something*. As in what would eat us at the end of this march."

"Not anymore," Nathan returned. "You and the others take off. Get back to your home."

Lyta narrowed her eyes. "I intend to find out what these animals wanted to do with me."

Nathan glowered at her. "You're not in condition to come with us."

"She could be," Thurpa spoke.

"Help the others gather supplies," Nathan snapped at him.

Thurpa frowned. "They're doing well on their own."

"Then stop convincing my cousin that she has to risk her life," Nathan hissed harshly.

Thurpa looked between the two. "As if you risking yours is any better?"

Nathan rubbed his brow. "I've got an advantage."

"What?" Lyta asked.

"None of your—"

"The snake-headed staff that Nelson Longa owned," Thurpa spoke up.

"Snake-headed… Is that why you're interested in it?" Lyta asked.

Thurpa shook his head. "It's an artifact, from the dawn of time."

"It's too complicated to explain here and now. You're hurt. Exhausted…"

"And free," Lyta responded. "Why would you deny me the chance to find out why my home was attacked? There've been so many people killed…"

Nathan grumbled. He gripped the strange walking stick, one she remembered from when Uncle Nelson had visited her so long ago. The object was as tall as Nathan, who was a shade under six feet, and it was one central ebony rod with strange designs inlaid along its length, wound about by two metallic serpents whose heads poked straight up. Lyta glanced at the space between the ominous snake heads and saw that there was a space for another object up there, braced or locked in between them.

Thurpa walked closer to Nathan, whispering into his ear. She couldn't make out what was being said.

"I don't know," Nathan replied. He seemed crestfallen, looking first to the strange staff and then toward Lyta.

"Just give it some thought," Thurpa said.

"Could I get some assistance?" the woman, Brigid, asked them. The two men walked away, leaving her be.

Lyta felt hands on her shoulders, sitting her down. Petroleum jelly salve was spread over her neck and shoulders. The ooze was an important supply for a militia on the move to deal with blisters, cuts and abrasions of all forms. As soon as the balm was spread across her raw back and about her wrists, she began to feel better. There were several jars of the stuff for the militia, so there was more than enough for the prisoners. Bandages from the Panthers' first-aid supplies were also put to good use to protect the ravaged flesh.

Lyta accepted a shirt and a web belt. The shirt was long enough on her to act like a minidress, but there was enough air around her bottom to make her feel self-conscious until a pair of men's briefs was provided for her from the militia's laundry.

Clean clothes, after being naked for so many days, were wonderful. A bottle of water was also provided for her, and she took several deep pulls before passing the bottle on. Fresh water, clothes, she didn't even mind the cooling of the evaporating wetness on her shirt. Boots, unfortunately, were in short supply, but Lyta didn't mind. Most of the people in her town didn't have much use for footwear, and the soles of her feet were only slightly less tough than rhinoceros skin.

Finally, Lyta got a weapon, two of them actually. One was a machete that looked rusted and pitted, but it was still heavy and felt good in her hand. The other was a .45-caliber pistol. Since the weapons of the Mashona were mostly stolen from the Zambian and Harare armed forces, she knew this pistol. She dumped the magazine and saw that it was loaded. She pulled back the slide and noted that the chamber was empty.

Lyta would keep it that way. She wasn't sure about the safety on the pistol, and she wouldn't carry one with a hammer on a live round. It would take a moment to slingshot a fresh round into the breech, if necessary. Both came with sheathes, so she put them onto the belt that tugged the long uniform tunic about her hips snugly. She rubbed her hand across her bare scalp, wishing that she still had her hair and idly wondering how she looked. Right now, she felt wonderful, but she was certain that a glance in a mirror would show her the truth of her ramshackle appearance.

Here you are, covered in bandages and the clothes of dead men, and you're wondering if you're hot or not, she thought, trying to hold down her disgust.

"It sure beats being raped and dead," she muttered. "I look human again."

"Are you all right?" It was Brigid, the beautiful woman from America, from the place she called Cerberus redoubt.

"Just trying to get my mind off of my vanity," Lyta replied. "Can I join your group?"

Brigid looked taken aback. "We're on a dangerous journey, Lyta. I don't know if it would be wise."

"Wisdom comes from mistakes," Lyta replied. "And I know this could be a big mistake, but if I survive, I'll at least know what awaited me. What was on the other end of this journey."

Brigid's brilliant green eyes looked the young woman over. She took a deep breath, pursed her lips, then nodded. "I'll see what my compatriots have to say."

"If it's any help, I'm a resident of a frontier town in Zambia. We all receive firearms training," Lyta added. She looked at the other prisoners. Though dressed, bandaged, rehydrating from water bottles and gobbling down random bits of food left behind by the Mashonan militia, they were ragged. They were unmistakably former prisoners, gaunt, wounded, eyes darting at the slightest sound.

"Not that it seemed to help us," Lyta amended, frowning.

"Does anyone else want to see where the Panthers were taking you?" Brigid asked.

"I have to see to my family," one man said. Others nodded, muttering in agreement. "If there's any left."

Brigid glanced to Lyta, and the young Zambian woman bit her lower lip, trying not to show any emotion. That effort translated into exactly what she tried to avoid as Brigid laid a gentle hand on her shoulder.

It was a warm, comforting action, and she looked worried for Lyta.

"I want to know what was worth the life of my mother, my fiancé," Lyta admitted.

Brigid nodded.

"I'll see what we can do," Brigid replied.

Lyta watched her head to the tree line. Her spilling curls of golden-lit crimson provided a beacon by which she could be seen in the light of the moon and stars above.

Kane mulled over the whispered Commtact message from Brigid, then looked toward Grant's position. He was a hundred yards away, barely a silhouette picked up by his night optics.

"Grant, you have an opinion on this?" Kane asked.

"The girl can use some closure," Grant replied. "And if we send her back, she'll just break from the group and follow us, maybe make a mistake which gives us away. At least we can keep an eye on her."

"Baptiste?" Kane inquired.

"She has a powerful desire to know. And when something like that hits, it's hard to resist," Brigid responded. "She'll definitely end up following us. We can keep her out of trouble."

"Pretty much my feeling, too," Kane said. "We might actually have some luck bringing her with. She seems smart and determined."

"Any sign of the Panthers regrouping?" Brigid asked.

Kane swept the forest. It had been twenty minutes since they'd driven the militia away, and their footprints had cooled to the temperature of the surrounding foliage. The blood of the injured was still only a few degrees warmer than the background ambient heat, showing signs of where the gunmen had escaped. Scanning between the trees, using the telescopic optics in conjunction with infrared and light amplification modes on the shadow suit hoods, he couldn't see any sign of them returning. Even so, he and Grant had moved along their path for a good distance, keeping their eyes open and scanning as far as the advanced suits would let them, but also making time for the rest of their senses, as well. Infrared tracking could be beaten, especially with the use of a shield of "room temperature" woven foliage that blocked out the heat signatures behind it.

For all the advantages that the two former Magistrates possessed, there were still ways for the enemy to sneak past them. Caution and alertness were the order of the day.

"Nothing so far, but I still want those people on the move to someplace safer," Kane said. "I noticed a couple of vehicles in the camp that they could use."

"We've fit as many as we could, those with the least ability to walk back," Nathan explained over the shared frequency. "Tell me we're not going to bring my cousin with us."

"She's family?" Kane asked him.

"Yeah," Nathan responded. "I'd rather not have her join us. Unlike the rest of us, she doesn't have any innate advantages like experience, cobra scales or a mystical artifact."

"No, but she does have frontier militia training," Brigid spoke up.

"Fifteen rounds a month shot at a paper target on a wall," Nathan countered.

"Her advantages don't matter," Kane said. "She seems dead set on joining this expedition. So let's have her with us, rather than tripping over her."

Nathan grumbled, "I guess that makes sense."

"Don't pout over it. Our job will be a little trickier, but she's the one who asked to come with," Kane offered. "She knows where we're going is dangerous. We can only hope to survive *with* her help, just like she survives with ours."

"All right," Nathan answered. He sounded much less sullen. It'd take a while for him to be comfortable with the idea of having a cousin along or their journey, but, in the end, Lyta was determined to join them.

"Kane," Grant warned over the Commtact. "I've got contacts. Seventy-five yards out. Three, no, five. Armed, moving low to the ground."

"Test force?" Kane asked.

"Maybe. Maybe not," Grant said. "None of them appear wounded. They don't seem to have any night optics, so they might not be expecting us to have the same."

"Don't engage unless they make the first move," Kane returned. "Keep an eye on them."

"Right," Grant said.

"Baptiste, they're early," Kane told her.

"Already back to the group," Brigid answered. He could hear her shouting orders for the prisoners to pack up and start moving out. In the distance, Kane could hear the low rumble of engines starting. He was glad that it was the audio sensors in the shadow suit hood. Still, he kept ready for Grant to tell him that the enemy were reacting to their vehicles powering up.

At the same time, he continued to sweep for signs of other foes in the forest. There might only have been five left uninjured after the initial assault, but Kane didn't feel like he was that lucky. If anything, they wouldn't put all their forces in one spot, especially not in the flanking maneuver that Grant observed.

Something else was happening. His nerves were on edge.

"Grant, status on the group moving up."

"They appeared, but they only advanced about twenty yards," Grant returned. "Then they hunkered down. Every so often, they look back, but that's it. Why?"

"There's something going on. I can't put my finger on it, but those guys have backup on the way," Kane explained. "I just can't see it."

"That void chick, Neekra?" Grant asked. "She could be oozing in?"

Kane thought about it. That's when he began to feel the vibration. He looked down at the ground. "Grant, get out of the forest. Get back to the truck."

"Shit," Grant hissed, and Kane could hear his effort at running, his increased breathing, the thump of his body as he landed on the ground—all conveyed via vibration over the Commtact. Unfortunately, Grant seemed to be moving in slow motion, just as Kane was, in relation to the rising throb of forces seething beneath the earth. Kane charged through the forest.

"Baptiste!"

"Go!" Brigid shouted loud enough to make Kane's inner ear ring. She was in full command mode, scooting two dozen noncombatants from the area. There were two trucks in the camp, enough to carry about sixteen people, tightly packed, so there were going to be people still on foot.

Running from a force that shook the ground and filled Kane's spine with ice-water terror.

"Kane!" Grant bellowed. "The ground split ahead of me!"

"Double around!" Kane returned.

Then Kane realized Grant's dilemma firsthand. He skidded to a halt as suddenly the ground split all around him. He threw himself down, reaching for the far edge of the ever-growing chasm, and he clawed at the ledge, but only for a moment. He hadn't rooted himself on rock; he'd grabbed a handful of soil. It crumbled beneath his grasp, and gravity sucked him down the face of the cracking cliff.

In free fall, Kane felt absolutely helpless, but that stopped a moment later when he slammed hard against a crag. The sudden alteration of the kinetic force kept Kane from bouncing off the ledge, but even so, every inch of his body throbbed, aching from the abuse it'd just absorbed. He clung to the side of the chasm, listening as the rumble suddenly stopped.

The earth beneath Kane disappeared into inky oblivion. Kane would have used the optics on his shadow suit hood, but somewhere along the way, the seal that kept its faceplate on had failed, probably when he'd planted into the wall while tumbling in flight. He couldn't find it anywhere, and he realized that most of his equipment was gone.

Sitting up slowly, taking deep breaths and forcing himself not to vomit, Kane brought himself back to a semblance of clearheadedness. He scanned the darkness, one hand absently digging for a flashlight. He clicked it on, and it spilled only a modicum of light.

He ran his fingers over the surface. The lens had been shattered. Likely, several of the LEDs embedded in the lens had been similarly knocked out by his plummet.

Now he knew why he felt like a punching bag for the gods. He'd likely rebounded from cliff face to cliff face, spiraling down the chasm until everything in his inventory had been smashed or torn from him. Even his right arm didn't feel right, as if it were too light. He shone his torch and saw that the hydraulic holster's arm brace was there, but the Sin Eater was gone, torn off completely. There was no Copperhead to be seen, either, at least not on the ledge with him.

Kane dug his fingers into the cliff face, taking advantage of what light there was from his torch to mark his territory. The ledge was a long one, disappearing out of the spray of LED-emitted light at about twenty-five feet.

He also realized that there was a small lip along the ledge. Slowly it continued to rumble, rising until it stopped, a slender barrier of stone three feet in height. Kane limped over to it, examining it. Over the stone railing, the abyss continued beneath him. He glanced upward, but the night sky was gone. Invisible.

Had the earth shut again?

He checked the floor of the ledge again and noticed that it had a tile-like pattern on its surface.

Kane realized that this was not a random formation along the chasm wall. This was constructed, but he couldn't tell by which force. He'd seen the rail rise before his eyes. He turned off the light in order to conserve its battery.

Nothing was around for him to see. Whatever had fallen off him had missed the ledge entirely.

And the way my luck goes, that's not happenstance,

Kane mused. A force must have guided me here. That bitch queen who played with my subconscious only a few days ago.

Kane sneered, then checked himself all over. He was relieved when he found that his web belt was still somewhat intact. He'd only retained two grenades and the Colt .45 he'd brought to back up the Sin Eater and the Copperhead. It had only one magazine in it.

He felt for the pouch and found the other magazines; their steel shells were bent and crushed by impacts. Kane figured he could pry shells from the damaged pair of clips to feed the one already in the gun, which meant that he was good for about eight shots before needing to retreat and spend minutes thumbing bullets into the remaining magazine. He checked the pistol for signs of damage, but the frame of the gun was thick enough not to have bent or warped under his impacts against the chasm walls. The grip was splintered on one side, though.

Luckily, Kane still had some duct tape in his kit. He wound it around the splintered wood, evening it out. He made sure the tape didn't interfere with the magazine release or block the magazine well, but other than that, his pistol was much like himself. Battered, held together by a reliable wonder material, but still ready to fight.

He also had his knife in its leg sheath. The one part of him that felt like it hadn't been swung at with a sledgehammer was his leg below the knee, where the fighting blade rested.

A knife. A gun. His shadow suit, sans optics. Two grenades. A flickering LED flashlight.

He touched his face. The Commtact plate must have been jarred loose when the face of his shadow suit hood had torn off. He patted himself down, reaching down the neck of the suit, but he couldn't find the contact plate.

Maybe it was better this way.

Brigid and Grant had shadow suits, as well, clothing that could have cushioned their plummet down the chasm.

But that was an advantage denied to Nathan, Thurpa and the new girl, Lyta.

He looked up. The sky was gone. Had the earth closed up? And had it been only he and Grant who had fallen? Indeed, had Grant fallen? Or was he still trapped aboveground, kept from advancing by the rift that had opened ahead of him?

Alone in the darkness, Kane knew that there were two ways to go. Up the inclined ledge, toward the surface where his friends may or may not be, or down, deeper into the belly of the underground, where he was certain the trouble originated.

His enemies were likely ahead of him. That meant going down.

Kane descended into the abyss.

Chapter 6

Neekra rode in Warlord Gamal's skin. She'd carved his psyche out using the telepathic equivalent of a rusted fork, hurling the man's personality into the void. His body, despite the loss of a foot when his truck-bed platform imploded on it, was more than sufficient for her needs.

Neekra infected his body, occupying his nervous system and limbs, consigning the original mind of the man to a hellish oblivion. She felt a disjointed sense of pain as she took the flesh from one part of his anatomy and turned it into a new foot for her. The effort and the laws of matter conservation had stolen inches of height from Gamal's skeletal structure, but it also provided her with more room to play with and forge him into a brand-new shape. She took his manhood and much of his muscle and transferred it to fat, to curves, to feminine bits.

Once again Neekra had a body, and it befit the body of the seductress, the queen of the damned who drew men to their doom. Gamal had been one of her first consorts in a good hundred years, mainly because she didn't find that much ambition, that much grandeur, in the lesser men scurrying past her tomb. Her telepathy projected from where the Annunaki overlords had interred her, but it could only stretch so far. In all that stretching, all she'd encountered were desperate men whose thoughts were living to the next dawn, whose desires were a mere crumb of food, to slay or elude their enemies.

The warlord Gamal was different. He'd organized the Panthers of Mashona into a teeming army, built on a bedrock of terror and brutality. Gamal had the promise to expand beyond being a mere robber baron and seizing the world by the reins. Unfortunately, there were others who had arrived on the continent, others who had their own agendas that were attractive to her.

And Gamal? He'd made the mistake of hurling his might against a set of opponents whose will was simply too much for him to overcome. His failure, even bolstered by his militia and swarms of winged mutates, cooled her interest in the man as a lover, as the savior who would raise her from her tomb. But Durga had been correct in retrieving the fallen warrior from the battlefield.

Neekra now had a skinsuit, a hunk of flesh with which she could interact with the world, even as she flowed through his cells like quicksilver, shaping him into a blood-skinned goddess.

And as her host, as her consort, she had a dozen snake men and their prince, a king cobra who had dared to challenge even the god who'd entombed her, far from man, entrapped without a hope of freedom.

Prince Durga of the Nagah was part of a race of genetically altered humans, spawned by Enki, brother and rival of Enlil, and kept vital for millennia by the cobra baths that could transform human to Nagah or back again, using cellular manipulation similar to what Neekra used on Gamal's carcass. Durga had cut deals with Enlil and then the Millennium Consortium, in order to cement his place as the emperor of the Nagah's underground kingdom. His plan would have worked had it not been for the resistance of the other man Neekra had been drawn to. As it was, Durga's attempt at domination was undone, but not before a thousand had died and he'd wrecked Enki's fountain of genetic alteration.

Durga had come to her, to Africa, because he sought the means of returning to health. He'd barely survived an immense explosion, thousands of bullets, grenades and knives hacking at him. Durga had abused the cobra baths, utilizing them to make himself into a living juggernaut, but even that invulnerability paled in the face of the efforts of Kane, her other target, and his allies from North America.

Kane, Neekra mused. I tortured him, ripped him from his friends and family, did everything in my power to shatter his spirit. And yet, when he had me on the ropes, he offered me mercy.

Mercy was a concept that Neekra had utilized before; she'd manipulated it in foes who assumed she was a mere mortal, a weakling. She'd appealed to the mercy of others to draw them into her trap.

But for all she had subjected Kane to, he'd stayed his hand and offered her a chance to walk away from the battle. As far as he was concerned, he'd won, and that meant he had no need or desire to murder her cold. That was something she'd never encountered, at least in her memory. At her current age, she wasn't quite certain of her earlier days, when she had still been mortal.

Neekra would have had no problem with Kane putting the finishing blow upon her. The peace of oblivion would have been just as fine a reward for her as freedom. Anything would be better than confinement within her prison. Right now, inside Gamal's head, she was only a sliver of what she had been, despite her ability to effect his cellular structure.

In her own body, alive and free, she was nigh unlimited, rather than being a ghost shredding minds on the mental plane or pulling parlor tricks with musculoskeletal reformation. Her senses were dulled, as if she were interacting with the world through a woolen blanket. Trapped in human flesh, she couldn't even reach out to touch Durga's consciousness, let alone reach out to locate Kane, the mighty and the merciful, the attractive human who had drawn her to his nobility and strength.

To corrupt such a figure would be delicious. To do it and retrieve her body, to become the goddess she was meant to be, not a corpse buried in concrete, that would be the ultimate. To attempt it, to fail and to be utterly destroyed by such a warrior would be the end of her imprisonment, her torment.

Either way, it was win-win for Neekra.

"My queen," the prince spoke softly, awakening her from her reveries. "The other has arrived."

Neekra regarded Durga, realizing that he made no secret of his disdain and jealousy of Kane and her newly spawned interest in him. She smiled at him. "How do you know?"

"The Panthers of Mashona have arrived with their tribute to your servants," Durga stated. "And now they are under attack. They retreated."

Neekra pursed her full, lush lips. The face she'd molded was a near approximation of her true beauty, but it was as nothing to her original self. She'd had to deal with mere human flesh, and, as such, it could only hold so much of her majesty. She recalled the tales of Zeus, and one in particular, how even at his most diminished in power, a glance upon his visage by a human turned them to ash.

She wondered if modern man could withstand her true beauty.

"Then send up my children," Neekra told Durga. "Open the earth, and let them take those on the surface."

"You would have those things kill Kane, after all the moony eyes you've cast his way?" Durga asked.

Neekra smirked. Durga had spirit. Certainly, he had positioned himself as enchanted by her sexuality and her promises of power, but he still retained his own individuality, an unflinching fear of stating his mind in contrast to her wishes. "They will not kill those who I do not wish to harm. I control them."

Durga barely concealed a shudder of revulsion. When the Nagah had first come to this underground city, encountering the minions within, he had been disgusted by their translucent, wormlike flesh. However, they were among the layers of warriors for the city of Negari, which she'd ruled for centuries until the arrival of a black-clad European. He had traversed Africa, seeking out a young woman, a relative of some other man to whom he owed a debt. In the space of a few days, the traveler had brought the city down, wrecking it completely, causing the death of the pitiful human shell she'd used at that time and bringing dark slaughter to the cultists who'd clung to her.

Neekra could not help but recognize a small spark of that dark, grim Puritan within Kane. She even sensed an echo of the man's voice within the wails of the tortured twenty-second-century adventurer, as well as a flash of familiarity with his profile as he rose from his psychic dungeon, armed for battle.

She closed her eyes and extended her consciousness to the minions.

They would rue the day they'd come to her city.

BRIGID BAPTISTE WATCHED as the earth that the prisoners had occupied suddenly began to crack open, then slanted down as if on a ramp. At first her mind reeled. That was exactly where the dozens of captives would have been had they not been freed; they'd be rolling down a slide of stone. The change of the terrain was sudden and dramatic, and as the dust and dirt tumbled down the preconstructed ramp, she realized that this was an ancient design.

She looked as the ramp disappeared into an arched entrance and segments of the floor slid and crunched out into the open. It all slid together with uncanny precision, producing one smooth inclined plane that stretched down into the darkness and out of sight. Even more boggling to her was that as the floor extended, she could see little lips of stone rising, forming a railing.

"What the hell?" Nathan muttered, gripping the artifact Nehushtan tightly.

"It's an entrance to hell," Lyta spoke up. "They brought us to the city of the damned…Negari!"

"Negari?" Thurpa asked.

"It was a realm which was thought to be made up by authors in the early twentieth century," Brigid spoke. "A hidden city, ruled by an eternal…queen."

Brigid kicked herself. This was the void entity that Kane had described as his tormentor, the one who'd plucked out his mind, taken it to another plane and tortured him on multiple levels.

"Neekra," Thurpa snapped. "That blood-skinned bitch!"

Brigid nodded. "That was who was spoken of. She is real, unfortunately. And we've encountered her machinations already."

"There's movement," Nathan said. He clicked on a

light, but the beam, despite an intense brightness, could not reach the edge of it.

And still there were movements visible in the gloom beyond, odd flickers of shapes.

Brigid knew that she had the ability to get a closer look at whatever glimmered in the inky blackness. She swiftly tugged her hood up, feeling her long flowing curls bunch against the base of her neck, but it was something that she could endure for the time being. She swiftly adhered the shadow suit's faceplate on, switching to night vision and image magnification.

Immediately, her stomach twisted with revulsion as she spotted the creatures rising from the depths. They whipped out their hands, which stretched out on pseudopods, not arms. Stretching out, hurled like lariats, the hands snapped shut as they gripped the walls. It was an obscene parody of how she'd seen amoeba attack and devour their prey.

Her photographic memory flashed back to the story Nathan had told of his father, Nelson, and Nelson's death. The disappearance of the murderer through a hole that no man with a skeleton could fit recalled a similar "stretchiness."

There were a dozen of the things, and they were moving toward her, Nathan, Thurpa and Lyta as swiftly as they could. Her mouth went dry, but she whipped up the Copperhead and peered through the low-powered scope atop the compact submachine gun. They were quick, but she anticipated the path of one of the beasts and she cut loose with the Copperhead, spitting high-velocity bullets toward it. The rounds slapped into it, and her shadow suit's optics extended, picking up on the thing seemingly blowing apart in chunks.

She pivoted the gun's muzzle, aimed at another and fired.

"What?" Thurpa asked.

"Monsters," Brigid said. She ripped off a burst into the third of the creatures, but even as she did so, she could see the first of her targets reassembling itself. It'd been hurt, yes, but she was firing into gelatin-like bodies that could reassemble themselves.

Thurpa shouldered his rifle and looked through the scope. He let out a grunt of dismay at the image of the newcomers. "Enki help me."

"They're bulletproof," Brigid shouted. "Move!"

Thurpa grimaced and triggered his weapon.

"I said—" Brigid began.

Thurpa glared at her. "That little gun doesn't have the punch this does. I can at least break them up, stun them."

Brigid glanced back and saw that the creatures that Thurpa had struck were down. They still showed signs of life, but the heavier rifle that the Nagah expatriate had used on them had left them stunned and confused.

She glanced after Nathan, who was leading Lyta away as quickly as his legs could carry them both. Thankfully for Brigid, they weren't enhanced by the ancient staff's power. She could catch up. "We both go, now."

Thurpa kept shooting. "Aim for their center line. That seems to disturb and stagger them the most! I'll hold this line as long as I can…."

Brigid grimaced. She took off, realizing that she could not allow Nehushtan to fall into the wrong hands.

Durga and his queen, Neekra, were definitely the *wrong hands*.

She sent a silent prayer of hope to Thurpa, knowing what he was risking for their sakes.

The big rifle kicked hard against Thurpa's shoulder, and he knew that each bullet he put into one of the strange creatures coming up the underworld path bought more yards, more seconds for his newfound friends and allies to get away. He didn't want to think of what horrors would befall him once they got to him, but, dammit, the fallen prince Durga had led him astray, pushed thoughts into his head and brought him to this countryside.

He dumped the spent magazine from his gun, pushed another one home and worked the bolt. Even as he did so, he realized that two of the things had survived his rain of lead. Technically, they'd all survived, but these two had avoided his shots and had not been slowed. They were only thirty feet away, and they showed no sign of slowing down.

Thurpa let out a roar of frustration as he tracked one of the slippery pair of translucent, stretchy foes, firing bullets to chase it down. As he did so, he felt a hand grasp him by the throat. Within moments, he was sailing through the air toward one of the underground horrors. Thurpa tried to scream, but the elongated limb around his throat cut him off. The strength of the creature was such that it pulled him through the air, feet airborne.

Those fingers clutching at his throat were as strong as iron, and he struck the ground behind the pair of gelatinous assailants. Thurpa blinked, struggling to bring his thoughts back into line, to get his limbs to respond to commands.

The two leapers continued on their path, having forgotten the cobra man after they'd unceremoniously dumped him on the ground. He twisted himself, rolling from his back to where he could get his hands and knees beneath him. Even as he did so, a hammer blow struck him between the shoulder blades, and his face was mashed into the ground, dirt digging into his nostrils. He turned his head, exhaling and clearing his airways, but another rubbery paw pressed down on his cheek and neck.

Out of the corner of his eye, Thurpa could see it was one of the horrors. It had fissures through its flesh and cracks on the surface of its skin. It looked vaguely male, but inside bones hung like pieces of fruit in dessert gelatin. His nostrils were assailed with the sickening, ugly stench of copper and salt, a cloying reek of decaying and drying blood.

The creature's face lowered nearer to Thurpa's, and it seemed to sniff.

"No," came the order from another. "She says…no."

Thurpa felt a moment of relief, but even so, the slimy, clammy grip on his neck and face was steely, rigid, unforgiving.

"Lucky," Thurpa's captor growled. "Lucky you."

Thurpa wanted to say something, but he knew better. These creatures had some intellect, but they were following the orders of another. Someone who wanted living captives.

If the shimmering monstrosity hadn't been resting its weight on his shoulders, neck and head, he would have been able to move, to shift the creature's weight atop him, but the thing was either too well balanced on him or it had somehow laid down roots to make any motion on the Nagah's part impossible. Seeing glimmering pseudopods digging into the dirt before his eyes confirmed his second suspicion, and he realized that he was a prisoner, pinioned and helpless.

He watched as translucent legs raced past, heading into the forest after Brigid Baptiste, Nathan Longa and Lyta.

Thurpa's stomach churned with regret that he couldn't protect the young woman.

GRANT HEARD THE RATTLE of gunfire and grimaced. He was separated from his friends and allies by the rift in the earth. Kane was gone, down through the pit, and while he was concerned for his friend, he knew his partner was wearing his shadow suit and had the devil's luck when it came to surviving bad situations and the same devil's cunning when that luck was not enough.

Right now, Grant knew that Brigid and the others were in combat. With what, he couldn't tell, but everything he observed told him that this was not the work of a simple militia, even one with as much manpower and firepower as the Panthers of Mashona. This was more akin to the work of the Annunaki or the Tuatha de Danaan, ancient technology, and perhaps a subterranean city. He'd encountered many such hidden societies. One was lodged within a bubble in the basalt that separated the surface of the earth from its molten, fiery interior, a true lost world of dinosaurs, cast-off pan-terrestrial humanoids and ancient horrors.

Whether in the depths of space or at the center of the world, there were millions of secrets still strewn about the planet in multiple forms, and most of what they had encountered was deadly and dark.

Grant looked up and down the rift between him and his friends, and he saw that there was a tree, tottering with its gnarled roots showing out over the drop-off.

The trunk of the tree was thick enough for him to walk on and long enough to use as a bridge. Running in either direction, looking for a better crossing, would eat up valuable time while his allies fought against the unseen force.

He rushed to the tree and hurled himself at the trunk with all his might. The shadow suit helped protect his shoulder from potential dislocation by the amount of force he'd thrown at it. Dirt broke and cracked, and he listened to the snap of roots.

One blow and he'd loosened an already half-uprooted tree. He immediately wrapped his arms around the trunk and pulled back. The tree rocked toward him, more cracks, more snaps echoing the distant gunfire, reminding him of the countdown he fought against. Grant surged with all his muscle, weight and leverage, and he felt the tree begin to loosen.

Pushing the tree down straight across the chasm wouldn't do much. All it would do was rip out the tree by its roots, and perhaps send his only bridge toppling into the depths of the rift. Toppling the tree "inland" would take the ungraceful roots and make them into a grapnel, then leave the upper branches and trunk to rest on his side of the improvised bridge.

Grant moved nimbly out of the path of the toppling tree, letting it crunch down. Boughs were reduced to splinters if they weren't simply bent out of the path of the falling trunk. There was a crook that he could use to drag the tree out and across the crack in the ground. Using his prodigious strength, he tugged the trunk. Luckily, the bent branches formed runners, taking up much of the weight. With a final powerful tug, he jammed the roots into the far side of the chasm.

He'd aimed the tree right; the roots shoved into the

chunk of ground where half of its roots had been torn out in the splitting of the earth. Grant turned and leaped behind the crook and pushed, throwing all his might into lodging the bridge into the recess on the far side. He then got onto the trunk.

In four strides, he was across his improvised bridge, leaping over the roots and onto the far side just as the roots gave way. Grant glanced back and watched the tree slither off where he'd rested it, sucked down by gravity.

"Kane, Brigid?"

Nothing on the Commtacts. He frowned, realizing that he was alone.

He raced faster to reach Brigid and the others.

Chapter 7

Nathan Longa looked back as the roar of Thurpa's assault rifle died out. His stomach took an ugly flop, and he clutched Nehushtan, the ancient artifact of Moses and King Solomon, tightly until he could feel his knuckles crack. He turned to Lyta.

"Take this stick, and don't let go of it. Run and hide!" Nathan told her.

"What?" Lyta asked as he shoved the staff into her arms.

"Don't be dense," Nathan hissed. "You need to keep this stick out of their hands. It's our only chance right now."

"If it's our only chance, why not *use* it?" Lyta asked.

"Because I've been asking it and asking it for the past five minutes," Nathan growled. "I'm getting no response. But we cannot let those things capture it!"

Nathan pushed her, and the shove made her stumble back three steps. She glared at him, halfway between anger and disappointment. He knew that she was his cousin, but he'd only just met her. His father had barely mentioned her, so she was a stranger. And now he had to trust her with an ancient tool utilized by heroes of myth and legend to battle the worst demons on earth.

Lyta took another step back as Nathan turned and brought up his rifle. Brigid Baptiste was bounding up the game trail they had taken, and she had her gun out and ready for battle. When she saw Nathan standing his ground, she skidded to a halt beside him.

"You're letting her have the stick?" Brigid asked. "Good idea."

"Protect her," Nathan pleaded with the Cerberus archivist. "I'll do my best to slow these things down."

She chewed her upper lip for a second, then nodded. "All right."

Nathan didn't care much for how quickly she acceded to his request, but the woman had shown brilliance and quick thinking. Perhaps she would come up with some ploy that could protect the stave and its new bearer. "Good luck!"

Brigid gave him a pat on the shoulder, then followed after Lyta.

Brigid already had a plan, and that entailed pulling Lyta along toward the pickup truck that had been lent to them. The girl kept up easily despite the ache and torment of the past week. Brigid didn't say it out loud, but she suspected that Nehushtan was speeding Lyta's recovery along.

They reached the truck, and, from there, Brigid opened the passenger side door and pulled out a pair of flexible conduits, entwined against each other and fastened off by metal belts. Lyta looked down at the conduits, then at her own staff. The girl's eyes lit up with instant recognition as Brigid retrieved a long black section of pipe. With one hard shove, she perched the conduit cables atop the pipe, then affixed two bulbous heads on the ends of those conduits, plugging tail ends. Suddenly, a collection of spare parts was assembled into an imperfect version of the artifact. A second bar formed the cross at the top, pushed through the curves in the conduits.

"You planned for this," Lyta said.

Brigid nodded. "I did. This ruse won't work much, but I will give them reason enough to make them believe this is the real deal, giving you time to hide."

"And then what?" Lyta asked.

"Then you try and locate whoever escaped," Brigid ordered. "We've been scattered, and I can't reach anyone."

"It's going to be that easy?" Lyta asked.

"With the staff, yes," Brigid answered. "It's already given you back enough stamina to keep up with us as we ran from those things. It'll give you hints, intuitions."

"It can think?" Lyta pressed, holding the strange staff tighter despite her growing fear of it.

"I don't know what form of sentience it possesses. It could just be an automaton, nothing more than an autopilot, or it could be something much more. It's helped us immensely so far, and it will help you. Now run!" Brigid ordered.

Lyta swallowed as the flame-haired woman made certain she had items in her belt pouches.

She turned, and, despite every emotion telling her she was being a coward, she ran into the forest of the night, leaving Brigid to her task.

Brigid Baptiste knew she didn't have much time, and so she was glad that her faux artifact had been so easy to assemble. Durga and others had shown an interest in the ancient weapon, and the Cerberus warriors all knew that having a false copy would buy them some time and effort.

Brigid just hadn't expected this to occur so soon. She was doubly confounded that the amorphous, pliant monstrosities were so quick and aggressive on the task of bursting from the ground. Certainly, the things had shown properties of the murderer that Nathan had mentioned, but she had not anticipated that the Panthers, or Durga, would have had such swift and easy access to them. And yet the militia brought prisoners for these creatures.

Brigid could only feel a brief taste of relief that they had not encountered these gelatinous beings alongside the Kongamato, the huge mutants whose strength enabled them to weather gunshots, tear steel doors from their hinges and pull the limbs off grown soldiers as if they were mere insects.

Brigid realized that if the murderous abominations were fighting *alongside* the brutal, powerful, *winged* Kongamato, the Zambians would have been exterminated, and she doubted that she and her allies from Cerberus would have fared much better. These creatures broke apart, were stopped and stunned by gunfire, but because of their strange anatomy, they seemed to regather their burst forms and stagger back to life. Her Copperhead at two hundred yards did little to them. Thurpa's rifle proved to be a little better at stunning them, but his gunfire had died out.

Brigid threw a silent prayer to whatever being might be listening that Thurpa had been taken alive, but her stomach churned at the ominous quiet. Nathan's rifle blazed in the distance now, which meant that he saw their opponents, the grim, determined beings who ignored direct hits from bullets and continued on, stretching and bounding through the night, seeking out the living.

At first, the concept of octopus-like abilities among the monsters seemed incongruous to any mythology that Brigid was aware of, but then she thought of all the creatures with seeming preternatural speed, or the ability to cling to walls or disappear in plain sight, as well as apparently being unharmed by most weapons. One thing she could count on was that human perception was unreliable, especially as these entities operated in the darkness. Brigid had only been able to make out their physiology thanks to the advanced optics installed on the faceplates of the shadow suits.

Nathan's rifle now fell silent, and Brigid strained her ears, waiting for any sign that he had suffered a mortal injury. The audio pickups in the hood were nearly as good as the optics, but, thankfully, she didn't hear a death cry or the sound of shredding flesh. That much was good news. But these things seemed to operate on the same scale as vampires, draining blood. Those elongated limbs could also be keenly utilized at strangulation.

The first of the monstrosities bounded into her line of sight, and Brigid "aimed" the false Nehushtan and fired.

What she actually used was a 12-gauge shotgun whose shells were loaded with mini-grenades. It was incorporated into the girth of the pipe, with a trigger on the side. The micro-grenade leaped across the distance between her and the first of the pliant terrors, and when the shell struck, it blasted the creature into a fine mist of mucus and rubbery, flapping skin.

She spotted things falling from the creature's burst form, but she allowed her subconscious mind to sort through the details of her surroundings. The monster's allies were present, and she whipped the muzzle of the improvised grenade launcher toward a second and fired. The miniature grenade speared toward the thing, but its extending pseudopod deflected the shell; the tentacle itself spiraled out of control to the ground. The tumbling high-explosive slug cartwheeled through the night and struck a tree trunk, detonating.

Broken wood and splinters flew wildly, and suddenly Brigid picked up on keening wails of terror among her opponents. Instantly, one part of her mind brought up the common "solution" to a vampire menace: the introduction of a wooden stake or the thorns of certain trees. Given the balloon-like nature of these beings, wooden splinters could be seen as a threat. Another section of her intellect correlated certain resins or the cellulose that made wood so firm and hard having a negative interaction with the biology of these beings.

She was also reminded of the creatures that Kane and Grant had mentioned: mollusk-like creatures in which a sentient "virus" had been trapped. Snot-like octopoids that had not been seen on the planet—horrible things that had also served as parasites on humans once released into the Wiregrass forests of Florida. While it was possible that those octo-slugs could have been a form of submarine life undiscovered even by twentieth-century science, these creatures bore many similarities.

They could have been from the same world.

The Annunaki had deposited those things in an inaccessible ocean-floor research center called the Tongue of the Ocean, one of the deepest places on earth.

For good reason, Brigid mused. The octo-slugs could have been aquatic versions of the standard subterranean species she was dealing with here.

All these thoughts raced through Brigid's burning brain. She was trying to quantify and identify these organisms, find their strengths and weaknesses, but in the forefront, she was all action, thoughts whipping at the speed of light even before she brought up her TP-9 and aimed for the odd, off-colored lumps floating in the soupy carcasses of the beings. She shot a creature through what she assumed was a brain, pumping rounds into it as fast as she could work the trigger.

The vampiric blob squirmed under the impacts, retreating as clouds of murk erupted from the burst sac within its anatomy. As it sought escape, Brigid swung the base of her false Nehushtan around and drove the tent stake base of the staff into what she figured was its heart. Impaled, the gelatinous form let loose a horrific cry, something akin to the most shrill woman's scream she'd ever encountered. The audio pickups were a moment too slow in modulating themselves and dampening the earsplitting wail.

The blob exploded into another spray of viscous gel.

"Staked a vampire through the heart," Brigid mused. "Digs the Vampire Slayer."

She spotted movement and struggled to bring around the faux staff, but extended arms snatched at its length. Brigid lifted her TP-9 and fired at the opponent coming straight toward her, knowing that she couldn't win in a wrestling match against two of these things, maybe not even one.

Brigid shot this attacker through the heart, and that slowed it drastically, but the wounds were nothing like a big long piece of steel—or wood, she amended—piercing its heart. The sudden reflexive spasm of the vampiric creature bought her a moment that allowed her to turn the gun against the two that grasped at the fake Nehushtan.

She shot them, knowing that she couldn't kill them immediately, but her gunfire blazed through them, stunning, disrupting them for a moment. Brigid lunged, grabbing her fake Nehushtan from the weakened tentacles, wresting it free with her leverage and momentum.

So far, so good. Moving with every bit of speed and skill she could muster, she also knew that her reserves of strength were fading. Battling multiple monsters was difficult, energy-consuming.

Even so, Brigid was counting Lyta's steps. Measuring her stride. Imagining how far she could have gone.

She'd bought plenty of time. And she'd made these things assume that she was armed with a powerful weapon, the very artifact that they'd been sent for. A stick with thunderous power, which had proved to be the death of two of their kind.

A pseudopod whipped around her neck, the tentacle pulling tight on her throat. The non-Newtonian nature of her shadow suit took the sudden flux of pressure and stiffened against it. She wouldn't be strangled, now with the polymers having transformed into an iron collar to protect her neck and windpipe. She was lifted bodily from the ground and pulled into the darkness. Another limb lashed out, grasping her wrist.

The mollusk vampires reached for her, a dozen tentacles snatching at her, grabbing her other wrist, her ankles, around her thighs and upper arms, about her waist. Brigid twisted, pulling with all her might, trying to tug herself free, but those odd limbs had suckers on them. She could feel the pokes and prods of dozens of tiny needles, trying to push through the shadow suit, and she grit her teeth, pulling herself to freedom.

No good. While the suit provided protection from the crushing grip of the monsters, their combined might was just too much. She was immobilized, held fast.

A pseudopod slapped against her faceplate. With a yank, the seam between her hood and the rest of the suit parted. Another tug and the cool night air was on her face and her golden-red curls tumbled free in the breeze.

In the darkness, she may have felt some consolation that the creatures were not visible, that she could not see the gelatinous horrors seizing her. But Brigid's photographic memory added in details that she'd noticed in the battle while she'd had the suit's faceplate optics. A smooth tentacle rubbed against her cheek, and she recoiled from it.

"For our queen," one uttered, its voice coming from nothing resembling a human mouth. It was a warbling tone, air burped past a gaping hole, which was as alien to a vertebrate as anything on earth.

The tentacle wasn't slimy, as she'd imagined, but soft, like the skin formed on top of a pudding, slightly tacky, since it was in contact with air. And it was cool, unnaturally so. These things possessed no internal body heat. Brigid pulled on her arms, trying to wrest free again, but nothing happened except that the shadow suit's seams between her sleeves and gloves came apart. That was how strong their grip was.

"No fight," the horrible voice said. "You live."

Brigid swallowed hard. She didn't know which unnerved her more, the relative sentience of these things, or that they were following orders to take her alive. She also wondered if Nathan and Thurpa were still among the living, especially since it was highly likely that they wouldn't give up without a fight.

"Comply?" the thing asked.

"I will comply," she answered.

"Good." Their ability to speak more than one syllable was problematic, but it wasn't from a lack of vocabulary. It was simply a matter of anatomy that limited them to terse phrases.

"Bros..." It was another of the things, one without a tendril in the group that restrained Brigid, even though those long, sinewy limbs were no longer clutching her as tightly.

She was defeated, disarmed. No guns, no belt pouches of explosives and no faux Nehushtan. Just herself.

Brigid Baptiste, however, still had her wits and her incredible wealth of knowledge, an eye for detail second to none. They'd only stripped away the merest of tools that she'd brought with her.

The real weapon was her brain, but she didn't want them to know that. They would have no clue about the kind of power she really had.

"Bros," the thing said again. It was calling its brothers, and they turned their attention toward it, though none had a head with which to turn, per se. Brigid squinted, trying to pick up the figures in the shadows now that her light amplification was gone.

"Bodies," came multiple grumbles.

"Later!" the one who'd spoken to Brigid snapped.

Brigid smirked. She could tell by the gibbering excitement among the gelatinous monstrosities that they were excited at the presence of corpses.

Her mind pulled up "facts" about vampires.

In medieval times, and closer to the present, when a vampire was suspected, the freshly dead were dug up. When a corpse appeared not only too fresh, but *flushed* and *bloated with blood,* the townsfolk knew that they had their vampire. They staked and decapitated the corpse, ensuring its eternal death.

These creatures, as much liquid as anything else, loved wearing the bodies of the dead, she figured. The bloated with blood bodies were actually places where these vampires nested for the night. Sometimes, they might even have been a form of armor, or at least a disguise, a means of moving about the world of humans.

As those bits of information turned over, calculated, digested by her intellect, Brigid had a new idea of what these creatures truly were, what they were capable of. She smiled, even though she was their prisoner. She was guided back to the subterranean entrance by the creatures. Nathan and Thurpa waited there, bound, heads hung low, equal parts exhaustion and defeat, sadness and embarrassment.

They were alive. That was all that mattered to Brigid right now. The bruises on their egos would actually prove even more useful in surging them from this emotional and physical nadir. Shame could quickly be turned into anger, and anger into the will to fight. These two young men had battled the hopeless odds of Warlord Gamal's hideous Kongamato, and they would be spurred to take on these vampiric horrors.

Brigid's intellect brought up another point.

The prisoners had been left to the point of near starvation and dehydration. The semiliquid beings would be able to utilize their forms more easily. The nearly dead prisoners would be grabbed, taken over, consumed and subsumed to form new hulls for themselves. That was the point of the death march, and Brigid and her allies had arrived just in time to save them, to spare them the horrific fate of these things injecting their gelatinous essence into their bodies.

Brigid didn't know how terrible that would have been, but considering the volume of the amorphous beasts, and the fact that what remaining fluids and organs within the body would not fit…

The mental image of her brain bursting through her ears, nostrils, mouth, even tear ducts…that was a grisly fate.

Brigid fought the urge to shudder.

Even when she saw the tall, hulking form of Grant stagger into view between two of the bodiless vampires.

"Grant," she subvocalized, hoping that her Commtact could connect her with him.

Nothing. Grant's Commtact plate was in place, and she could feel her own.

Someone had jammed them.

Brigid's lip curled.

Austin Fargo was around. He'd interfered in their communications once before, utilizing the odd nano-machines that had become a part of his brain. Now they were deaf and quite likely blind. Cerberus redoubt would have already known that they'd lost contact with them.

Cerberus Away Team Beta would likely be on standby for any other form of threat, but one thing that Kane and Lakesh agreed on was that having both Beta and Alpha Teams in one place was not a good idea. If one team was overwhelmed, the other would be able to protect Cerberus and engage in battling threats to the world on its own. If both teams were wiped out, there would be no fighting team trained and available to respond to emergencies.

Certainly, the Tigers of Heaven, the warriors of Aten, even the Gear Skeletons of New Olympus could be enlisted, but, ultimately, they didn't have the concentrated experience and training in dealing with the likes of the Annunaki overlords or other threats of their ilk. Even Domi had nearly died when the mad Tuatha de Danaan Maccan had attacked Cerberus redoubt while wielding the Hand of Nadhua.

Brigid had no delusions of her, Grant's or Kane's infallibility, but she did know that they had forty-eight hours to effect their own escape. She knew that she was already picking up clues and information about these horrific creatures. As well, Lyta was free, armed with the real Nehushtan. Grant looked a little scuffed up. His shadow suit's top was torn off, and he stood, shirtless, in the dark.

Grant nodded to Brigid, his forehead wrinkled with concern.

No sign of Kane. And no communications signal.

Kane did not die easily. He still roamed free. And Lyta had escaped with an artifact that had already reached halfway across the planet to find the man once before.

Brigid knew how to kill these monsters. She'd already killed two of them.

They had a chance.

Things were dark now, but Brigid held the spark of hope.

The four people entered the underworld, accompanied by creatures of myth and horror.

Chapter 8

Kane spotted a faint glow a hundred yards away. It was the only form of illumination. He'd left his compact flashlight off in order to stay hidden from anyone else in the underground cavern and to preserve the rechargeable batteries. He directed himself mainly by running his fingers along the stone railing. When he actually saw what was across the chasm, he knelt by the wall and peered across.

There was a single torch among a group of many. He cursed not having the faceplate on his shadow suit, but, even from this distance, the height and breadth of Grant's backlit frame was unmistakable. Kane frowned.

The glimmer of firelight off Brigid Baptiste's hair also indicated that everyone who didn't tumble down into a split in the ground had been picked up by the enemy who called this subterranean realm home. He couldn't get more than a hint of the form of their captors, but he *did* recognize the silhouette of Thurpa. There was only one more human shape, and, considering that all four walked under their own ability, Kane calculated that either Nathan or Lyta had escaped.

Unfortunately, the bastards seemed to have captured Nehushtan; one of the captors wielded the ancient artifact. Kane gritted his teeth.

Neekra undoubtedly wanted to get a hold of that artifact…

Wait, Baptiste had made a fake, Kane remembered. He glanced at the ground again as they trundled down the distant walkway. He couldn't tell from this distance, but Brigid and Grant seemed to be calmly going along with their captors. Neekra's minions, whoever or whatever they were, didn't seem to exert any control over them, but his partners did look bound. Kane set his jaw and checked back the way he'd come. There was an entrance on the far side of the yawning gap between himself and the others. He peered over the rock ledge, keeping his profile low so as not to give away his position.

Below, deep in the tenebrous pit, was a single sliver of light spilling through a doorway.

Someone who needs vision is down there, Kane thought. Durga? Fargo? Some other pawn of Neekra?

I'll figure that out when I get down there, Kane promised himself.

Even as he was curious about what was at the very bottom of this chimney, Kane kept his eye on his captive allies. Right now he needed a way down, and Kane wasn't certain of the path hewn into the wall of the hole. If he had the light amplification optics from his shadow suit, he'd have been able to see the layout. He didn't know if they were all on one spiral or if there were multiple planes, especially given the gradual incline of the path under his feet.

If he moved too quickly, he might end up running into the group ahead, and while he would conceivably have a chance in a fight with the captors, that they'd taken Brigid and Grant was a telling sign Kane would be outnumbered and outclassed. As things stood, they were currently unharmed, which meant that Durga or

Neekra wanted to know more about them and perhaps get hold of the artifact that Brigid had mocked up.

Kane also knew that there was little control men such as Durga possessed when it came to boasting and gloating over a defeated foe. There had been plenty of opportunities missed by Kane's opponents when they should have simply blown his brains out rather than suffer him to live, break free and escape. Perhaps it was a delusion of power, or maybe it was the need for the approbation of those they defeated, but Kane was still alive.

Unfortunately, more than enough of those powerful enemies still lived, as well. Durga among them, despite the outcome of their initial battle, the detonation of a fuel-air explosion that overwhelmed the enhanced abilities and added biomass that had rendered the Nagah prince a superhuman. Kane also tried to forget that he'd actually put his life and mind on the line to bring the murderous being *back* to health.

I may have been too merciful, Kane thought, but then he remembered that Durga had saved Kane while they'd invaded the cloning facility that produced Kongamato. The Annunaki threshold gave them the ability to transmit their bodies into the distant facility, send out the control signal for them to return to their nest and then detonate the laboratory, turning the place into a gigantic firebomb and then a tomb to bury the few survivors.

The plan was simple. Follow the group that kept his friends prisoner. Spy on them. Evade the security this place possessed; then put together a break-out plan.

Simple. Kane remembered something Brigid had once told him. *Simple is not easy. It's simple to lift the pyramid, but nearly impossible to apply the right force. It's easy to digest an apple, but the biochemical pro-*

cesses involved took millions of years to develop, and a man could starve before he could even finish the genetic and chemical codes to do so.

In other words, putting tasks into terms such as *easy* or *simple* was mental busywork. Kane moved, trying to keep up around the curve. It wasn't difficult for him to follow the rail of the stone pathway he trod on, and the procession of prisoners wasn't moving too quickly, so he could keep their torchlight in view easily.

Even so, Kane kept his pace slow and his profile low. If he could see them this "easily," then there was the same chance that they could spot him, notice his movement behind them. He still could not make out the details of the things that held his friends captive, so he didn't know if they were human or not.

Kane didn't have many doubts about the nature of his enemies, or their access to things that were more than human. He also had been paying attention when Brigid spoke of the potential for vampires, as she'd gone over suspected abilities they possessed, especially ones that seemed logical. Unfortunately, without getting close enough to these things that they could more readily notice *him,* Kane had no idea of their anatomy.

Not knowing the capabilities of your opponents was a sure path to being overwhelmed and killed.

Then he stopped. He heard the scrape of a foot on dust-fine gravel.

It took everything in his will to prevent spinning around and firing a shot from his .45 at the being behind him. A single gunshot would bring enemies running. Instead Kane's hand dropped to the handle of his combat knife in its sheath.

If only the opposition hadn't already called ahead, alerting its masters to Kane's presence....

LYTA HEARD THE EXPLOSIONS, heard the gunfire. When it finally died out, cut off swiftly, she clutched the black staff tightly. She could feel its warmth and an odd sensation, as if things crawled on its surface. She looked down at it, but there was not enough light for her to see the ebony skin of the artifact.

They called it Nehushtan, and it resembled the caduceus, an international symbol of health and doctors, at least at first blush. Lyta had seen enough of the medical symbology to wonder at the change in its name. Even as she handled the staff, the two heads of the snakes wound about it seemed bent out of shape. Had she damaged it while scrambling for cover?

The heads, once separate, now were pressed against each other. She wanted to slap at it, try to knock it back into alignment, but as soon as the urge arose, she was frozen in place. She could hear the horrors taking Brigid prisoner, alive and unharmed.

She recognized their voices, and noticed how inhuman they appeared. Lyta felt the force holding her in stasis release, but she remained quiet and still.

How close could those things be? Lyta felt as if she'd run for hundreds of yards.

The darkness seemed to fade, and she could see far more clearly, as if it was growing lighter. Of course, it was still the middle of the night, and there was no sun in the sky. However, the moon and stars glowed with a ferocity she'd never experienced before.

She returned her attention to the staff in her hands.

"You're doing this—aren't you?" she whispered.

The artifact didn't speak, or think, but she felt it warm where she touched it. She grew calmer.

Lyta listened to Brigid surrender to the creatures; she could hear them across what must have been two hundred yards. She followed the movement as they retreated, obviously heading back toward the hole in the ground from which the odd creatures had come.

Lyta followed, staying back and trying not to make any noise. She found that it was oddly easy not to disturb the undergrowth. Her steps came much more surely now, and no twigs broke; no stems crackled as she walked through the forest. It was an eerie, unnerving silence that had come down around her, made all the more strange by the fact that she could hear almost everything around her. The universe was painted across her mind's eye in sonar images.

No wonder she didn't want anyone else getting a hold of you, Lyta thought toward the staff. Even so, she continued slowly, carefully. It was almost as if she were on an autopilot, aware of what was around her with uncanny hearing and vision, knowing where she had to go, but scarcely needing to concentrate. It was as if she were a puppet, but she couldn't feel the influence of marionette strings guiding her.

Closing with the subterranean cavern entrance, she slowed to a halt. The others were prisoners, too, the giant named Grant, her distant cousin, Nathan, the snake-man, Thurpa. None of them showed any sign of distress, though the enhanced vision granted by Nehushtan allowed her to make out scuffs, bruises, torn clothing on all of them.

Brigid's uniform was disheveled, but the creatures had only stripped her of the all-concealing hood. Grant, on the other hand, was bare chested. Sheets of muscle rippled beneath his dark pelt of chest hair. Oddly, he still had one glove on; everything else had been pulled off him.

It was the right-hand glove, and she seemed to remember that Grant was one of the pair who carried some form of high-tech forearm holster there. That was gone. Only part of the sleeve and the glove remained where it'd been shorn from him. The creatures were far from stupid, having the presence of mind to strip their prisoners of weaponry and equipment.

There was no sign of the other man, a slightly smaller but no less powerful-seeming white man who'd also had a forearm holster for the amazing folding gun that they'd stripped from Grant. His name was Kane. At that thought, Lyta felt the urge to look away from the small squad of rubbery monstrosities, and she cast her gaze in the another direction.

Her instincts kicked into gear, telling her that the ancient artifact wanted her to head that way. Lyta felt torn for a moment. This cavern, and the slope that extended downward from its mouth, was in a direct line of descent to wherever the monsters came from, and where her newfound friends were being taken.

Kane. The name repeated in her mind, beckoning her in the direction she now wanted to go, despite her observation of the underground marauders and their prisoners. As soon as the name popped up again in her brain, she began walking. The staff, just like Brigid had told her, was giving her the direction to find whoever was free, and it was the man who was built like a muscular wolf.

Lyta moved with a silent grace and purpose of movement. Once more, her footfalls were silent, coming down in just the right spots and not creating anything more than the soft rustle of a breeze on a blade of grass. Whatever magic this staff worked, it was something far beyond her experience, and she was a young woman who had an interest in learning, educating herself in the ways of science, her intellect ever reaching out for more knowledge.

The fact that she thought of the staff as "magic" stunned her. Lyta was a practical person, a believer in rational explanation rather than mythology. And, yet, magic was not so outré now that she'd not only looked a hybrid of man and cobra in the eye, but had seen the abominations who had taken Brigid and her allies captive. She closed her eyes and took a breath, trying to dispel the crazed superstitions that lurked in the darkest reaches of her intellect, but the reality of her situation was that *some* legends and lore had a basis in reality. This was science, but it was science that operated on an entirely different level from what she knew. She'd read about the theories of things such as time travel and concepts even beyond that—multiple universes, quantum physics—but those were terms that were so far beyond human technology that they might as well have been fiction in a novel rather than reality. And yet she was here, experiencing the stuff firsthand.

Lyta finally reached another hole, one that was large but not as big as the massive cavern that could take a group of ten easily through its entrance. This was slimmer; perhaps two people standing shoulder to shoulder would fill it completely. Even Lyta, at five foot nine inches, needed to stoop to avoid bumping her head against the entrance. She levered the artifact sideways so that she could fit its entire length through the cave.

Once more, she was surprised at how much she could see; her eyes adapted to the murk with uncanny quickness. She remembered reading that the human eye was able to see only 3 percent of the entire electromagnetic spectrum. Otherwise, the universe was invisible to people. Lyta admitted that made sense. The air she breathed was invisible, and yet it was real. It had weight, it had pressure, it had texture when she ran her hand through it at speed. It could even move of its own accord.

If air was invisible to the naked eye, there were far more things in the universe than what she could imagine. Nehushtan had granted her vision beyond the norm, and she was thankful for that, even as she walked down the corkscrew incline and emerged into the open, able to stand with the staff standing on its pointed end.

Below, in the distance, she picked up movement. She could see the glowing torch of the group who had the four newcomers prisoner. Lyta's eyes picked them up quickly and easily. Even though they were a hundred yards distant, as she focused, she could make out details of the rubbery-skinned things who held them captive.

They were odd, hulking figures, with most of their mass in their shoulders and upper chests. They didn't have defined separate heads like humans; rather faces were embedded in the bulbous mounds of torso between the creatures' shoulders. Their limbs were long and slender in appearance, at least in comparison to the rest of their frames, but she could see that their arms and legs had the same thickness of a grown man's arm. They probably also appeared more slender to Lyta by dint of their proximity to the mammoth Grant. She was surprised that their legs, translucent and slim, could hold up the rest of their bodies, but for some reason they didn't look as if they actually had that much weight in them.

As she scanned them, there was a movement out of the corner of her eye. Lyta turned, and, as she focused her vision, the artifact zoomed her in on the man's face. It was Kane.

He seemed to be two or three loops around the corkscrew down, which made her wonder if all the circles descending the capped "chimney" they were in were connected. Lyta concentrated, trying to pay attention to the grade of descent, to see where they would go out of sight on the far wall and where the path would emerge. It took her three minutes to figure it out, especially as she watched the prisoner group go into one entrance and then appear again lower.

There were two different paths twisting around the subterranean atrium. Looking down, she could see where both ended up on the ground floor. Lyta also noticed a small assemblage of buildings, one of which was lit from within, occupied. She could hear whispers, but these were out of range of even her advanced hearing. She also heard the scuff of feet on the path. Lyta mentally traced, and saw that Kane was going down the same ramp she was. She needed to get to him.

Brigid had told her to do so, and, so far, the damned stick was actually pointing her in the right direction, even going so far as to shine a light in the darkness that only Lyta could see. She hurried along, taking ground-eating strides. Her feet were bare, so she didn't have to worry about the clomp of heavy boot soles on the flag-stones of the ramp. She did wonder at the slap of her steps, but those remained quiet, as well.

It took her little time to catch up with Kane. She eventually slowed to where he remained crouched at the stone railing, peering toward the mixed group of captors and prisoners in the distance. As quiet and stealthy as she was, though, her footsteps less than whispers even to the artifact-boosted hearing she possessed, Kane suddenly reached down to his belt for a knife. His movements were swift, and he whirled, facing her in an instant, gleaming steel rising toward her.

Lyta blinked, her conscious mind gone blank, and

with a suddenness that stunned her, the head of the staff came down on Kane's wrist, driving it to the flagstones at their feet. Kane grimaced, glaring blindly in the dark, but that was only for a moment. Kane stopped fighting against her and Nehushtan, and she relaxed the pressure on his arm. He turned his hand around and gripped the shaft of the artifact along with her.

His eyes went from unfocused darkness to staring at her.

"We haven't met formally," Lyta spoke up. "I'm Lyta K'Wonga."

"Nathan's cousin. A variant on Longa?"

"Yes," Lyta returned. "The main language around here is English, but each of the tribes within the two nations have their own dialects."

"The Longa clan have traveled some," Kane mused.

Lyta looked down at the stick. "It might have something to do with this."

"I figured as much. This staff has one hell of a heritage," Kane said.

For an instant, she had a mental flash. At once, it resembled Kane—tall and powerful, dark haired with slender features—and yet his clothing was different. He wore a black leather fencing vest, a tough canvas shirt, folded-down thigh-length boots and a slouch hat. Kane's belt was adorned with ancient pistols and a fine blade, akin to the ones that Lyta had seen fencers use, the ones with bent steel forming a protective basket for the fingers of the wielder.

In an instant, the image was gone, and she saw Kane once more in the eerie full light that apparently could only be seen by the two people holding Nehushtan.

"This isn't the normal spectrum we're seeing in. Our brains are translating it as the normal spectrum, but we're probably looking at something akin to infrared or ultraviolet. The colors aren't real," Kane pointed out.

Lyta nodded. "So, there's no glow giving us away."

Kane shook his head. "By the way, my name is Kane. No first name."

"That's unusual," Lyta returned.

"It's how I was raised. When I was growing up, boys who were in the Magistrate program were stripped of their other names in order to reduce their individuality," Kane explained. "It almost worked."

"Almost," Lyta repeated. "No more Magistrates?"

"No more villes utilizing Magistrates. We're still around, and many of us are actually still protecting the communities we've settled into," Kane said. "Grant is also a former Magistrate."

"Hard to limit his individuality," Lyta noted. "He's a large man."

Kane glanced to the side and saw his friend in the distance. "He's a good man, too. We need to free my friends."

"I know," Lyta agreed. "I just hope this stick is enough."

"I'm not going to rely on the staff," Kane said. "I've been to this dance before. While the stick can help, I'll rely on my wits."

Lyta nodded.

Kane looked away again, eyeing the strange beings who held his friends prisoner. He studied them, looking for weaknesses.

Lyta felt her blood chill at the Magistrate's intensity.

The rubbery horrors were going to pay; that much Lyta could tell. She didn't need a magic staff to see the raw, bloody hatred in his eyes.

Chapter 9

Grant was not a man given to ebullience; indeed he was infamous for his grouchy attitude. His current frown, though, was a false mask. These rubbery little freaks with the stretchy limbs and bodies that seemed composed of balloons and gel were strong and fast, but he had swiftly come to find their weakness. He'd actually killed one of them before the elastic bastards brought him down.

Grant noticed they had amazing healing abilities and were able to regather themselves when punctured. Their skin was not very tough, and they had less than a third of the weight of a full-grown man. Even with that minimal body mass, their elongated limbs aided them and gave them superior leverage when battling him hand to hand. There were two masses of darker fluid inside of them, and, judging from the positions on their ersatz humanoid frames, they correlated to a brain and a heart.

Grant shot through those "brains" and "hearts" with the powerful Sin Eater. But despite some disruption and spreading coloration within the fluid mass forms, the creatures recovered. Grant had ripped one entirely up the middle, but the dry, stretchy flesh had closed back on itself and the masses of odd internal organs had re-assembled. Even so, he could tell that the creatures had a window of vulnerability when struck in those areas.

They were stunned, and that bought Grant moments to fight the others off.

Only one of them had died, never to recover from the injuries he'd inflicted. Grant picked the thing up by its torso, uprooting its "feet" pods from the ground. With a powerful surge, Grant aimed the creature at a tree trunk with a snapped branch on it.

Speared through the heart, the creature had unleashed a horrible keening wail that had made Grant's teeth vibrate inside his skull. However, the death cry was its last issuance, and the body had burst apart and flowed into the dirt, unable to rise again.

That mortal howl, however, had pinned Grant's feet to his position. Pseudopods and tentacles had snapped out, lashing at his arms and chest. With every ounce of his might, Grant had fought to tear himself free. Rather than breaking the grasp of the semifluid beings, his shadow suit had split.

Panels of the shadow suit had fallen away with each shrug of Grant's mighty muscles. When his bare flesh was exposed, the creatures had seized him even more solidly. When their skin touched his, tiny grabbing needles pierced him, adhering both together, and a numbing toxin reduced his strength. Grant had pulled and tugged, fighting for as long as he could with the sedative flowing through his body. He couldn't shake their incredible grip, a sign that the needle pricks were anchors that could not be broken even by a man as strong as Grant.

Finally, Grant was still. The toxins didn't interfere with his ability to breathe, and his senses were clear. And he could stand; he was just unable to pull and thrash against his imprisonment. He was already putting together the truth of what these things could and could not do.

There was something with either complete transfix-ion by a spear, or perhaps the nature of wood, that caused these creatures to burst, incapable of reforming. Maybe it had something to do with the two major "organs" in their bodies.

Either way, he knew one weakness was there, per-haps two. He looked at Brigid. Her uniform appeared in less distress than his, but then he doubted that she had the raw bulk and strength to have caused such rend-ing and tearing in conflict with the sticky creeps. She had tears in the shadow suit and it was missing panels and parts.

And, like him, she was without the hood and face-plate that would have made seeing in this darkness a piece of cake. As it was, the torch, a token that could be considered an amenity to those without night vi-sion, actually made things worse for him and the oth-ers. The proximity of the flare at the end of the torch was enough to make all four people squint, and if it was bright enough to make them squint, then it was bright enough to make their pupils contract. And with those contracted, they couldn't gather any of the ambi-ent light, even if it reflected off faraway objects. There could have been a hundred of the rubbery freaks stand-ing just outside the spill of light from the fire, but with the proximity of the torch, they were swimming in an inky sea of blackness, eyes automatically shielding themselves from the blaze on a stick.

Grant almost felt dejected about the current situa-tion, but then a dim sliver opened in the distance. It was either a tent flap or an opening door. The weak band of brightness was immediately eclipsed by the shadow of a figure. Grant blinked, trying to accustom himself to the dim conditions, but as soon as his eyelids peeled back, the torch caused his eyes to react, and he was blind to anything ten feet from his nose.

But the very fact that someone had come out of a lit room could mean only one thing.

The prisoners were being received by the master of their current captors. Grant's lips formed into a tight smirk. He was in store for a grand bit of self-aggrandizement, gloating and posturing by the villain or villainess of this particular hole in the ground. Grant took a deep breath and made a wish for it to be a villainess. After all, if he was going to listen to tired old boasts he'd heard a million times before, he'd prefer it from the luscious lips of a sultry queen bitch like Lilitu or the new devil slut, Neekra.

There was a husky, feminine chuckle.

"Your dreams have come true, Grant," came the soft, silky words from the wide-hipped, long-haired woman who entered the periphery of the firelight from the torch. She drew closer to him, and Grant could see her in the flesh. Kane had described the amorphous void witch as ultimately being a curvy, full-figured female, and Grant could see the dangerous swoop of her hips and the gentle jostling of pendulous breasts, unhindered by a stitch of clothing.

Grant sized her up. She was nearly six feet in height, with long black hair and skin that, trick of the flames or not, seemed as red as any devil's. He looked her in the eyes and saw only two deep voids of shadow, not even a glint of reflection of the torch she looked into. Lips large, soft, sensual, turned up into a smile.

"I'm glad you approve, Grant," Neekra spoke again.

"Keep rooting around in my thoughts, honey," Grant snarled, but his scowl quickly returned to a smirk.

Neekra stepped forward, brushing her fingers along

his skin. "Your thoughts are the only thing you can get up right now, darling."

"The paralytic toxin is the only thing protecting you," Grant replied. "I'm fairly certain that the rest of my friends feel the same way as me. Except for Brigid. No boner for her, just cold-blooded hate."

Neekra pursed her lips, her kiss looking like the flower of a rose, eyebrows wrinkled in mock hurt. She even let loose a soft purr of a pout before stepping away from him to address all the prisoners.

"Welcome to the city of Negari."

Grant sneered. "Maybe you could turn on the lights. All I smell is ass, and all I see is some bitch too dumb to throw on some pants."

Neekra shook her head.

"He's got a point," Brigid spoke up. "Frankly, everything about this city is boring. Including its queen."

Neekra narrowed those midnight-black "eyes" into slits of concentrated hatred. "I am not concerned with your boredom, Baptiste."

Brigid reacted to the inflection of her name. Grant could feel it, too. It sounded exactly like Kane, especially when he was in a short-tempered mood when referring to her.

That meant this woman knew everything about them that Kane did, at least as far as her captivity of Kane a few days before went. Grant pursed his lips.

Of course, she seemed to be able to skim thoughts off the surface, and Grant realized that any of his thoughts to date, any plans percolating in between his ears, were hers to spy on.

"Well, hello, honey," Neekra said, stepping closer to Thurpa. "Good to see you again. I wondered why you didn't show up with Durga."

"Get stuffed, bitch," the young Nagah man said.

She cupped his cheek and leaned in closer. To his credit, Thurpa tried to lean away. Unfortunately, the numbing toxin that made Grant's arms hang like limp string kept him from moving much. Grant glowered at the scene, and he felt his fists clench at the end of his insensate arms. He could even hear the pop of tendons, and then the rubbery beasts slapped his shoulders, his biceps, his forearms again, and his fingers loosened.

"No getting cross with me," Neekra whispered in Grant's direction.

"Then quit bullying the boy," Grant returned.

Neekra released Thurpa's cheek and strode toward him. As she grew closer, Grant could smell the stink of rot on her breath. He tried to place the all-too-familiar odor, but it took him a moment to get it. She stank of dried, coagulated blood. He glanced at the things on either side of him and was able to place them, as well.

"Your things are made of blood, aren't they?" Grant asked.

"Smart man," Neekra replied. "They're not *strictly* blood, but they are close enough to revitalize a corpse. In fact, lads, you found some bodies up above?"

There were burbling, guttural sounds that had no right resembling any language spoken by a human, but Grant realized that he didn't need to understand. Their thoughts were apparent to their mistress, and that was all that they needed to have understood.

"You're figuring out so many secrets. Aren't you, big man?" Neekra asked. She ran her fingers up his naked chest, and he could feel his skin prickling, growing number with her icy touch. Just casual contact between her and him spread the same numbing toxins to Grant, and he shuddered at the growing discomfort stitching from his navel to his clavicle.

"Not casual, actually," Neekra said. Her whispers were the promise of seduction, despite the bone-chilling numbness that made his chest tighten to the point that his back ached. "I'm doing this all so you know what this *devil slut* is capable of, even wrapped in this puny excuse for flesh."

Grant's jaw ground tight. He glared at her, but instantly he put himself into the Zen mind-set of *kyudo*. His thoughts were gone. It wasn't the easiest state to attain, but he'd pushed himself into it. All that ran through his mind were sensations, sounds, sights, smells. He was in the moment, thinking of neither the past nor the future. Nothing was put into phrases or words, except for the meditation-like concentration.

Grant wasn't new to meditation, but his martial arts training alongside Shizuka had helped him achieve such a clear, unrestrained mental state with greater facility.

Neekra wasn't going to pry anything out of his brain in the foreseeable future.

Unfortunately, that kind of protection wasn't going to be afforded to Thurpa or Nathan.

So, whatever luck that the Cerberus group could rely on, it was going to have to come from a blindside. Grant fought every instinct to turn his thoughts to the man he called his brother.

PERCHED ON THE RAILING, still eighty feet from the bottom of the shaft, Kane peered down on the assemblage, his vision augmented by his contact with the pre-Biblical artifact they knew as Nehushtan. Kane was a little perturbed at the change within the staff's appearance. The twin snakes had shifted in their relation to each other, and now with the way they had combined what had once been two serpentine heads was a cat, one with all-too-human eyes. The appearance of it stank of ancient blasphemy, and its glassy stare unsettled Kane.

The change in mien, however, made the staff more familiar to Kane on a subconscious level. He recalled his discomfort at an earlier incarnation's reception of the staff as a thing of black magic, but only initially. It also was sleeker, seemingly taller and more adapted to use as a mere walking stick, albeit one that could be pressed into service as a spear or club if necessary. Perhaps it was Nehushtan's gambit to disguise itself, meaning that Brigid Baptiste *had* succeeded in putting together her imitation stick.

Not that Kane should have been surprised. The girl, Lyta, stated that Brigid had pressed the original artifact into her hands and bid her to escape. She'd stayed behind and fought against the pursuers, at least until she had picked the time to surrender.

Kane dropped down, listening to Grant and Neekra go back and forth. They'd been in these straits so often that they had the ability to seem bored and unimpressed while at the same time picking up as many details as their enemies would accidentally provide. So far, there wasn't much that Grant or Brigid gave away. In lieu of Kane's presence, Grant took the lead, bumping egos against the thing shaped like a woman.

The "blasphemy" of Nehushtan and its change were second only to that which he could see in the entity of Neekra. It was as if he were looking at a double exposure, the woman as she wished to appear, and then the poor thing that she had usurped, hijacked, demolished.

She unfortunately had to look like former Panthers of Mashona Warlord Gamal, standing naked because

Neekra felt as if she were wearing enough "layers" by sheathing herself in the skin of a man. Kane grimaced at the knowledge that she'd taken over the man, despite all his crimes.

What was worse was that he could see, through the power of Nehushtan, that Gamal was still in there, still conscious, still alive and in terrible agony because she'd taken every muscle, every bone, every cell and wrenched them out of place to change him from a tall, muscular man into a voluptuous, sexy woman.

She had not been gentle in changing Gamal's plumbing.

And then, to rub salt in the new wound between his legs, Neekra had tried out her sexual organs with Durga. The tales and scars on the current queen of the Nagah, Hannah, were evidence that Neekra had little regard for her body. Or maybe she didn't *feel* the body the same way a normal human would. She'd taken up residence in Gamal's meat and bones, but "feeling" through him must have been like interacting with the world in a biohazard uniform—numb, detached. And, thus, by exposing her puppet to the kind of cruelty and ferocity that only the brutal Durga could provide, she was able to *feel* her lover.

And for that to happen, she needed to override that filter, subjecting Gamal's carcass to enormous stresses and agonies.

Or perhaps, what she considered pleasure *was* agony.

Kane shuddered at that thought.

Neekra had played with him, forcing him to endure psychic horrors that left him emotionally exhausted. Had the trauma she'd inflicted on him in her psychic attacks been one iota of reality, he didn't think that his body could have survived the shock.

Kane had dealt with those who had warped perceptions of right and wrong, of pleasure and pain, of good and evil. But he recalled the alien feeling of how she was inside his brain, how he'd barely been able to conceive of her until she grew more and more willing to give him a form to imagine.

What if that was just a ruse, a false face?

What if she'd crafted that just to lure him in, to provide something, someone to sympathize with?

It wouldn't be the first time that someone had utilized arcane means to draw the attention of the Cerberus redoubt group. So baited, the explorers were drawn in by a vulgar trap merely for the purposes of eliminating them, as had been attempted by the barons or their more evolved forms, the Annunaki overlords. However, other times they had been pulled in, as a tool, a blunt instrument utilized to smash a rival, as in the case of Lilitu's attempt to eliminate her brothers.

That fiasco had ended with a gigantic, living starship swatted from the heavens above, and the deaths of at least a few of them; others had been scattered to the winds, ultimately leaving the earth even more vulnerable to a son of their leader, Enlil.

Kane stilled his thoughts.

Neekra had proved to be a powerful psychic entity. She'd literally trapped him and Durga into a shared consciousness, isolated from control of their bodies. Together, they had been seemingly cast across a universe, into the space between dimensions, but it was all a ruse, a waste of mental energy and time. And where Kane had been told by Brigid Baptiste that dreams, no matter their depth and their seeming duration, occurred only within a few seconds of hyperkinetic brain activity, Kane realized that he had felt the length of centuries as he'd struggled across the faux multiverse constructed by Neekra. And then he'd suffered agonies across more millennia when they had burst the illusion and been drawn into psychic battle with her void form.

The thing that struck Kane right now was her seeming lack of knowledge of his presence. His mind had touched hers, and over the past few days, Kane had been hearing her whispers, perhaps mental shadows, traumatic memories of the time he'd spent as her prisoner, perhaps her way of keeping in touch with him in the present. She should have had some kind of scent of him.

He glanced down to the old staff. Nehushtan, in addition to enabling him and Lyta to see in the darkness, was creating a hole in the devil queen's perceptions, allowing them to get this close. Even so, he had no urgency to go any further. Almost as if when he took one step closer, the bubble of comfort that the ancient artifact wrapped him within would burst and the hordes of Neekra would rise, screeching from this infernal pit, rushing after him.

Kane glanced at the stick once more, and he realized that the staff had reconfigured itself to keep Lyta and him safe. When they'd first met, the staff had been styled like the Caduceus, providing health and healing to its users. Now its head resembled a cat and appeared to mirror more closely the tales of the ancient traveler Solomon Kane, whose juju-stick was purported to have been cat-headed. He and Lyta were now stealthy and able to see in the pitch darkness where their enemies could not. Making use of the eyes of a cat, figuratively or literally.

"We need to back away," Kane murmured softly to Lyta. She nodded.

"You can't talk to them anyway," Lyta returned. "You all seem to have lost those cheek plates."

Kane nodded. "We go any closer, Neekra will see...."

There was a warbling that silenced Kane, and they ducked back from the railing, crouching low.

Arms snapped past their level, reaching up and snagging the walls above them. The pliant, stretchy subhumanoids hurtled up through the pit, gibbering in excitement.

Kane could not imagine what could give those creatures their enthusiasm, but then he thought of the corpses above. If these creatures were anything like their mistress, then they would seek out bodies to usurp. And, thanks to Kane and his allies, those monstrosities would have an embarrassment of riches. He grimaced at the thought but was thankful that it was a group of dead men who would enslave innocents, rather than the emaciated, helpless prisoners that they'd formerly held.

Of course, with their new bodies, they would come back down. And who knew what kind of senses they possessed? Even worse, what if they were being sent out to hunt for Kane and Lyta. Neekra might have peered into the minds of her prisoners and seen they were missing. As underarmed and under-equipped as the two of them were, Kane didn't relish the concept of going toe-to-toe with reanimated corpses under the command of a body-stealing demon deemed too dangerous to leave free by the Annunaki.

Kane also had an additional chilling thought. The overlords must not have been capable of killing her. Or perhaps they'd had the idea of weaponizing her.

Kane remembered the "living weapons" in the undersea Tongue of the Ocean base, the horrors within which the spirit of Kakusa had hidden.

The similarities to the mollusk-like sacs of coppery blood who'd just surged past were too great to ignore. Kane clenched one fist, wishing to hell that he hadn't been stripped of his gear.

No. Wishing for things to unhappen was a waste of time.

Kane had plenty at his disposal, and he started thinking of what he could do to go one-on-one with Neekra.

Logistics be damned, Kane was the last line in the sand against the body thief. And utilizing every ounce of his resourcefulness in a foreign land and nearly alone, he had to do what Enlil could not do with his legions of Nephilim and star-flung technologies.

Kane hoped that he wouldn't have time enough to entertain a single doubt.

Chapter 10

Lyta followed Kane, the two of them linked together by the length of the staff Nehushtan. Its uncanny powers allowed them to see perfectly in the dark and their footsteps to land no louder than the wing beats of a butterfly as they raced toward the surface entrance. They were heading to another opening in the earth, where they hoped that the vampiric horrors wouldn't be gathering bodies. And if they were…

Lyta would face that challenge when she came to it.

As it was, the healing power of Nehushtan made the past week of arduous marching and minimal subsistence fade away. Lyta wasn't certain how this was, but considering the nervousness that Brigid had in protecting the staff, it was certain that the object possessed incredible power. Whatever energies were held within the stick, she no longer felt thirsty, hungry, not even sleepy or achy. Lyta's medical background was limited to bandages and rinsing out wounds, basic first aid that was of use on the frontier of Zambia's wilderness. But she did know that she'd lost body fat, which meant that she'd also lost a lot of moisture in her body. She didn't see how any stick could undo such damages, but she was certain that whatever energies it was pumping into her, they must have come from an incredible power source.

She just had no idea how that energy could be transferred, let alone stored or even directed in terms of increasing her visual acuity as well as her relative health.

Lyta didn't want to think about how she'd "known" that Kane was down the path she had taken to the underground. Just as the staff was a power source, it also appeared to be some manner of intelligent organism. It even felt warm and alive to the touch, and it had changed right before her eyes.

Then again, she and Kane were running from creatures that had no skeletal form and seemed to be interested in the corpses of the men Kane and his allies had slaughtered to rescue her and the others.

And since these things were tough enough *without* human form, surviving gunfire and explosions, the thought of them reinforcing themselves with the bodies of others was terrifying. Like Kane, she had seen what Neekra truly was—physically and spiritually. She saw that Neekra had molded, warped, *raped* the warlord Gamal's flesh. Neekra had torn him apart cell by cell, nerve by nerve, ripping him asunder and recasting him as a woman.

It was not a pretty thing. Again she felt disturbed that she had received this information from Nehushtan. The stick proved able to fill her in on the back story, gave her a taste of the physical horrors inflicted on Gamal's flesh.

She could also read the discomfort in Kane as he looked on the thing that used to be Gamal. Nehushtan was giving them a warning not to be taken in by the appearance of the woman.

Kane had also informed her that the rubbery beasts were most definitely some basis for vampire legend. They utilized their near-spineless abilities to invade people' homes, as if they were made of mist. Seeing the horrors swing up the shaft of the underground chimney, Lyta had little doubt that the creatures were swift, deadly predators.

Moving as quickly as they could, they kept the staff as a tether between them because of the silence it bestowed on them and the ability to see in the dark. A stumble would give them away, make them vulnerable to Neekra's minions.

Even if there were no more of the creatures than what they'd seen, she and Kane were outnumbered. And Lyta figured those must have been let free because there were others down there to guard their new prisoners.

And so she and Kane ran, making their way to the surface, Lyta feeling the uncanny eeriness of eyes watching her from the shadows. She didn't dare to look back over her shoulder to acknowledge that presence. She bore down, put one foot in front of the other, taking long strides, keeping wary of cracks in the flagstone path corkscrewing its way up from the depths of the chimney shaft. Even though she moved, able to see everything, she was filled with doubt. Was this real or was this a dream? She had abilities that had been granted her by a magic stick, so was this an illusion, or was she actually keeping her footing because she could see in the pitch black as if it were the brightest noonday sun?

Lyta tried to fight the doubts, fight the nerves that jangled within her brain. Doubt was the enemy, and if she lost her concentration, she was certain that she'd doom herself and Kane. She'd gone from a world of men preying on their fellow humans to a realm where goddesses sculpted human flesh as if it were clay, and where liquid beings took over corpses and turned them into unliving warriors at that goddess's beck and call.

Each stride brought them closer to the surface, and

Lyta could see the light at the end of the tunnel. Her heart skipped a beat, and her grasp loosened on the artifact. As she did so, the world dimmed immensely; her eyesight returned to normal human parameters. Her feet slapped the ground harshly, bare soles as tough as elephant skin crashing to the ground again and again. Kane whirled and grabbed her by the hand and once more the darkness was pushed away. The light of the alien staff was picked up by her optic nerves.

"Come on," Kane grumbled through gritted teeth. His grasp was as strong as iron, and she felt as small as an eight-year-old girl, pulled along by this tall, muscular warrior. They continued rushing, and the oppressive pressure of the underground realm lightened about them. Cool air wafted into her nostrils, caressed her skin, promised her relief from her fears.

And then a single figure landed in the mouth of the tunnel, a black shadow defined by the starlit night sky behind him. His stance seemed wrong, as if parts of himself were broken, bent out of place.

Kane growled and released Lyta's hand, then grabbed the pistol in its holster. He came up, triggering the .45, pumping slugs into the shape ahead of him. Lyta, plunged once again into the blackness of the tunnel, didn't see a single reaction from the impacts of those bullets.

Lyta hadn't been alongside Kane for long, but she didn't think that he could miss a man-size figure, not from under fifty feet with his vision enhanced by the ancient artifact he grasped in his other hand. The .45's three mighty blasts were the only ones issued, and Kane paused long enough to return the gun to its holster. He then grasped Nehushtan in both fists.

"Stay behind me, Lyta," he snarled, stepping forward.

Kane saw the man drop to the ground, right at the mouth of the tunnel. Thanks to the powers of the artifact he carried, he could make out details of the horror. It was more monster than human, and he could see where a knife had laid open the flesh beneath its jaw from one ear to the other. Its head listed over one shoulder, a sign of how he hadn't died from massive trauma to the arteries that fed blood to his brain, but from the brutal wrench of neck bones.

Kane recognized his butcher's work, and he had no guilt over it. Men like the one before him had been dragging unarmed, naked and helpless humans to be sacrificed so that Neekra's minions could have flesh to occupy. That he himself was now a husk for such a monstrosity was a fitting punishment. Though Kane was glad that he'd killed the man before he could suffer the agonies of being conquered while alive. Even so, he had no hesitation in pulling the Colt automatic from his hip holster again.

A flick of his thumb as the front sight rose, and the pistol was alive. He squeezed the trigger. The hammer snapped down, igniting the primer and setting off the powder charge within the cartridge. The bullet, a fat, nearly half-inch miniature cannonball with a blunt, flattened nose, snorted out of the muzzle at hundreds of feet per second. The recoil worked the slide, feeding another fresh round under spring pressure from the magazine. Kane rode out the recoil, lined up the front sight and fired a second round as soon as the gun was on target.

Everything was moving fast, but Kane was in the zone. He knew each step of the weapon's function, and with an odd detachment, he ticked them off. The swiftness with which he analyzed each must have been a side effect of the same powers the cat-headed staff Nehushtan granted for night vision. He could feel the steel and wood buck against his palm; the forces of recoil pushed the gun up while his forearm muscles flexed to snap it back down on target. He watched as each round smashed into the bloodied militiaman's chest. The first two slugs struck in the center of mass, just as he'd been trained as a Magistrate.

Two slugs in the chest, and the man didn't even stagger in reaction to their impacts. Kane rode out the recoil for the second shot and pushed the front sight of the pistol up. He aimed for the bridge of the man's nose where it rested at an odd angle on his blood-slicked shoulder. Kane didn't need much imagination to see how people could equate the walking corpses commanded by the boneless creatures with invulnerable undead. The third round struck the man in the face, in the triangle between eye sockets and the tip of the nose, where the skull bones were thinnest and most fragile, all the while sitting right in front of the clump of nerves that connected the human brain to the spinal column.

His Magistrate training told him that a single shot there would bring down any man, even if body armor protected the heart. The third shot snapped the thing's head back, and a fine mist exploded from the impact zone. Kane held his breath, continuing his advance toward the lifeless sentry to the surface world.

Then the bullet-smashed face rolled forward, eyes alight from within with demonic glee, even though one eye had popped from its socket under the force of the single .45-caliber slug.

Kane flicked his thumb again, putting the pistol on safe. No use wasting more ammunition on a foe who didn't feel the trauma of bullets.

He warned Lyta to stand behind him, even as he

replaced the gun in its holster. According to the oral history of the previous owner of this staff, Solomon Kane, the black-clad Puritan had utilized the ancient stick to slay vampires. Kane braced the stick in both of his hands, feeling the warmth and throb of Nehushtan's "pulse" pumping through his palms. The grinning, one-eyed corpse stepped forward. Its remaining orb glinted, almost as if it were filled with the confidence of its immortality in the face of a man whose gun didn't work.

But Kane was not defined by a hunk of lead-spitting iron. He'd fought for his life against all manner of forces, all forms of horror, utilizing anything he could get his hands on, his ever-burning mind seeking ways through obstacles, no matter how dire the odds. So the vampire thing ahead of him was bulletproof. With a surge of might, he lunged to take on the bestial corpse, face-to-face.

The animated carcass paused in confusion. Obviously, the thing had occupied bodies before. It seemed to be genuinely surprised that Kane was on the attack, not cowering in paralyzed terror at something immune to bullets. Too bad for the vampire that it was standing against a man who had seen his bullets bounce off or be absorbed by more enemies than he could count. If one form of combat was ineffective, then it was time to switch to another.

Kane pivoted with the staff, bringing the newly formed cat head across the jaw of the flop-necked horror, knocking the head to the other shoulder with enough force to send him staggering to the wall of the tunnel. Kane pushed in hard, snapping the other end of the staff into the ribs of the thing, listening to bones snap under the impact of the ancient artifact. The black surface didn't register a single mark despite the scratch of shattered rib across it.

The vampire folded over the bar. Its core was made from orichalcum, meaning that it was a nearly inde-structible length of alien-designed alloy. Kane looked toward Lyta for a brief heartbeat.

"Go!"

The girl, to her credit, did not hesitate as he returned his attention to the African vampire, whose head was now straight on its neck. Its loose eyeball had been sucked back into the socket, and the tattered lips be-neath the .45-caliber's entrance that used to be its nose peeled back to expose a death's-head grin. Suddenly, Nehushtan had another pair of hands on it, and they possessed enough strength to easily lift Kane until his feet could only kick at empty air.

Deprived of leverage on the ground, Kane swiftly adapted to the situation and brought up both knees, slamming them against the vampire's clavicle. There was a grunt of escaping breath, but that proved as much of an impediment as a bullet through the face. The vam-pire chuckled.

"You cannot stand long against me, bone sack," the creature taunted.

"How about standing on you?" Kane asked. His knees jammed onto the thing's shoulders, and he now had the leverage to wrench the staff out of his oppo-nent's steely grasp. The vampire's grip was strong, though, and the most that Kane could manage against that might was simply twisting his own torso atop his foe.

"Nope," the dead thing returned. With a sudden surge of might, Kane was hurled from the walking corpse's chest, and his broad shoulders slammed against the far wall of the tunnel. What was left of his shadow suit was enough to keep the Cerberus adventurer from shattering his spine against the stone. Unfortunately, the impact on the far side of the tunnel still knocked the wind from him, and the artifact tumbled from his numbed fingers.

The vampire chuckled at the sight of Kane slumped on the ground. "I have to admit, you show a lot of spunk for a bone bag. Too bad you're facing one of us."

Kane looked up, realizing that the monster before him had once more settled into an attitude of superiority. And it seemed to be recovering its facial features. The nose wound was rapidly closing, and lips that had been torn and bloody solidified, making its smile appear a little more human. It walked around Kane, studying him as he got back to his feet. Kane reached for his knife.

"Your gun failed. Your magic stick didn't hurt me. Now you're going to try that?" it asked him.

With speed that would have overwhelmed a less experienced fighter, the vampire surged forward, gnarled fingers snatching for Kane's knife hand. However, the dead thing was a heartbeat too slow, and it clutched at empty air. Instead of disarming the Cerberus explorer, the vampire found itself overextended in reach.

Kane brought up his elbow under the dead creature's armpit, hooking the thing with one smooth, swift motion. All the strength in the world was a great thing, but the vampire still only possessed the weight of a normal human being, maybe a few extra pounds for the entity that shared its lifeless mass. Kane easily hefted the vampire up, pivoting, then slammed his foe onto the flagstone floor. Bones snapped and popped like the sounds of distant gunfire, and the vampire looked up with bulging eyes.

Kane stepped back, wound up with one foot and kicked down hard. The sole of his boot stamped into the dead humanoid's face, producing another wet set of crunches. Kane took the brief second of the vampire's vulnerability and dazedness to hurl himself toward the staff. He hit a shoulder roll as he scooped up the powerful artifact.

The vampire sat up once more, then surged to its feet. It spun around with uncanny speed, and this time, it didn't move with the laconic assuredness of an unmatched predator. The dead horror moved forward with the suddenness of a lightning arc. Too bad for the vampire that Kane was no slouch in the speed department. Even as he came up with Nehushtan, Kane swung the staff around so that its pointed bottom was held up like a spear.

The vampire let out an agonized scream as the ancient staff's unyielding point burst through its shoulder and tore out of its back. There was the horrible shriek of a thing on fire, and the damned corpse writhed on the end of the stick, hands clubbing at the shaft to try to pull free. Kane saw the panic, felt the heat of the artifact increase beneath its blackened surface. Kane pushed forward, bowling the monstrosity off its feet, slamming it to the ground.

"No!" the vampire shrieked, impaled on the staff of Moses, the scepter of Solomon. It seemed the myths of the vampire's vulnerability to holy artifacts had the whiff of truth. Kane could smell it as the thing let off steam from around the edges of its wound, a rancid, putrid scent that stunk of white-hot brass.

"Why not?" Kane asked, wrenching the staff free from its shoulder wound.

This time, the vampire didn't show any haste in rising back to battle. Perhaps the touch of the relic was too much, too poisonous for its remarkable parasite to heal it, to continue this fight. Either way, Kane wasn't sticking around. He turned and followed Lyta out into the open.

And stopped cold. Others burst from the woods. Where there had been one, there were now a half of a dozen. Kane clenched the staff, knuckles white with the adrenaline surge that came with near-abject terror. Kane was not immune to fear; indeed, he relished the ability to be scared. That was the trigger for the body to increase its efficiency, flushing the bloodstream with extra oxygen, extra strength surging through his muscles. It made him quicker, more powerful. All the better to fight, or to flee if necessary. Only the fused-brained worst burn-outs, unsuited for any contest of survival, would show no emotional response to being outnumbered.

Here, Kane was surrounded and outnumbered by six more examples of a creature who'd shrugged off gunfire, withstood some of his strongest blows and only felt pain at the touch of a product of ancient alien technology.

Even with the relic grasped in both of his hands, he'd just came off a battle that had left him rattled, his skull pounding. Nehushtan might not be enough to turn the tide of this ambush.

He choked up his grip on the artifact, holding it more firmly.

If Kane failed, it would not be for lack of effort.

A snarl curled his lip. "Bring it, you freaks."

Chapter 11

Lyta, once more in the open, could see the vampiric figures staggering in the darkness, and her hands were no longer preoccupied with staying in contact with the staff in order to gain night vision. She saw the six figures leap and land about her.

And, unlike Kane, she had not been disarmed. Brigid Baptiste had made certain that she had avoided capture and kept her slung rifle and handgun. Even as she was urged to race past Kane and his reanimated opponent, she was taking the rifle off its sling, gripping it in both hands, stock tucked up against her shoulder. Even a woman as slight as she was had a much better chance hitting a target with a rifle than a handgun. The handgun was an unsupported, lightweight piece of steel that was far less efficient than the long stocked rifle in mediating recoil or aligning sights. Most especially, the rifle had much more ammunition capacity and stopping power than even a large-bored pistol.

Kane was out. He joined her as the vampires circled them both, hemming in the subterranean tunnel entrance they'd originally come through. The man from America had traded his handgun for the staff, and he tightened his grasp on the long weapon, looking around. The dead puppet carcasses kept equidistant from each other. Attacking more than one at a time would be difficult for them and there was coverage in case someone tried to escape between them; two attackers would fall on any victim trying to cross their line in the sand.

Kane edged closer to Lyta until they were back to back.

"Any plans?" Lyta whispered.

"Make it costly for them," Kane growled.

That response wasn't the most heartening of military stratagems, but at least Kane wasn't ready to lay down arms and be dragged into the depths of the earth before Neekra. Lyta ground her molars, dark eyes flitting from vampire to vampire and keeping tabs on them in her peripheral vision. The rifle she carried wasn't fully automatic, but at this range, against normal human opponents, it unleashed some serious damage.

Against normal human opponents, she mentally repeated.

Despite the lack of stopping power of Kane's .45-caliber handgun, the Cerberus explorer had hit the vampire right in the spot where a normal human would have instantly dropped. A bullet through the thinnest bones of the skull, burrowing into the medulla oblongata, the deepest reptilian parts of the human brain responsible for controlling heartbeat, breathing and other motor functions, was a kill shot, no matter what. That was what she'd been taught in her training as part of her town's militia.

Even though she didn't expect much of an effect on her enemy, she snapped the rifle to aim and fired as fast as she could pull the trigger, starting at center of mass and letting the recoil guide her fire upward. The gun boomed, poked against her shoulder, brass spinning out of the breech across her vision, and she watched as her target staggered in a deadly dance of hammer blows that made its arms windmill in a wild effort to regain its balance.

When the vampire finally toppled, she realized that Kane was no longer at her back. The sounds of battle were on, the thud and crunch of fists on flesh, staff against bones, and Lyta turned toward the second of the creatures on her side of the melee, tearing another salvo of bullets into its face and upper chest, grimacing as this one struggled upstream of her gunfire even as chunks of its head were blasted away.

The third of the vampires lunged at her, and Lyta barely had time to twist out of the way of its snatching fingers. Unfortunately, the thing grabbed hold of her rifle's barrel and squeezed hard; metal whined under inhuman pressure. As the carcass crushed the rifle's business end, she heard the bones shatter and splinter in a hand not designed for producing that kind of force. The horrific things that subsumed the dead bodies had little concern for the corpses they operated. It was as if they felt no pain, and they had little fear of irreparable damage.

After all, they could find another more intact corpse to inhabit once they'd finished killing Kane and Lyta.

She pulled the trigger on the rifle, despite the bent and crushed barrel. As soon as the round struck the obstruction, the damaged tube ruptured, turning the vampire's hand into a ragged mist of blood and fluttering pieces of tissue and shattered bone. Lyta didn't let go of the damaged weapon, but pushed on the attack, ramming the stock hard into the side of her foe's head. Bone crunched as steel met skull, but the vampire swatted out with its remaining hand, hurling her a dozen feet across the ground, where she skidded to a halt.

That was *not* comfortable, and she realized that her

left arm was raw from where her sleeve had torn and where the pebbles and gravel in the dirt had torn off the top layer of her skin. Lyta gritted her teeth and rolled to a sitting position. Her hand dropped to the .45 in its holster.

The handgun hadn't done much when Kane had used it, but Lyta refused to roll over and quit just because she didn't have the right tools on hand. She stiff-armed the pistol and fired at the vampire that had tossed her aside so casually. The impacts of her bullets drew its attention away from something just out of Lyta's peripheral vision, and the creature snarled at her. Then it tumbled backward, struck by something large and heavy.

In an instant, she realized that it was one of the other vampires. She shot a glance toward Kane, who was still in mid-spin, slashing across the chest of another of the reanimated corpses. Lyta saw that he didn't use the staff as a sword, rather more as a club, but even with the hammering strokes, he certainly had more than enough force to keep the horrors at bay.

Lyta looked back toward her two adversaries and saw one of them making for her, slavering hunger in its dimly glowing eyes. She triggered the pistol, grasping the weapon with both hands, holding it as tightly as possible.

At least one shot stuck, dimming one of those reddish lights glinting in the face of the awakened corpse, and the thing clutched at its broken head. Lyta took that as a brief moment of victory, and then Kane grabbed her by the wrist.

"Move it!" Kane grunted. His breath came rapidly, in harsh wheezes; his hair was matted damply to his forehead. This was the look of a man who'd been through the exertion of a lifetime, and there was a spark of emotion in his eyes that spurred Lyta quickly to her feet. She wouldn't give up the fight, but if there was the call and the room for retreat, she wasn't going to hesitate, either. She took off, racing into the forest, into the direction that Kane pointed. Her legs thrust, sending her into two yard-long strides, legs kicking her toward the depths of the jungle. Kane's own feet stomped through the forest behind her, staying close, a comforting presence.

The trouble was, with Kane following her, the vampires would be able to track them much more easily. Any comfort that she'd gained from his presence disappeared swiftly.

All her firepower had been utterly useless against them. Kane's use of the ancient artifact that Brigid had demanded *not* fall into the hands of Neekra and the vampires had barely held them at bay. And now they were on the run from creatures who showed incredible speed without the benefit of solid-limbed bodies and who had nearly overwhelmed them in the space of a few moments.

Nearly overwhelmed—emphasis on *nearly,* Lyta thought as she charged through the forest, weaving and moving as quickly as her legs could take her. She bounced off trunks, and her legs tore branches and long grasses. There were moments when she felt as if she were a human pinball, banging through the jungle. Luckily, with adrenaline surging through her bloodstream, she didn't feel the bumps and bounces, didn't worry about sticks or stalks slicing her shins, and she was keeping loose and limber so that rather than colliding, she rolled along a trunk rather than plowed right into it.

Lyta would be hurting later, but so far she'd escaped a broken bone, maybe because she wasn't so much charging ahead, regardless of obstacle, but flowing. Any bit of resistance, she rolled to where she was deflected and continued on.

The explosion hammered at Lyta's ears, and for the first time in what felt like a year, but actually was more like twenty seconds, her footing failed her and she plowed into the ground, all scraped palms and jarred knees, spitting out leaves and bark from where she'd gone went through a shrub face-first trying to arrest her fall.

Lyta glanced back and saw smoke billowing, watched trees sway, then topple and heard the horrible keening she'd heard earlier when Brigid had set off detonations. Whatever Kane had done, it must have been pretty good, because nothing scampered through the smoke. Could the lone blast have peeled off the pursuit?

Kane didn't appear to want to hang around and find out. He hooked her under her arm and dragged her to her feet, and they were on the move again. This time, she watched her step better. When a tree came up between her and Kane, she shrugged herself free and ducked around the trunk, meeting up with him on the other side. Neither of them stopped as they ran.

Lyta finally sagged against a low-hanging branch. She flung her arm over it and used it to support her as she gulped down air. Kane's longish hair matted down on his face, which was a mask of perspiration. Yet even as he rested, he watched the forest, blue eyes cold, sharp, alert. The exertion didn't show in his ragged breaths, just in the sheen of sweat that glimmered as the first rays of the dawn cracked over the horizon.

"Sunrise," Lyta gulped. "That's good, right?"

"If you believe the legends," Kane answered. His voice was strained, the only sign of exhaustion other than his wetness as he struggled to maintain even breathing and replenish any oxygen spent from his bloodstream in the rapid departure.

"How long—"

"We've gone maybe two miles," Kane answered.

Lyta nodded.

Kane finally allowed himself time to relax, leaning against the trunk of the tree. He brushed his forearm across his forehead, shaking off droplets. He squeezed his eyes shut, swallowed, then stood up. "We'll need shelter and water."

Lyta nodded. "And more grenades?"

Kane looked down. He still had his handgun in its holster, but the rest of his belt was barren, save for the remnants of torn pouches.

"I snagged one off of one of the reanimated thugs," Kane told her. "Figured it couldn't hurt to try one. They stopped."

"Brigid scared them, hurt them, by blowing up a tree, too," Lyta mentioned. "I heard it. They screamed when splinters blew out of the tree."

"Splinters. Shrapnel," Kane mused. He didn't feel like heading back the way they'd come. It was still too dark, too shadowy, and the chances that the vampires might not *need* to hide from the golden rays of the sun was still too untested to be certain.

"Maybe wood hurts them, at least when they're not in their corpses," Lyta said.

Kane nodded. "It makes sense. They definitely cried out in pain."

"I'm not really sure now, but when I was touching that staff, I was able to hear things. It was like I could see things as they happened. I know that Brigid impaled one on a splintered tree branch," Lyta said. "At least, it was certain in the sense of a dream. Now…with the sun coming up…"

Kane looked at the staff, still firm in his left hand. "Yeah. This stick does that to you."

"Makes you doubt yourself?" Lyta asked.

Kane nodded. "Why did it choose *me?*"

"Maybe it knew you wouldn't abuse it," Lyta returned.

Kane curled his lip. "Too damned trusting."

Lyta, however, glad to be alive, didn't agree one whit.

THE CRACKLE OF GUNFIRE, spread across a half of a minute, maybe more, fell down the corkscrew hole into the depths of the earth, reaching Thurpa's ears and raising his attention. Grant, Brigid and Nathan took notice, too. No one uttered a sound, but they knew that somewhere above, at least one of their companions was alive and fighting. None of the vampires that had been sent up were returning to sound the alarm, and the prisoners waited, biding their time.

There was silence.

Thurpa was tempted to hold his breath until the other shoe dropped, but he didn't want to pass out and look like a fool. Besides, if he held his breath for a response, for a sign of vampires crawling back with either captives or excuses, things would go more in his favor the longer he had to wait. It would mean that Kane and the girl, Lyta, weren't overwhelmed.

And if they were free, then those two could come back.

It also meant that the gelatinous horrors were *not* invulnerable, invincible. They could be beaten, and the four prisoners could stage their own escape.

As long as there was no news, there was hope.

So Thurpa stayed quiet. He didn't look anxiously toward the others. Rather, he stilled himself, meditating, giving himself a chance to better attune his eyes and ears to the surroundings. He looked for ways out, weaknesses in those guarding him.

And then he noticed the silhouettes stalking just beyond the firelight. He made out the amber, snake-slit eyes of his brethren. Durga, the fallen prince, had not come alone. Others had come, and a cold dread slithered through Thurpa's veins, down his throat, slowly constricting his belly with icy strength. Thurpa had thought he was the only one who had been sent on ahead to Africa to coordinate with the Millennium Consortium, but these men had the unmistakable eyes and heads of Nagah.

The Nagah had been fashioned in a semblance of their Annunaki gods, most especially Enki, who'd crafted them into the beings he wished to follow him. As such, the cobra, a respected part of Indian society, had donated genetic material to the hybrid between man and god.

Unlike the lobotomized Igigi of Enlil, named the Nephilim, the Nagah were to live by their own morals, not the whims of their master, not in a mental limbo of robotic existence with his whispers in their mind. The Nagah were at once fearsome and beautiful, and they were viewed as a benign race in the mythology of the region. Their wisdom was matched by their speed and strength, and their bites were a match for any demon. The cobra men were mighty warriors and wise council at once.

And yet something seemed off about the figures standing in the darkness, huddling in the shadows. None of them stepped forward. Not one of them approached Thurpa, wondering why he had turned against his prince.

Indeed, they stood at quiet, perfect attention.

Thurpa frowned. Nagah warriors had discipline and could stand easily in silence, but this seemed eerie, unnatural.

"Are you fretting over the behavior of your brothers?" a familiar voice whispered in his ear. Thurpa turned and met Durga's cold, unblinking glare at a range of mere inches. Thurpa tried not to show how startled he was, but his reflexes betrayed him, and he jolted a step backward.

"I don't think those *are* my brothers," Thurpa said. "You chose men who would follow you, not zombies."

Durga's smirk was sly, almost imperceptible, but Thurpa spotted it readily, even in the dim light thrown off by the underground hut's small lamp spilling its orange and amber glow through the doorway.

"Durga wouldn't choose people who could think for themselves," Grant said. "I mean, a few minutes with us, and you showed us much more humanity than he'd want."

"Silence, ape," Durga snarled. He pushed Thurpa back and walked closer to the hulking Cerberus captive. "If I wished for your opinion—"

"You don't wish for the opinions of humans," Grant countered. "So come down off your high horse."

The corner of Thurpa's mouth twitched with a smile he tried everything to dispel. If there was one thing that the young Nagah could appreciate, it was Grant's turn of phrase.

"It will be interesting to see at which point your bravado dies," Durga mused, circling Grant.

Grant followed Durga with his eyes. The Nagah

prince's intimidation sloughed off of him. The droop of the man's gunslinger mustache enhanced the deepness of his frown. There was a flicker of disdain in Grant's eyes, but there was also a wariness in his stance. Thurpa could make out that Grant's feet were perpendicular to each other, allowing him to brace himself with just a slight movement or to hurl himself into action.

Even without his hands being free, Thurpa had no doubt that Grant could unleash prodigious damage with a shoulder block, a snap of his knee or even a head butt.

But Grant held his ground. They were surrounded by the things that Durga wanted to pass off as Nagah. Thurpa had seen the Kongamato clones, and obviously Durga had made these drones, Nagah in form only, not in mind or spirit.

If Grant made a hostile move, those mindless thugs would fall on him, and each of them was equipped with deadly fangs, loaded with venom, maybe even stronger than what a normal Nagah would have. After all, Durga had had no compunctions about altering his own physical nature when he had access to the source of the cobra baths. "Improving" on the basic Nagah is what Durga would see as necessary while alone on the continent, no matter what his goddess promised him in terms of power.

Just the same, if they went after Grant on their own, which Thurpa doubted they would, they'd end up being torn apart by a skilled, dangerous man who didn't fear chains or fangs. Still, Durga had wooed Enlil, and, according to Brigid's stories while they'd traveled, Enlil had supplied Durga with Nephilim, who he had refashioned to resemble Nagah, and whom he'd had murder helpless people in a wave of terror that kept Durga's name alive.

Thurpa tried to tamp down the seething anger he felt for Durga. The fallen prince had abandoned him, left him to take near-fatal punishment.

And why?

Even Brigid couldn't come up for a reason for that.

Thurpa's nerves were raw from abandonment, just as his body was sore from his recent capture. So the young Nagah outcast held on to that anger, that negative energy. He could turn it into strength, hone his nerves into an edge, to keep himself ready to escape and fight for freedom. But he'd hold his temper, bide his time. He'd wait for Grant or Brigid to make the first move, to provide leadership for their escape.

Thurpa prayed to Enki that it wouldn't take that long.

Chapter 12

At noon, with the Zambian girl Lyta in tow, Kane returned to the Mashonan militia's camp. There, they scrounged for weapons. Along the way, they checked out the area where Kane had thrown his grenade the night before. They saw that he had struck a tree, blowing off a two-yard stretch of bark and splinters.

It certainly would have created enough wooden shrapnel to cause harm to their vampire pursuers. So, the things didn't like wood. But was that vulnerability applied to their naked forms, without the shell of human flesh they appropriated? Or did it apply to their stolen skins, as well? Kane didn't think so, not unless that wood somehow transfixed the blood vessels that the creatures accumulated.

Blood vessels, or the chambers of a dead heart and/or brain.

A stake through the heart or decapitation were known methods for returning the dead to their eternal sleep, perhaps because of the entities that took up residence within those vital organs. It made sense to Kane. If you were to control a corpse, the two places where you could animate it from would be the nervous system and the circulatory system.

Again, Kane's thoughts returned to Kakusa, the disembodied entity whose cellular strain was trapped within a series of simple yet gigantic monocellular organisms that resembled unholy hybrids between octopi and garden slugs, or, as Grant had pegged them, gigantic balls of snot.

These particular balls of snot, however, had managed to wrestle three grown men and Brigid into captivity. And one of those three was Grant, six foot four and heavily muscled, with even more combat experience than Kane himself.

They were under the command of an alien entity who could wear any human's skin and remold herself into whatever she felt was the standard of attraction. And Neekra's new body was indeed beautiful, alluring and frightening. She'd been the purest of darkness and inhumanity while she'd rested between his ears, psychically imprisoning him. It was only when his will had surged to the point where he was about to utterly destroy her presence in his mind that she'd morphed into something that could elicit a modicum of sympathy from the vengeful Kane.

Kane had realized that it was a mistake, but she was already inside and had plucked that string, that bit of humanity that saw a chance for redemption in others. She'd also aroused his natural human desires, his interest in her as a powerful mate, one who could provide for him as much as raise his status. It was ancient code wired into the male mammal, nothing that would appeal to his higher consciousness, especially since he knew the true horror that was Neekra.

Kane was not unfamiliar with femme fatales. Indeed, he'd encountered enough of them to know that selling the female of the species short was a quick ticket to an early grave. Some of these "hell bitches" might not even allow enough remains to throw into a grave. From the charismatic and draconian Erica van Sloan to the dark goddess Lilitu, Kane's respect for opponents from the "fairer sex" was high, at least his respect for their deadly skills and powers, if not their ideals and methods.

Over the morning, on their walk back toward the Mashonan camp, Kane had filled Lyta in on the journey that had brought them to this deadly tableau. Kane was rarely certain how any of the information he provided to newcomers about the adventures of the Cerberus outcasts would be accepted, but the young woman with him had just encountered gelatinous creatures whose existence hearkened back to the darkest legends of vampires and demons. The concepts of cloning facilities, a network of matter transmission units scattered across the planet and that there was an ancient race trying to reconquer the earth were all accepted, albeit with some stunned blankness in her features.

Survival, for now, was a more important priority for the girl than wrapping her mind around the quick rundown Kane had given her. Her rifle was gone, and she wanted a new gun, as well as a refill of the ammunition she'd expended from her pistol. Kane also needed more gear. While conventional firearms seemed to do little in terms of permanently downing the vampiric horrors, they at least slowed them down, with proper shot placement.

As well, Kane calculated, the vampires might not be the only minions to whom Neekra had access. Grenades, Lyta reported, also seemed to work quite well against the unsheathed snot-balls, if only to slow them down or to spray splintered wood and cause them burning pain.

"Baptiste caused a couple of these things to scream in agony?" Kane asked.

Lyta nodded. "Maybe she'd caused it damage with a significant piece of wood."

Kane scratched his bristly chin. "Vampire myths state a wooden stake can kill, or at least incapacitate, one of these creatures. They must be staked *and* decapitated...."

Lyta narrowed her eyes. "You're getting an idea?"

"Anchor it, maybe with a biological-based pin. Then divide it from its other section, its second nucleus," Kane mused. "We saw that the blobs had what appeared to be two organs within them."

"One which would be in the heart, one in the brain?" Lyta asked.

Kane nodded, slowly at first, then picking up speed. "One could be seen as the heart and the brain of the actual organism. The thing is, these are likely single-celled organisms, comparatively."

"Like amoebas?" Lyta questioned. "We're twenty-third-century Africans, and during the twentieth century, we learned about germs and bacteria in water which could make people sick. So, the creatures have two nucleus nodules...but if they're single-celled, why do they behave so intelligently, almost humanlike?"

"Just because they don't use conventional cellular structure does not mean that they aren't complicated organisms," Kane said. "Baptiste told me, while explaining what Kakusa was, that an entity could be stored as a living, extended protein molecule. In fact, cellular structure is loaded with protein molecules in which is stored fantastic amounts of information."

"DNA," Lyta responded. "The stuff of genes."

"Multiple gene structures could be arranged to create a brain as complex as a human's," Kane said. "Just like Kakusa."

"That was the thing trapped in the octo-slugs you fought in Florida, right?" Lyta asked.

Kane nodded. "We've also encountered microscopic technologies. Nanomachines which can move and even perform programmed tasks on a scale below cellular. Those machines literally rebuilt a friend of mine, making him from a withered old freezie into a man of forty years."

"Is that normal human technology, or is it from the Annunaki?" Lyta asked.

"Humans have duplicated it from, I suppose, Annunaki influence," Kane answered.

As they searched the camp, both kept an eye on the tree line. It was high noon, and there seemed to be no indication that the vampires were up and about, stalking within the forest.

Even so, they remained quiet and cautious, their conversation barely above a whisper, and neither letting the other out of sight. Neekra and her vampires must have been certain of their invulnerability, because food, water, weapons and ammunition were still prevalent throughout the shattered Mashonan camp. Lyta and Kane were able to eat and drink, replenishing lost calories and fluids from the night before. A good splash of water in the face also helped Kane feel better. Instead of his shadow suit, he was wearing a uniform shirt packed as a spare in one of the dead militiamen's tents. It was snug about his shoulders but hung voluminously about his slender waist. He tied that off with a web belt that he'd stocked with gear he'd need for the upcoming conflict.

Kane knew that he couldn't replace the Sin Eater lost when he tumbled through the breaking ground, but perhaps he could locate it later. He picked up a

Sterling submachine gun. The weapon was an older design, but it was as simple as a brick; it fired a lot of 9 mm bullets quickly and it didn't take up a lot of room when it was on a sling. The grip angle even matched that of the Sin Eater, so he didn't have to worry about adjusting his aim.

Kane also decided to take a folding stocked AKM rifle. The creatures showed some hindrance when they were hit with a lot of big bullets, and the compact rifle was designed to put out big bullets at high speed, both in rate of fire and velocity of those bullets. It was also easier to carry than the big FAL that Lyta had replaced. However, since Kane was loading up with a pouch of grenades and his sidearm was going to be the Sterling, he didn't feel under-equipped in terms of firepower.

"Do we try to take them now?" Lyta asked.

Kane shook his head. "No. We don't know if they'll be up and about. We'll wait until night."

"And then sneak down," Lyta said. "Most of them will be out looking for us. But can we hide from them?"

"We definitely can. We hid almost in plain sight of the blobs as they climbed up the well from the city. There was nothing between us and the creatures as they scurried from wall to wall," Kane answered. "We settle in, find a good hiding spot and bide our time."

"Maybe get some rest, too," Lyta said. "I never got a chance to sleep last night."

Kane nodded. "We'll sleep in shifts."

Kane scanned the area. He'd counted the dead the night before, and he noticed that there were now about fifteen corpses missing. That was a hell of a force to be facing down, but the vampires weren't invulnerable. He had Nehushtan, as well as the rest of the equipment he'd scrounged. His allies needed his help, so waiting until dark to make a rescue was all he could hope for.

Fifteen guards who didn't require sleep and shrugged off bullets would be unbeatable as defenders. Kane needed them spread out thinly, on the hunt for him and Lyta to even those nearly impossible odds. And once he got to Brigid and Grant, his chances would increase exponentially. Those two were likely studying the vampiric horrors, and had probably gained a lot of data from their initial conflict with the entities. Kane was dead certain that they would have their own ideas of how to deal with this opponent.

Whether their queen, Neekra, would share the same weaknesses and vulnerabilities as her minions was another question. Kane had his own thoughts, more like desperate prayers, but he'd cross that bridge when he came to it.

Who knew what kind of other beings were down in that city? Kane had only gotten glimpses down the corkscrew shaft, sighting elements of buildings, as well as a camp. He still had Durga to account for, and perhaps the millennialists or cobra men who he hadn't committed to the siege at the Victoria Falls power complex. Being outnumbered was nothing new for the Cerberus explorer, but he had no delusions that he could take on an army of undead, let alone perhaps a platoon of gunmen, either soft- or scale-skinned.

And that brought Kane's worries to the two young men who had accompanied the Cerberus expedition. Nathan Longa was the former bearer of the ancient artifact that Kane held close to his side. That youth from Harare had crossed miles of deadly African wilderness to bring himself into contact with Kane. All of this had been at the subconscious urgings of Nehushtan, a device that was intelligent enough to steer Nathan to the one facility for miles where he could communicate with Cerberus.

Then there was Thurpa, a young Nagah who had served as Durga's liaison with the Millennium Consortium mercenaries who'd joined the fallen prince in his quest for African artifacts. Thurpa had been nearly killed in what initially had been a means of bringing the Cerberus warriors closer to Durga, but the cobra outcast had found himself identifying and collaborating with the group of humans who cared for his wounds and protected him. Thurpa, in turn, had risked his life to protect the Zambians who ran part of the Victoria Falls power complex. As a stranger on a strange continent, Thurpa, with his Indian background and posthuman appearance, knew that his best chances were alongside Kane, Grant and Brigid, despite the gratitude of the Zambian soldiers he'd rescued.

Thurpa missed the Nagah city-state of Garuda, and even though he realized that his prior allegiance to Durga would be damning to him on his return, he still hoped to be among his people again. He'd accept whatever punishment he'd receive, just to put aside his crushing loneliness.

Kane felt for the outcast Nagah. Kane was an exile, as well. All the people of Cerberus were outsiders, strangers in countries and times that were not their own. Kane himself had begun as an enforcer for a megalithic city ruled under the iron fist of a post-human hybrid baron—the nascent incarnation of what would soon become the Annunaki overlords. Everyone in the base known as Cerberus had been cast out of their homes, in the feral wilderness, on a long-frozen lunar colony or preserved in suspended animation from the twentieth century.

If there was something that Kane could identify with, it was being an alien in a world you thought that you knew. And now Thurpa risked his life. If Durga were at the bottom of that pit, Kane feared for the young Nagah's safety. Durga was not a kind prince, and the depths to which his lust for vengeance dived were dark and brutal indeed.

The sooner Kane could get to them, the better he would feel.

BRIGID BAPTISTE WOULD have felt much better if she had had more room to maneuver. Durga guided his faux cobra men to separate his four prisoners.

None of them were allowed to talk to each other, only to speak to their captors. What was it about the maniacs that she and her allies battled that made them so willing to gloat?

Durga and Neekra had the wherewithal to keep the Cerberus members from communicating with each other, to the point of taking off their Commtact plates to prevent private, subvocal transmission between them.

Now Brigid stood in a five-by-eight cell. There was little room to walk, and she could sleep on a bare floor. The room was unadorned except for a small candle in a barred and meshed hole in the wall. She bent and observed it and saw that it was against a door. Even if she could slip her slender fingers through the bars, without being stopped by the wire mesh, the steel hatch was thick and reinforced. The slit for the candle wasn't much thicker than the thin column of wax itself. Thus, the prisoners could see, and the candles could be replaced with an absolute minimum of vulnerability for the guards.

It struck Brigid as odd in this dungeon, but then, from what she could make out of the architecture, it most assuredly was from an actual civilized society. She examined the candle and noted that it would last approximately eight hours. She wondered if it would be replaced by a new shift of guards, or if she would be plunged into Stygian darkness for the remainder of the day.

With no features to provide a distraction, Brigid could easily keep her intellect occupied, but the closeness of the walls, coupled with oppressing darkness, could be a form of torture. She touched the mesh, running her fingertip along it. She could feel the sharp edges of the wire scrape and slice at her skin from the slightest pressure. Any effort to dig into the mesh would end up scouring skin from her fingers. Getting leverage against the bars beneath was even tougher.

Brigid passed on that particular opening and looked toward the back of the cell. Ancient musk wafted up through a small hole. She grimaced at the tiny toilet and knew that she didn't want to stay around to see how well it drained.

Her thoughts about how civilized this underground city had been in its heyday were scrubbed as she realized that these prison cells were the bare minimum. Brigid saw a small slot for food, but it was not large enough even for a bowl, just a shallow plate. She didn't think that chunks of meat or bread would be shoved through. Or, worse, they *would* be shoved through the hole. She could see scratch marks on the floor where hungry prisoners could easily have worn in the floor, trying to scoop up broth or crumbs or even just slop in an effort to maintain the calories needed to live. Brigid caressed the marks and realized that they made an indentation on the floor. It was an inch deep, meaning that prisoners had to lap up whatever came through the slot.

It was also in the darkest section of the cell; the soft glow of the candle created a night-black shadow over the food. Whether they received clean or dirty water, gruel or some other hideous semisolid stew would only be known the moment their tongues touched the slop-spattered floor bowl. Prisoners became animals. The thought made her stomach start to turn.

Brigid touched the walls. They were dry, solid stone. A hard scrub of the surface didn't dislodge granules. Human nails wouldn't make a difference on the featureless slab. There were seams where the stones were pushed tightly together, but they were too thin to get more than a fingernail stuck in them. She even wondered if something like a pocket knife could do anything to the wall. Then again, maybe the stones were actually soft enough to damage, but the prisoners didn't have enough food or water to make an effort.

Ignoring the prospects of malnutrition and dehydration, Brigid reached her bound hands under her waistband and down into her black suit leggings, pulling a small, flat sliver of metal that had been stuck to her skin. The small shank was nonferrous, so it wouldn't show up on magnets, and flexible and low profile enough that even the most lustful of gropes along her leg wouldn't betray its presence. When pressed on the flat, the metal gave easily. When used as a knife, edge on, however, the object was a sharp, capable cutting edge, or it could be used as a screwdriver.

Keeping a few items as backup was a tactic that Brigid had always found highly useful. Her skin was protected from the knife's edges by layers of athletic tape. Brigid turned the sharp little device around and made short work of the leather bindings, remnants of belts and gear from the dead militiamen that the gelatinous sub-vampires had used to tie her up. She wished that the others had been kept restrained by just the straps, but Durga had correctly assumed that Grant could stretch and burst that leather easily. He must have underestimated her. The others' chains were suspenders to back up the belt that kept a six-foot-four, highly trained combatant from busting loose and turning his cloned Nagah into luggage.

SCRAPING THE KNIFE along the stone wall, she confirmed that attempting to carve through the stone would be an arduous process and would likely result in her skinning her fingers to the bone. Brigid looked at the wire screen protecting the metal bars. Digging the bars out would be equally tough. The stone was thick and hard. She frowned. It was also unlikely that she could carve through the mesh protecting the grid of thick metal. However, the tiny square would give her a slight advantage if she were up against a faux Nagah, Durga, the undead creatures or their queen. The square was only two inches long and a half of an inch wide with sharp corners, but Brigid was keenly aware that a vast majority of surgery was done with scalpels far shorter than the blade she carried. She'd also read that an unusual number of police officers were severely injured and killed by disproportionately short knives or simple razor blades. Jugular veins and carotid arteries were well within the striking range of her little tool, which was why she'd specified that particular length. Small enough to go completely unnoticed, but still big enough to kill if she needed it.

With or without an improvised handle, the metal rectangle was a good tool and a better weapon than an angry word. She had the ghost of a chance right now. Brigid settled in with her back to a wall, halfway between the door and the toilet hole. She used every moment to scan the featureless terrain, seeking out the slightest weakness in the prison.

For if she failed to find a way out, and if Kane was somehow captured, Durga and Neekra would come to their senses and execute their prisoners. In fact, Brigid wasn't certain that the bloody goddess wouldn't transfer from the warlord Gamal's mutated, carved body into that of a true woman.

Brigid cleared her mind of what *could* happen. It was time to think of what she was going to do.

Chapter 13

Grant and the other men were put in chains, while Brigid was allowed to remain in the leather straps that kept her wrists held tightly together. The chains were an obvious concession to the kind of physical power that Grant had demonstrated before Durga. Even though the Nagah prince had been elevated to superhuman durability and power by a corruption of Enki's technology back in the cobra people's city, Grant still had managed to survive a couple of blows in hand-to-hand combat with the elevated being.

That Grant's survival had been a combination of his own extraordinary stamina and physical conditioning and the impact dissipation of the shadow suits was amazing. The big ex-Magistrate didn't remember feeling all that incredible, especially with battered ribs and torn muscles in the wake of the punishment he'd received. He'd long since recovered from the abuse he'd suffered at Durga's superhuman hands, but his Nagah captor wasn't going to make any mistakes when it came to Grant. However, Grant was certain that it was a mistake on their part to keep Brigid in something that could be cut. If anyone planned ahead, it was the flame-tressed genius. Hell, she'd made a backup personality just in case someone took control of her mind, the one thing that had kept them from being utterly overwhelmed by the son of Enlil, the monstrous stone godling Ullikummis.

Grant had shown himself to be a remarkable physical presence, though, and the chain links were more than the powerful man could envision himself bursting. Even concentrating on one link, the chains were too well made to even damage the seams on one of the links. The manacles themselves were in good condition—of new manufacture—and there didn't seem to be a spot of rust on them.

He frowned, but then he realized that someone out there was either recycling metal or mining new resources. Then again, Africa was a major continent ripe with untapped mines and fuels. Pre-skydark, very few countries were worth blowing apart with nuclear weapons, but it had a thriving economy when it came to diamonds and other metals.

The big man had seen where patinas of rust had been on the manacles of the prisoners that he, Kane and Brigid had freed, but that was due to interaction with corrosive human sweat and blood, things that could turn even the smoothest of steel surfaces into harsh, pitted terrains of oxidization. The corners of the manacles were just sharp enough to begin rubbing on his skin, causing him a little bit of discomfort. With enough time and effort, though, Grant could see his skin eroding away. He'd only been in them for two hours since being shut into the five-by-eight Spartan cell, complete with crap hole burrowed in one side of the cell and a small dish for gruel and water underneath the door.

Grant adjusted himself to where the manacles were the least likely to dig into his forearms, but that was a little difficult as there were only a short few links between the belt around his waist, keeping his mobility to a minimum. Grant wondered at the hole in the back, especially as he had no slack in his arms in order to pull down his pants to use the toilet. He frowned, realizing that his captors had little interest in feeding him, or even less care if he soiled himself.

Not interested in sharing his pants with his own waste, Grant got to work thinking of how to get out of the cell. He was tempted to take out a spare Commtact plate he'd hidden on himself, but he wasn't certain what kind of communications technology Durga or Neekra had. He didn't believe that the vampires relied on electronic transmissions, but Durga was smart enough to have taken whatever equipment was left over from the Panthers of Mashona Warlord Gamal and the Millennium Consortium expedition. As the cells were separated, his captors certainly wanted to keep him from communicating with the other prisoners. There wasn't much space around the doorway. Even the slots for the candle and the feed tray through the door were barred by hatches that allow no light to get through. Grant leaned in close and tried to feel for any breeze around the entrances, but they were airtight.

Grant frowned. He didn't think that any sound would get through the doors or the stones. Indeed, the walls were almost seamless, and they were set close enough that he didn't think a piece of paper could slip between the blocks. Using a tool on the stone might work if their captors left them alone in these cells for a long time, but Grant knew he'd only have three days to work before he became too dehydrated to live. If they did provide moisture, but no food, then he'd have longer—a month. But that was only if they provided more than mere subsistence water.

Steel chains and stone walls didn't make an unbeatable prison, however. For now, it was a place for Grant to rest. He'd been up all night. Sleep was a gift to him, if only for a few moments. He could recuperate from the fight with the militia and his subsequent capture by the vampire blobs. He let his head rest on the stone of the wall, closed his eyes and drifted off.

Recharging his batteries came first. When he awoke, he'd attack his imprisonment with renewed alertness.

DURGA ENJOYED stretching, moving his limbs. He loved the feel of the burn in his muscles as he worked his *musti-yuddha* boxing practice. Utilizing the near-lifeless form of one of the failed militiamen who had not escaped the assault by Kane and the others, Durga worked out his tensions while returning vitality to his body. The sensation of flesh billowing upon impact, the feel of bones crunching as he drove an elbow or forearm into ribs, that was a long-lost joy that he was glad to engage in. The dying African, elevated by his wrists from a hook, was slick with blood from the powerful punches unleashed on him.

Durga stepped back and looked to see that Neekra's "children" were present. They looked at the dripping form hanging as if it were raw meat. In a way, it was, and the vampiric things looked with rapt attention at the drenched, fading human.

"My children have worked up an appetite in their effort to capture Kane," Neekra said. "And here you are, splattering their favorite foodstuff."

Durga looked down at his bloodied arms and fists. The Indian boxing he engaged in was a native art of the Nagah, one they had taught to the people of Varanasi in northern India, an art that was recorded in the Eddas when mythic legends battled with bare hands.

Its focus was on punches and gouges, but it spread to knee strikes and standard kicks, as well.

With his scales and physique returned to the prime of his health by Kane's artifact Nehushtan, he was deadly against a human. His knuckles and forearms were akin to razor-studded clubs, so taking out his vengeance on soft skin was going to be like using a cheese grater on it.

"I might as well have dipped myself in sauce, then," Durga mused.

"They want his blood," Neekra said, pointing to the failing slab of humanity.

Durga shrugged, then stepped away. He'd done enough of his workout for now.

The reanimated corpses lurched forward at Neekra's nearly imperceptible nod.

Durga looked at the woman, remembering what she had done to Gamal. He'd watched as she'd taken a grown man and burst and abused his flesh to the point where he resembled nothing that he'd been born to be. Despite what he knew she'd originally been, he had taken the skin-sculpting queen as a lover. Their bodies had entwined, surging against each other with all the strength and power they both held.

Durga had always been a violent lover, but Neekra didn't care. Indeed, she relished it, as if every ounce of discomfort that he inflicted in the name of his own pleasure added to hers. Durga realized that she was as much a psychic as physical "vampire" queen; she'd subjected Kane to endless agonies while they had been drawn into her telepathic trap. Durga had enjoyed his sojourn in her realm of reality, where he was not a prisoner or a little mind lost on endless universal planes.

Neekra had spoiled him, giving him every fantasy he'd ever desired, drawing on his cruelty and pleasure as much as she feasted on Kane's despondence and pain. When they were lovers in the physical sense, she kept that up, bathing in the glow of his psychosis, mixing hatred and lust. There was no way that Durga could permanently harm her new body. Every cut, every bite, every bruise healed at her whim. It was almost as if Neekra didn't feel it, but Durga didn't doubt that the pain went nowhere.

Gamal was still inside, trapped in the mutilated and mutated remains of his own body. And when Durga unleashed suffering on Neekra's shell, Gamal was the filter, the funnel through which she gorged on pain, drinking his agony as if it were ambrosia.

Durga was flabbergasted when she'd become "pregnant." Her belly had swollen with swiftly growing eggs. She'd passed them out, little translucent orange beans of dense, odd gelatin. Durga had been about to reach out and touch one when she ordered him to stay his hand.

"Despite appearances, this egg is not of your seed," Neekra warned. "And to touch it…"

The eggs smelled sweet, and Durga wondered briefly at that, but then came small rodents, attracted to the scent of food. And as they came closer, as they nibbled at the shells, the eggs suddenly reacted violently. To Durga's eyes, it seemed as if they were balloons, bursting, but that "burst" was actually the gel-like material of the eggs expanding, snapping shut around what rodents showed up. Trapped in the enveloping tendrils of Neekra's spawn, the rats screeched.

The suffering of the small mammals lasted only a minute or two before their furry little bodies disintegrated, breaking down as they were turned into nutrients for the slowly growing creatures.

No longer small beans of jelly, the blobs quickly

went out hunting, seeking new warm blood and flesh. Neekra kept them from targeting either Durga or his cloned Nagah soldiers, but she wanted humans, both for herself and her children.

Durga was surprised when the first shipment of "tribute" arrived just the day after she'd conquered Gamal's body. Neekra had thought ahead, getting her other seduced lover to send out troops to bring her what she'd known she'd need.

Durga frowned at the thought that he was merely a stepping-stone, a future meal or a future set of clothes for this ancient goddess. Lover, mating subject, piece of food. That was all that men were to her.

But then Durga wasn't known for being straightforward. He'd made deals with plenty of devils; indeed, his efforts that first brought him in contact with the men and women of Cerberus redoubt had been a ploy pitting Enlil, the Millennium Consortium and those selfsame explorers and heroes against each other. The impatient prince knew that asking any *one* party to assist him in gaining control of the Nagah's city-state would lead to that ally screwing him over completely, making his bid for power an exercise in futility. However, asking several different entities for help, allies who would be at odds with each other, gave him an opportunity. He'd specifically held off on his plan until he'd found the means to bring in a noble fourth party, one whose interest was not conquest, but justice and liberation. Kane and his allies lived up to those prerequisites admirably, and it was only Durga's own greed, basking in what appeared to be unlimited power potential, that had made him overreach and try to destroy Kane and company after they'd valiantly and decisively sent Enlil and the Millennium Consortium packing.

That misstep had left Durga in need of the power of ancient artifacts to return him to the realm of those who could walk under their own abilities. And once again, the exiled prince was working as many angles as he could. And those angles had changed drastically. Where once he had the Panthers of Mashona and the Millennium Consortium—still useful and easily manipulated—he now had the vampiric queen before him. For now, she didn't show any interest in him as food, merely as ally and a living sex toy, but that could change quickly. Neekra had inserted herself into Durga's quest, and though she was indeed an attractive ally who had tended to more than one of the prince's needs, he maintained vigilance.

Enlil had sealed the goddess into a tomb for a good reason, trapping her body in an effort to keep her away from the outside world. Neekra made no bones about the fact that, even with her vampiric children, she needed him to help her out of her prison. And Durga couldn't discount that somehow she might have been hedging her bets, drawing Kane and his allies along with them. He'd seen how Kane had relented in his attack on her psychic avatar within his mind. Durga could see her take the form of a helpless female, begging for mercy, preventing the human from crushing her once and for all.

"Damned fool," Durga muttered.

"Speaking of Kane and how he spared me?" Neekra asked as she watched her children feed.

Durga glanced at her. "I don't have to answer that question."

"You don't quite trust me," Neekra mused. Her bemusement stretched her lips into a smile beneath her dark, smoldering gaze.

"Nor do you trust me," Durga responded. "You're

keeping Kane's allies alive. They're your hostages. And when he comes…you'll do what? Pit us against each other for your amusement?"

Neekra shook her head. "Nothing so provincial. Enlil hid my true form away. You think that an Annunaki would trust merely stone, even tons of it, sealed airtight, to hold a goddess who could read minds and telekinetically sculpt flesh as if it were clay?"

Durga frowned. "You want the two of us to work together. To defeat the security Enlil put in place against you or your rescuers."

Neekra nodded.

"And you think that holding his friends hostage will influence him? That he won't try every trick in his book to free them and leave you alone with me?" Durga asked.

"He does not know where I am sealed," Neekra said. "He knows of my existence now. My presence. My world-shattering power. He would not dare allow me to continue, even trapped within an Annunaki jail."

Durga's eyes narrowed.

"This is a demonstration for him. I am proving myself as a threat that he needs to chase down and nip in the bud," Neekra told him. "You do not need to fight at his shoulder. He will lead the way."

Durga nodded. There was still much that this goddess wasn't saying, holes in her strategy, holes big enough to swallow Durga and make him disappear forever, and Neekra wouldn't give a damn. In fact, the witch was probably counting on it. Anyone who possessed the abilities to assist her would likely be powerful enough to stop her, or at least inconvenience her. Durga knew that's what he'd do in her situation.

Durga kept these thoughts tightly under wraps. The

last thing he needed was to tip off Neekra over how much he had planned in case things went sideways for himself. He returned to his conversation with her. "Is this why your vampire men aren't running Kane down? Because you actually want him free and actively hunting you?"

"I've been in his mind, and yours, lover. I know what makes either of you tick," Neekra responded, as if to punctuate Durga's own fears about her ability to pluck at his surface thoughts. "Kane will want to hunt me down. If I endeavored to seduce him, he would be resistant indeed. I'd be skating uphill against the current misgivings he possesses about me. But if I can play him, I can get a grudging alliance."

"That's dicing with damnation," Durga replied. "I tried that game—"

"A game which lasted up until you got a taste of superhuman power," Neekra said. "That rush and your impatience left you wide-open for him to bring you down like a sack of bricks."

Durga frowned.

"You got greedy, overconfident. That is why you failed, why you fell," Neekra continued. "Unlike you, dear boy, I have the patience of millennia."

Durga brought down a curtain over the string of responses he wanted to utter, but the glimmering, bloodred goddess smiled and traced her fingertips across his cheek, smirking at the daggers sharpening in his eyes.

"Remember, for all the gifts Enki bestowed upon you and your race, you are merely human. You are soft and temporary, while I and the Annunaki are truly eternal," Neekra whispered. "There is nothing that you have that I could not plan for."

Durga continued to stew, anger bubbling and obscuring his deeper thoughts, the plans that he buried deep down, utilizing meditative disciplines that had availed him well in his telepathic dealings with Enlil. His angry turmoil was a good filter, a screen that prevented the thing before him from recognizing that she *hadn't* seen everything in Durga's plans.

The cobra prince's ace in the hole would remain buried deep within.

Yes, Durga had given in, *once,* to a moment of impatience and overconfidence. But that misadventure had burned patience into his mind. That lesson was hard earned, at the cost of his mobility, his capacity to live without being subjected to constant pain. And now he was an exile from a realm that was his by blood right.

No, Durga knew the patience of which Neekra spoke. He also knew better than to rely on any one man or woman, no matter how powerful they were.

Durga would survive, goddess of hell or not.

Chapter 14

It was closing in on late afternoon, and Lyta was finished going over her equipment. She didn't like the quiet, the lack of interest from the necropolis beneath. Kane had said that if it was an underground city packed with vampires, they had one name for it, drawn from historical myths—the undead city of Negari, of which Neekra was the queen.

"You heard this myth and we didn't?" Lyta asked. "I mean, I've lived in this region for twenty years and never heard one lick about any vampire cities."

"The myths were recounted by an American writer named Robert E. Howard," Kane answered. "And, unfortunately, the legends he wrote of had a strong undercurrent of historical truth."

Kane held his tongue for a moment.

"Something else 'true enough'?" Lyta asked.

"One of the tales, back then, was about an adventurer who went by the name of Solomon Kane...no relation. He found himself taken to the tomb of an imprisoned horror by chance when he encountered a slave train," the Cerberus explorer said. "Indeed, Solomon Kane seemed to be the lightning rod for most of these myths we've ended up chasing, from the stick itself to winged horrors such as the Kongamato."

Lyta nodded, remembering Kane's description of the nightmarish creatures controlled by Thurpa's former prince, Durga. Those things had come up recently in the news, sightings of the flying, apelike monsters slashing through the skies over the Zambian capital. Each was the size of a gorilla, though their anatomy was more like bats or pterodactyls, with their powerful arms the roots of long-stretched wings.

Kane had tied those horrific marauders to the tales of the Puritan wanderer.

"Luckily for you, when we found you, it wasn't because of a girl who was whipped to death," Kane concluded.

Lyta realized Kane's sudden unwillingness to speak about her condition. "I don't think I can thank you enough for freeing me and my neighbors."

"I didn't do it for the thanks," Kane replied. "I did it because it was the right thing to do."

Lyta managed a smile, wishing she knew how she looked. Kane was a tall, handsome man, exotic as very few whites were among the Zambian country folk, though "white" belied the rich hue of his skin, weathered by years of sun and the elements. She wondered if he had a woman somewhere, because despite his obvious affection for the redheaded Brigid, there was no spark of romance between them, no sexual tension, no flirting.

Then again, Lyta hadn't been with them for long. There could have been much more to their relationship dynamic, but Kane seemed far too no-nonsense for that. His urgency toward rescuing Grant and Brigid seemed rooted more in rushing to the aid of captured *family* then mere friends or lovers. It was possible that the pair could have been a married couple, except for the fact that Kane often referred to her by her family name, though in a deeply intimate manner for such a reserved form of address.

Almost as if Kane was either distancing himself from her or…

Lyta thought about it for a moment. Kane and Grant were only referred to by singular names, as well. They didn't seem to have first or given names, just the tag that came from their family. And with that, Lyta caught a slight glimpse. Brigid became "Baptiste" because Kane had accepted her into the same no-nonsense clique, the same ultimate level of trust that Grant had.

They *were* family, despite the sharpness of tongue and differences of opinion. They'd disagree, get on each other's cases or laugh at the other's expense, but only in good nature and humor.

Kane's attention seemed to wander, and Lyta found herself tensing up. If something drew the man's focus, then it was something important, worth that scrutiny.

Kane gave her a gentle nod, then stood up. "I'm going to take care of some business. Be right back."

"All right," Lyta answered. With that, Kane took a few steps toward the trees, and then he was swallowed up, disappearing despite the bright sun hanging low in the sky. The man moved with the speed and grace of a natural-born hunter, a sleek-muscled predator who had been both stalked and stalker and had always come out on top. Lyta hoped that his record would remain unbroken, because she didn't relish being alone.

Not when there was an underground city full of vampires a few dozen yards beneath their feet and other unknowns in the forest around them. Lyta slid her rifle into her lap, letting it rest on her thighs, hand not too far from the grip, finger ready to hook the trigger at the slightest sound of a twig's snap. The silence became preternatural, odd and enveloping. Normally, there would have been the sound of birds and bugs, small creatures communicating with each other, but the silence accompanied a strangeness, a deep-down quiet that unsettled the Zambian girl, as well as apparently the local fauna.

Lyta kept her big brown eyes wide, scanning for trouble.

She grimaced at her pride going so far as to think it could match a man whose instincts were enhanced by an ancient god-fighting artifact.

It was then that Lyta noticed that the staff still rested next to the tree, along with the rifle that Kane had picked up to supplement his sidearm. Her stomach flopped, and her heart felt like it had been splashed with ice water as she realized that Kane must be operating half-blind without the gifts of the strange stick. Against an intruder, that could turn out to be damning, crippling.

Lyta cast her gaze about, seeking out Kane, but he'd disappeared completely. She hoped that it was enough for him. She let out a sigh, realizing that she'd been holding her breath for several seconds.

"Please be careful," she allowed herself to whisper.

"If your companion is…" said a voice behind her. Lyta's nerves were wound tight, and she whirled, whipping up her rifle in a fast, fluid movement that staggered even her expectations of her reflexes. As she saw the front sight of her weapon intersect the silhouette of a stranger, the man was a blur. He stepped aside from the muzzle, hand pushing down on the barrel. Lyta let out a yelp of surprise as she triggered the gun. A bullet slammed into the dirt, kicking up lots of dust but harming no one otherwise.

"…who I believe he is," the man, another white,

wearing a battered Stetson and a well-worn khaki shirt, continued, not even fazed by the eruption of a high-velocity bullet into the ground. "Kane will be extremely careful. Chances are, he's already got me in his sights."

"No chance," Lyta said. "He already *owns* you."

"You show a lot of faith in a man you've known for less than twenty-four hours," the man replied. Other than redirecting her shot, he had not moved an inch. "My name is Austin Fargo. And I've known Kane for much longer."

Lyta narrowed her eyes. "And if you're trying to cast doubt on him because of that, you're mistaken."

"And now, another convert to his cult. Where he finds you little girls—"

Lyta swung up the rifle, bringing the muzzle around. It was a feint, and she immediately reversed the weapon, pushing the stock toward Fargo. Where she expected to connect with his chest, driving the wind from his lungs, she only pushed through empty air, much to her surprise. She turned, trying to reacquire her target, but the man quickly snatched the rifle from her grasp, taking advantage of her momentary confusion.

With a sneer, she backpedaled away from the man in the hat. "How are you so fast?"

"I have my own gifts," Fargo admitted. As Lyta studied him, she realized that the brim of his hat was drawn particularly low. She couldn't even see his eyes, but he followed her with little difficulty. He moved with unusual grace.

"So, you know Kane?" Lyta asked.

Fargo nodded. He wouldn't allow her a complete look at his face, and that made her ever the more curious. She was half-tempted to try for the pistol in its holster, but his swift reflexes had already stymied her twice. That kind of preternatural awareness might not be accompanied by patience. A third try at shooting or harming him might be met with than simple disarming moves.

So she kept her head, realizing that if she made the wrong move, she'd be dead, and that would make her worthless. Besides, Fargo was likely right. Kane had him dead to rights. It was one thing to disarm someone standing only a few feet away. Kane was a good shot, and pulling those swift kung fu moves from twenty feet away would not amount to much, not against a combatant like the one who had set a militia's survivors to flight.

"And how well do you know him?" Fargo asked.

"Enough that he's saved my ass twice in the space of a day," Lyta replied. "While you—"

"Prevented you from hurting yourself. Twice," Fargo interrupted. He took off his hat, and now Lyta could see what was so "wrong," what had made her suspicious. His forehead was swollen, but not as if it had been bug bitten. His brow had thickened, and it was smooth, unlined; even his eyebrows were missing. From under the shade of that massive forehead, Fargo's eyes glittered like moonlight off black glassy ponds.

"What…"

Kane stepped out from behind Fargo. "This man made a deal with the same devil responsible for Durga becoming a cripple."

Fargo turned. Kane was out of his reach, and no amount of enhanced reflexes could give Fargo an advantage over the man.

"You make Enki out to be a demon," Fargo replied. "He was a good, benevolent being. Otherwise, the others who staked their claims on this ball of mud would not deride him so."

"Still, it was not Enki who gave you that facial condition. It was a computer. The same one which gave Durga superhuman power," Kane countered. He kept his distance.

"Why did you leave the staff unattended?" Fargo asked, nodding toward Nehushtan.

"Because the stick has its own agenda, and if it doesn't want to be touched, then it won't allow itself to," Kane explained.

Fargo turned, walked toward the ancient artifact and grasped its shaft. He picked it up, looking it over.

Lyta turned to Kane, who seemed surprised at this sudden turn of affairs.

"Why isn't it repelling you as it did before?" Kane asked.

"Oh, I was repelled by Nehushtan?" Fargo asked, turning it, testing its balance. "Smooth. No glyphs on its handle at all. And the head has changed."

"You lied," Kane surmised.

"You were ready to blow my damn fool head off just for showing up in the wake of the Kongamato attack," Fargo responded. "And then I'm going to make it look like I'm able to interface with this piece of technology? Yes, that would have been a great piece of strategy. No. I stayed away from it because I thought it'd be nice to not be riddled with bullets."

Kane had his machine pistol in hand. "Put it back down."

Fargo rested it against the tree where Kane had left it. "Now, the staff *is* freezing me out. It hid its glyphs the moment I touched it. I cannot access it at all."

"Why do you feel safe unveiling your lie now?" Kane asked.

Fargo smirked. "Is Brigid around? Grant?"

Kane's lips remained a tight crack. Lyta could feel the brittleness of his self-control. She didn't envy Fargo's position. The man's cockiness had just rubbed a raw nerve on the tall Cerberus warrior. She was tempted again to reach for her pistol now that Kane was there to back her up.

Kane shook his head, looking at her. "We need what little help we can get."

Kane slung his machine pistol over his shoulder and walked closer to Fargo. "Emphasis on *little help*."

"Where is this coming from?" Fargo asked.

Kane glared. "You walked out on us when the Kongamato made their big push."

"Us. I seem to recall that you and Durga were both comatose," Fargo replied. "And yet you both roused and rallied, defeating the menace."

"No thanks to you," Kane remarked.

"Are you certain?" Fargo asked.

Kane didn't appear to buy it. Lyta could feel the seething disgust just under his surface, so close that a mere scratch would open him up, unleash the blazing lava of hatred onto Fargo. That Kane kept that distrust on a tight leash only served to impress the African girl.

It also conveyed just what kind of man Austin Fargo must be, if Kane was kept so close to apoplectic rage by his presence. The kind of fury emanating off of him indicated a killing mood, meaning that Fargo was likely guilty of more crimes than simply being an inconvenience to the Cerberus explorer.

Kane moved closer to Lyta, looking her over, as if for signs of foul play. "He didn't bring out his whip on you, did he?"

"I didn't need to," Fargo responded.

Kane glared at the newcomer.

"He whips people?" Lyta asked. Her skin started to crawl. She'd spent enough time, for the past week exactly, living in terror of the whip as the Panthers of Mashona had marched her and her neighbors relentlessly toward the underground necropolis of Neekra. Using such a tool against animals disgusted her enough, but seeing the horrors it had exacted on other human beings—especially her mother—burned the thing into her mind as a symbol of evil.

She leaned her head and saw the braided leather coils hanging from the back of his belt.

"Good way to poison her against me," Fargo murmured, his beady eyes narrowing. "I have not used this against a human being—"

"This year? You've flayed people alive, as recently as a year ago, when we first met," Kane grumbled. "So don't play innocent. You have blood on your hands, no matter how dried it is."

"Like you, enforcer of Baron Cobalt?" Fargo returned. "You are no babe in the woods."

"I'm at least making up for the harm I caused while being a Magistrate," Kane snapped.

Fargo turned his attention to Lyta, a smug smirk stretching across his lips. "He is now a saint, or at least feels he is in the same standing as one. He's the only one doing something to atone for his sins. No one else is as special as he."

Kane clenched his fists and took a deep breath. "I'm not saying that. But I am saying that nothing you have done since we first met has proven you to be anything but out for yourself."

"Well, you've proven yourself beyond any benefit of a doubt, Kane. How many cities have you left in ruins, not counting the villes? Not counting the swathe of destruction you tore through China? The wreckage of Garuda?"

Kane narrowed his eyes. "Your bombs were a part of that. We protected the Nagah. And mind you—you brought us there."

"To protect them."

"This is how you can tell that Fargo is lying...his lips—"

"Enough!" Lyta snapped. "Sunset is coming in less than an hour, and you two look like you've got enough piss to keep going 'til dawn!"

Fargo glared at the young woman.

"She's right," Kane agreed. "There's bigger danger beneath our feet. You probably know all about them, especially if you've been spying on us all this time."

Fargo nodded, tugging his Stetson back over his head, obscuring his obscene brow. "I know about Neekra and her vampire minions. But not because of interest in your pedestrian exploits."

Kane let his shoulders drop, breaking into a smile.

"That wasn't an insult?" Lyta asked.

Kane shook his head. "He's groping in the dark when he calls our quest run-of-the-mill, and he knows it."

"Had to disarm your animosity somehow. Making you laugh helped," Fargo responded.

"So, what do you know about Neekra?" Kane asked, strapping his rifle across his back. He leaned against the ancient staff, taking a moment to study its suddenly smooth surface. On contact with his palm, he felt the artifact's skin change. No longer in the hands of Fargo, it felt free to return to its normal mode.

"She was a great opponent of the Annunaki, not only here on earth, but across the stars," Fargo stated. "She had attacked their kin as they colonized other planets."

"Neekra had her own galactic empire to fight Kane's 'snake-faces'?" Lyta asked. She quickly added, for her own clarification, "No relation to Thurpa's people."

"You're familiar with the concept of a galactic empire?" Fargo countered. "Because for all her pomp and circumstance, Neekra was no more than the Norwegian brown rat sailing across the Atlantic with Dutch and British exiles."

Kane frowned at the analogy. "Those rats did pretty well in nearly wiping out Europe with a few plagues, let alone spoiling tons of food, helping out famines."

"That is why I used the rat as her analog in this description," Fargo said. "Neekra *is* dangerous, not only to the local fauna—that being humanity—as well as being destructive and disruptive to the Annunaki themselves. Otherwise, Enlil would have let her scions run loose as a natural predator for mankind. However, now, considering the tentative hold that they have on the planet, the fragmenting of what structure the overlords *had* put in place for themselves, there's nothing to stay one's hand in unleashing them as a scorched-earth protocol."

"There's an overlord operating in Africa?" Kane asked.

"I'm looking into it," Fargo stated. "It's why I became interested in Durga's escapades."

Kane's mood took a turn for the darker. Gone was his loathing of Fargo, at least as far as Lyta could tell. It had been replaced with concerns of other menaces.

"So, either Neekra was let loose…presumably to wipe out this planet's annoying pests…" Kane began. He motioned toward himself and Lyta when he referred to the pests. "Or Durga is working with another overlord in order to protect his planet from her."

"Or both," Lyta offered. "After all, didn't you two

mention that the aliens aren't all on the same page anymore?"

Kane and Fargo both nodded in agreement. He glanced at Fargo. "Of course, this story could be just a ruse for you to work alongside us so that you can accomplish whatever your twisted goals are."

Fargo smirked. "You have trust issues."

"Only with known and proven bastards," Kane responded. "You were still fairly chummy with Durga, even after being chased to the high hills out of India."

Fargo laughed. "You do have a good point. If I prove to be utterly useless to you, there'd be no reason for you to keep me alive. If I'm somehow working with your enemies, you'll hope to trip me up and find out what they are up to. The only time you'll be free to eliminate me as a threat, and avenge whatever crimes you accuse me of, is if I take leave of my senses and act openly against you. Which I will not."

"Someday your little game will tire my patience," Kane said. "You're just lucky I need all the help I can get right now."

Fargo nodded to the man, then bowed graciously to Lyta, handing her back the weapon he'd plucked out of her grasp.

"We have minutes before Neekra's children are free to stalk the shadows," Fargo stated. "I have a back door that even she cannot suspect."

Kane motioned for Lyta to go along with the man in the hat. For now, they were in a dangerous balance of trust.

Chapter 15

Thurpa had been alone in his cell for just an hour, his mouth still hurting from where he'd wrenched the hinge muscles in one of his fangs, his body battered by the gelatinous forms of Neekra's spawn. He'd been relieved that Durga, except for a few sneers, had largely ignored the former loyalist to the prince. It was for the best, Thurpa told himself.

Durga was a man of no small temper, and his spite would be a focused, special flavor of hell. Thurpa had seen those who had failed the not so noble Nagah. And Thurpa had seen Durga's negligent concern for the young man himself—it was the reason he'd thrown in his lot with Kane and the others.

Putting aside thoughts of the ache in his overstressed fang hinge, he considered his options for escape as he looked down at his manacles. The chains were firm and thick, as were the clasps that limited the motion of his wrists. He'd also been frisked down completely, any hope of tools hidden in pockets taken away, not that he had much in terms of clothing to have pockets. He was good with a bare chest and feet, thanks to his scales and his tropical upbringing. His scales were thick and hard, relatively immune to sunburn. All he had were some cargo pants that he'd cut off at the knees. Those pockets had been emptied and his belt taken away.

Thurpa looked at the manacle clasp and saw that

there was a spot for a key. He didn't even have to think twice about what long, slender tool he could slip into the keyhole. He had two hinged fangs. He simply had to bend his head down far enough to insert a tooth in and jostle the tumblers on the manacles' locking mechanism.

Sure, thank you, Enki, for giving us such great snakelike attributes. Everything except a spine that can fold and bend like string.

His neck ached, and the manacles were testing the durability of his forearm and hand scales. Thurpa's shoulders and biceps protested as he bent, holding up the weight of his cuffs and chains, all the while his lower jaw feeling as if it were pinned to the rest of his head by rusted nails. His tongue dried out, and the flexor muscles in his fang burned as he tried to hold his tooth steady, trying to jostle the tumblers in the manacles.

He felt the tendons freezing, refusing to keep his fang extended. The rust on the manacles scraped across his tongue, but he couldn't pull his head away. He needed to stay down in that lock, despite every instinct to spit out the flaked, oxidized iron.

Something popped between Thurpa's neck and shoulder, and something hot spread beneath. He knew it was a tendon popping as the heat crawled up and down his tugged, pained neck. And yet he could feel the progress being made. The dull clicks within the lock, tumblers being moved. The grind of metal on his tooth was maddening, and his scaled lips were growing ever more raw.

Every bit of him felt like it was being crumpled up more and more, and his muscles *begged* to be stretched out, the kinks pulled and popped, freed from this tension. He could feel the salty sting of a tear crawling down his nose, dripping off it and onto the metal. The tear stung his lip, and he fought off the urge to wince away from it.

Enki, I'm sorry for complaining. Please, I need to get out of these chains, he began praying after an hour and a half of effort. The strain on his neck had crawled slowly inside his skull, the coils of a boa constrictor winding around his brain and causing his head to throb. He'd close his eyes, and, under the lids, he could feel them spasm, twitch, rattling side to side as his orbs seemed to twirl free at the end of rubber bands.

Thurpa's will was draining, but he kept pushing, kept stretching to reach the keyhole. He ignored the split and cracking of his scales around his lips and wrists as the heavy steel yearned to obey the tug of gravity.

Biceps now had daggers poked into them, then slitting lines of fire up their centers. Holding up the chains was just too much.

Come on, you crybaby, he scolded himself. Lyta is half of your weight, and she survived six days with bindings like this digging into her. And she didn't have armored scales!

It took every ounce of discipline he had. Somewhere along the way, he'd lost track of time.

Suddenly, there was a loud click. And his left hand was free. No more was he grinding, bent, pressing his skin against unyielding steel. Blood trickled between his scales, and many of them looked burst on his dermis. He felt the urge to brush away the broken skin, but knew he'd only be aggravating whatever pain was now simply a dull ache.

He also only had one hand free. Thurpa licked his lips, feeling the jagged flakes of scale and rust mixing on his tongue. He barely had the moisture to spit, but he managed to cough and blow out the detritus in his mouth.

Thurpa lay back, resting his head against the wall. He blinked, taking inventory of his hurts, his discomforts. He ran his tongue over the fang, and found that it had been chipped badly. He also realized his venom sac was empty. He'd need to get a closer look at the fang in a mirror, but at least the tooth hadn't been broken off.

Rest, he told himself. They've left you alone for this long. Regain your strength. Maybe look for something that could be used as another tool.

"You know, maybe something showed up since you last spent an hour looking at everything in this cell," he spoke out loud. His words felt slurred, but then, this was the third time in as many days that he'd sustained damage to his mouth. This whole trip to Africa seemed to be one smash in the face after another.

He rubbed his forehead. Knuckles cracked from disuse. He'd kept his fists clenched as he'd gnawed, probed, turned his tooth inside the manacle keyhole.

Thurpa examined the manacle itself as he ran his tongue over the raw, aching roof of his mouth. The chains were fairly dense and heavy, but not so bad. He could actually grasp it in one hand, providing support for his other wrist. He looked to see if the opened clamp could provide some sort of tool to undo the other side.

He rested the apparatus in his lap and manipulated the hinge of one of the bracelets, looking for a way to work out the pin holding it together. There was no such luck for him. Each end of the hinge was capped in a heavy metal fastening. To get even one side off would take a saw or a ton of hammering. He looked around and he noticed that he had plenty of solid stone to work against. There was also the candle port. Wire mesh and heavy bars.

Thurpa examined the manacle and the chain, then crawled over to the port. Maybe he could keep the chains on, using them as a weapon or tool against the door. As he crawled, he noticed that water had been poured under the door, filling a depression in the floor.

"Oh, no way," Thurpa muttered. If they expected him to drink off the floor...

And, yet, he was parched.

Wrinkling his nose, sneering at his weakness, he stooped and lapped at the water. Grit scraped the inside of his throat as he swallowed, but even though it was full of dust and rust flakes adhered to his tongue and lips, he continued to lap. Thirst controlled him, and he hadn't replenished himself in so long.

Finally sated, he sat back up, breathing deeply.

Just a little more time resting, Thurpa mused. Then I can get back to breaking my chains....

Thurpa closed his eyes, brain working even as he nodded off.

NATHAN LONGA WISHED that he hadn't ceded Nehushtan, but then, while he was in charge of carrying the artifact, he felt less than helpful, no matter what abilities it imparted in him.

Of course, now he missed the presence of the ancient device. He could have used a surge of strength sufficient to snap the chains, but those were just pipe dreams for now. He remembered his father telling him once, "Wish in one hand and shit in another, and see which fills first."

Nathan couldn't hear any of the others. Maybe they were attempting to break free.

Maybe? Nothing maybe about it. Those people hadn't gotten this far, hadn't battled their way around the world without having the drive to escape when imprisoned.

Nathan figured at least one of them would have a tool hidden away.

He wasn't so certain that Thurpa would have a way out, but he'd known the snake for a shorter amount of time than he was familiar with the Cerberus heroes. But Thurpa had survived where others of the Millennium Consortium contingent had died, and had gone on to save the Zambians when he could have played possum and laid back, allowing a horde of monsters to ambush and overwhelm humans who would have no qualms about letting him die.

The two of them, Nathan and Thurpa, were young men who were far from home, and they had managed more than a little bit of camaraderie.

He'd spotted a pause in the young cobra warrior as he'd looked into Lyta's eyes. Nathan could identify the beginnings of an attraction, especially since she'd stayed close to him while the group was setting up for their further investigation. Nathan didn't care. Thurpa had shown himself to be a fine person, and Lyta was a distant, never-encountered cousin. He had others at home who had caught his eye.

Nathan looked over the chains. Maybe he couldn't pick a lock, but he'd been around the artifact Nehushtan, a device that had granted him the strength to battle gorilla-size mutates that seemed to shrug off rifle bullets like raindrops. He felt them, looking for seams or imperfections. Nathan didn't delude himself that any superhuman power he'd been granted would allow him to snap chains as if they were twigs.

For as strong or as swift as anyone had been while boosted by the staff, they still succumbed to injuries. Nathan knew that human flesh and bone were far more likely to yield when applied against steel than anything else. And so he felt a seam where one link wasn't quite welded true. He put his thumbs against the inside of the circlet and pushed.

Nothing. Nathan ramped up the pressure. He fought to bend the chain link, to break the weld. He kept going until he was certain his thumbs were going to break, and he stopped.

Nehushtan's influence over his body was gone. He'd need to find a different means to enhance his physical might. That added up to a tool, and he was completely disarmed. Nathan rested his head against the wall, closed his eyes and thought.

If only the staff could hear me, he mused. Brigid was captured, but she didn't have Nehushtan in her possession, only the improvised one. Chances are my cousin Lyta has it. And, hopefully, it'll lead her to Kane.

I did lead her to Kane.

The whispered thought was in his own voice, but it had come unbidden to him. He opened his eyes, feeling the skin on his arms prickle, hairs rising to produce sheets of goose bumps all up and down his flesh. Nathan gnawed at his upper lip, looking around. Was he starting to lose it, after only a short time of being confined alone?

No, you are not, scion of N'Longa.

It was the staff. The rod that had been attributed to Solomon and Moses, which had its origins even further back in the history of the universe, all the way back to, allegedly, Atlantis. He gritted his teeth and closed his eyes again.

"You're really there?" Nathan asked.

No answer. Then again, the staff had already provided its answer. He was not alone and still in contact with the artifact. The stave would not answer its question a second time, especially since Nathan knew in his heart of hearts that this was not imagination or fantasy.

"Let Kane know that we're in good sorts," Nathan responded.

He has seen you and your companions. He knows that you are prisoners of the devil's avatar and the errant son of Enki.

Nathan felt his blood chill at Neekra being referred to as a devil. The staff mentioning that her body was merely an avatar added to his discomfort. Recalling his education from his father, his studies of comparative religions, he knew that avatars were mere slivers, essences of the Brahmic pantheon's gods, which was where the term *avatar* originally came from.

So, Neekra was a mere shadow of her true self, and that meant her abilities were limited. Maybe that was why the four of them were now prisoners and not being hollowed out, killed and replaced by the gelatinous beasts that she referred to as her children.

Neekra probably needed them as bait.

To bring Kane and, most likely, Nehushtan itself.

"I'm trying my hardest to escape," Nathan murmured. "But I'm not strong enough. I have no tools or resources."

Faith, Nathan. They also serve who sit and wait.

The young man wondered what level of sentience the staff had. These transmissions could have simply been the equivalent of a standard computer's automatic responses, an artificial intelligence, or perhaps the staff actually had some form of life. Nathan had seen enough over the past several weeks to realize that the nature of life and existence around the world were far from the limited concepts he was familiar with, at least outside a science fiction novel.

Nehushtan seemed to have no answer for that thought, and, for now, Nathan didn't care.

All he could hope to do was try to save his strength and figure out another means of escape other than relying on the supernatural might of an ancient artifact.

It wasn't going to be easy waiting.

DURGA STEPPED AWAY from the door. Only the young African seemed to be doing nothing to escape. Sure enough, the two from Cerberus, the beautiful woman and the giant of a man, had been working with smuggled tools, items that had been missed by less than completely thorough frisks of their half-clad bodies.

Brigid had the easier time, her bindings being of leather, which she could slice through using a small razor blade. Grant, however, wasn't an expert lock pick, and his struggles with his manacles were increasing the frustration on his features. Durga was relieved that the big man simply hadn't flexed and burst the chains restraining him.

Durga thought he'd heard Nathan speaking, but the young man had grown quiet again.

And then there was Thurpa. The traitor Thurpa.

It must have been torture for that boy to pop the lock on his manacles with one long fang dug into the keyhole.

One free wrist, and then lapping water off the floor, like a dog.

Durga had not really offered him the promise of a

life of leisure in exchange for Thurpa's service, but the Nagah prided honor and loyalty.

That loyalty had shifted, drastically, to the very humans who had turned the cobra prince into a fugitive. All for what? A simple act of kindness?

Durga took a deep breath, watching his former minion lying on the ground.

The water was spiked. As much as Durga looked forward to seeing exactly how resourceful they were, he didn't want any of these four getting away.

Not yet.

Neekra strode down the corridor, her crimson flesh glimmering in the torchlight.

"What are you thinking of?" Neekra asked.

Durga rested his hand on the door. "My disappointment."

"Ah, the boy," Neekra replied. "I could try to woo him."

"No," Durga responded. "He is dead to me."

"And yet you're drugging him," Neekra said. "Why?"

Durga glared at her. "I do not want to have to deal with an escaped prisoner while Kane is still out and about."

Neekra nodded.

"I don't know what you're thinking, you're good at that, but I know that you are up to something," Neekra told him. She stepped closer.

"I'm protecting my ass," Durga said. "I've dealt with Enlil, the one you tell me imprisoned you. I don't trust so-called gods as far as I can throw the pyramids. So, forgive me for having something to keep me from ending up screwed to death."

Neekra smirked.

"You think you can protect yourself?" Neekra asked.

Durga kept his silence, kept his thoughts buried deeply.

"How do you think that you are special enough to handle me?" Neekra pressed.

"Because you asked *me* for help," Durga responded. "Right now, you're not at your peak. You need your original form, and you need someone to help you get back to it."

"So, you're planning to kill me?" Neekra asked.

"What would be the use in that?" Durga countered. "You promised me a great reward. I'll help you, until you decide that my reward is a shallow grave, if I get a grave."

Neekra looked him over.

"I'm looking out for myself. I'm also smart enough to know that planning to take you out of the picture is a good excuse for you to kill me. I want whatever reward, whatever power you're promising me, even if it's just more of you using me as your boy toy," Durga said. "Our relationship right now is good. You're not trying to kill me, and I'm going to keep my ass in one piece. In case you haven't noticed, my only friends here are the ones I cloned."

Neekra looked at the assemblage of cobra men. "Is that why you're showing such interest in your former minion? The one who showed confusion about me when last we met?"

Durga frowned. "Thurpa. What confusion?"

"He didn't know how to take me," Neekra stated. "It was as if he knew I were merely a psychic projection. He saw and heard me, but to him, something felt off. He could sense me within his skull."

"So, is he sensitive?" Durga asked, suddenly growing more interested.

"I believe so. He's not aware of what he is capable of, but then, most humans are not," Neekra explained. "And as far as I am concerned, you and he are as human as the hairless apes you're scuffling with."

"I don't care," Durga replied. "What I *do* care about is what your children are going to need to eat or whatever you need from 'sensitive minds.'"

"As in, do you think I want to eat your brain?" Neekra asked.

Durga nodded.

"Don't worry about that. I need more than blood or any biological material you are composed of," Neekra told him. "You are safe from being on the menu. As are any of your prisoners, if you wish to keep them alive."

Durga looked at the cell doors.

"You want to keep them alive," Neekra noted. "Why?"

"That is my reason to know alone," Durga responded. "But we both agree we need them for our own private purposes."

Neekra nodded.

Durga held out his hand to her. "Peace."

"Peace is always good," Neekra said.

Durga, though, could feel her thinking, her own little unspoken "for now."

He could sense hers just as he knew she could feel his own, despite the discipline hiding his deeper emotions.

Cobra man and vampire goddess, dancing around each other, looking for a weakness, knowing any failure on their own part would lead to their destruction. Durga was reminded of Kali, the goddess of destruction, herself a drinker of blood, and she who wove the dance of life and death. Was Kali another name for the entity standing before him?

Either way, Durga knew that he was walking on a high wire over the apocalypse. If she truly did get her way, whatever world Durga inherited would be barren and lifeless.

Chapter 16

The dreaded sunset fell, and Kane braced himself. Darkness would be when the creatures ventured forth into the night. It made sense to him, now, why they avoided the shining blaze of the sun, not for fear of its burning rays, but because night made the dead bodies they took residence in seem less out of the ordinary. He recalled the sight of these entities as they had clothed themselves in the flesh of the recently killed, and he knew that in the daytime, there would be little to hide their hideous mockery of humanity.

At night, as long as they kept to the shadows, they had nothing to fear of early discovery, until it was far too late for their unsuspecting victims.

And there one was, the first up to the entrance, wearing its disguise, formerly a man who had thought nothing of keeping other humans as slaves, like a suit that had been stuffed under a mattress and then slept on. The rumpled corpse *should* have moved jerkily, especially given the amount of tearing and stretching that its semiliquid owner had subjected it to, squeezing through wounds and orifices to set up shop. Instead, the snot-beast inside maneuvered with deft grace.

Kane had been up close in dealing with the prowess of the creatures, and, for now, he wanted to avoid that. No matter what kind of firepower he could assemble, the reanimates were swift and deadly. The artifact had provided a minor evening of the odds, as had grenades and bullets pumped relentlessly into them, but that took time, time the other killers could use to flank Kane and his allies.

While Fargo seemed capable of taking care of himself and Lyta was willing to fight, Kane did not want to risk the night, or the rescue of his friends, by engaging in an all-out gun battle. The noise alone would draw down far more trouble than Kane wished. No. Silence and stealth were going to be Kane's advantages.

It was bad enough that Neekra had preternatural psychic abilities, and they could only be shielded from her detection by the Nehushtan. As it was, Kane and Lyta were both touching the artifact, while Fargo relied on his own gifted enhancements to maintain his low profile.

At the same time, the three of them had made use of blankets, canvas tape and foliage during the day. They had hidden themselves in a small recess in the ground, behind the tree line outside the camp. In the rut and covered by handmade camouflage netting that they'd produced during the day, they should be invisible. Kane had taken the extra step of adding a thermal blanket to their cover, a heat-shielding square of foil and polymers that prevented body heat from being lost in the deepest cold. It would also reflect the broiling beams of the sun, keeping them from roasting the wearer. Even if the creatures had some form of infrared sensitivity, it would be unlikely that they would be seen from within.

As well, there was plenty of ground clutter and flora about them. They were off the beaten path, and no one was going to find them unless they were combing every inch of the forest.

Kane heard more of the vampiric creatures moving

about, and he closed the slit through which he observed them. They were coming out of the underground necropolis now, and Kane held his breath.

He glanced toward Fargo. However, beneath the blankets and the foliage and with bushes between them, he couldn't actually eyeball the man. But he knew where he lay, and he prayed that Fargo wasn't going to blow their cover.

Kane counted his heartbeats, waiting for any sound to interrupt, his fingers wrapped around the staff's shaft until he could feel the tendons stretch and the skin pull thin over his knuckles. Lyta shifted next to him, but she didn't dare speak. The tension under the tarp was growing unbearable, and, thanks to their mutual connection to the artifact, Kane and Lyta shared a vibration of each other's emotional states. She was worried, and it was mostly because of Kane's own concern. He wished that she wasn't so distressed, and, even as he did so, he realized that he had to calm his own doubts.

Kane was a warrior, a man of discipline. His focus had allowed him to survive in Neekra's telepathic hell. He centered himself, calmed himself, and in doing so, spread it to the girl lying beside him. She nodded, not enough to disturb their camouflage tarp but more than enough for Kane to notice.

An unspoken thanks surged through Nehushtan.

He returned his attention outward, opening the eye-slit, peering at the vampiric horrors loose among the forest. He waited. Fargo had promised that he would not move until Kane felt that the enemy had abandoned the scene and spread out to seek Kane and Lyta. Even if they did not have Neekra's impetus to discover and snare the man and his newfound companion, they had suffered at the hands of the two. Despite not dying from bullets and bashings, Kane was fully aware of the amount of pain they'd inflicted on the creatures. He'd heard their screams and squeals.

The "children" of the vampire goddess were in the mood for revenge, and though Kane was certain that he would not be killed outright, he was confident that if they got their desiccated hands on him, they would inflict as much punishment as they could on him.

After a pause of a few minutes, his eyes and ears probing as hard as possible, seeking out the slightest cue that one of the creatures could have held back in reserve to ambush him, Kane slid out from under his camouflage. He left Nehushtan behind, and Lyta. She was to be his backup, the ace up his sleeve, and she was crouched, unmoving, ready to come to the rescue, guns blazing if necessary.

Fargo rose from his hiding space, as well. The man had a whip on his belt, notched in a snap strap, ready to deploy with a flick of his wrist, and a powerful handgun on his other hip. Fargo had gone on far-ranging travels and had never felt the need for anything else to supplement his personal gear. Though, beforehand, his escorts had been armed consortium troops with machine pistols, and now he had the ability to blank out cameras and communications equipment.

He also seemed to have the reflexes to disarm a healthy, professionally trained young woman.

Kane didn't want to know what new tricks the man had learned. Actually, he loved having foreknowledge; he simply didn't want to learn those tricks with himself as the recipient. Fighting shoulder to shoulder with Fargo would give him insight but spare him the blunt introduction to whatever Fargo's powers unleashed.

Better to experience them secondhand and maybe learn how to avoid them altogether.

The two men moved in silence, walking parallel into the darkness. Kane crouched low as they reached the railing overlooking the underground shaft, the balcony of twin spiraling walkways down into the necropolis below.

Fargo's stealth was good, as fine and soft-footed as Kane's own, but the man from Cerberus was glad for the fact that he'd been able to recover a shadow suit faceplate and a fallen Commtact plate. These must have come off either Brigid or Grant, but at least now Kane didn't have to rely on the artifact to provide him with night vision. Though he could activate the pintel-mounted Commtact if he desperately needed to contact someone, the only one he thought of who would have a spare plate would be Grant.

Kane actually had both discarded Commtacts, as well as some of the other gear stripped from his allies. Most of it was packed in a war bag, hidden with Lyta, but Kane had decided to strap on Grant's discarded Sin Eater. He still kept the two other guns and a Colt .45 pistol with him, knowing that he'd have to arm the others in their breakout.

The Sin Eater, though, felt better. It was a familiar, comforting weight on his forearm. Sure, he'd gotten on fine without one, but now, he felt as if his arm was complete. That didn't mean he intended to get into a blazing gunfight. Kane was far too smart and experienced to allow himself to see the problem as a nail just because he had his favorite hammer back. Instead, he and Fargo continued their slow crawl down the spiral.

Every so often, he paused to listen. He and Lyta had set up a schedule, and, sure enough, within a moment, he heard a softly whispered "still clear" on his Commtact.

The girl would be his early warning system just in case the vampires sought to return to their underground home. Kane hoped the brief transmissions wouldn't be traced. The radios that they'd provided to their allies had been encrypted, as were the Commtacts, but Kane was fully aware that Durga came from a city that had some of the finest surveillance and intelligence machinery on the planet and had heard communications and details of Cerberus for years.

Kane didn't fool himself that Durga would give up such an advantage. He'd been present in Africa for a while, operating the cloning facilities that had created the Kongamato that had menaced them. Who knew what other technology Durga had availed himself of?

One mistake, and his rescue mission would end very badly. Kane was aware that Durga knew him. The Nagah prince had observed Kane's loyalty and willingness to sacrifice himself for the sake of his friends.

There was going to be a trap waiting for him. Kane only hoped that they hadn't expected Fargo, and whatever special abilities he was gifted with, to be alongside him, rather than Lyta.

It might not have been the greatest of surprises or weapons, but it was an advantage, and it could give him the edge he needed against whomever Durga held in reserve.

Kane paused, catching the heat signatures of three tall figures in the shadows at the base of the ramp. He crouched out of sight and peered down at them. The unmistakable sheets of muscle that formed the hoods between the sides of their heads and shoulders marked them as Nagah, but Thurpa had said that Durga had left most of his compatriots back in India, running the show and preparing for his return in full health. That meant that these might have been entities brewed up on the spot. Earlier, Lakesh and Domi had encountered manufactured agents, creatures who were, at their core, Nephilim who had been specially recrafted to resemble human or Nagah.

Domi had barely survived hand-to-hand combat with two of those monstrosities, and she'd won only from savagery, surprise and leverage, and the fact that neither of the faux cobra men had been armed with assault rifles or similar musketry. Kane could see the rifles gripped by the trio of Nagah warriors, and he also noticed that they had been allowed to stand naked. There was no fidgeting, no lack of comfort. These three guards were resolute, untiring.

They had to be clones, and that meant that Durga had indeed plugged the formula for full-grown warriors into the same facility that had produced the Kongamato.

What made Kane particularly despise these three was that Durga had hidden them from his young assistant, Thurpa. The boy knew that Durga was producing winged horrors in order to buff out an army to wrest a prize from the heart of Africa, but the Nagah soldiers were something that the fallen prince had neglected to tell him about.

That meant that Thurpa had been a sacrificial lamb from day one. The Nagah youth was a throwaway sympathy gainer, one that had faded from Durga's use.

Kane glanced at Fargo. The enhanced archaeologist nodded. They were going to need to be stealthy on approach to these men. Their attention was rock solid.

Kane's footsteps were whispers, and he was a shadow trotting lightly down behind them, knife in one hand, suppressor affixed to the muzzle of the Sin Eater in his right fist. He didn't look to see what Fargo was doing; he just had to focus on his targets and hope that he was swift enough to end the threat of these armed guards before they awoke the entire necropolis.

With a lunge, Kane was at the back of one of the Nagah soldiers, and he poked the cobra man in the back of his head with the blunt suppressor affixed to the muzzle of his Sin Eater. The instant he made contact, he pulled the trigger. Suppressor tube and flesh of reptilian guard formed a seal that swallowed the entirety of the gunshot, even as the gun bucked in his fist. The bullet struck skull, punching through sheet muscle and burrowing deep into the cobra man's brain.

Within a heartbeat, the Nagah slumped to the ground, his central nervous system destroyed, unable to cry out or do more than release a dying rasp as his lungs emptied.

The other Nagah turned at the sudden motion, the harsh breath, and as he did, Kane brought up his knife, spearing the point under the scaled chin. As the point plunged, taking just a little more force than usual to get through the snakelike hide of his target, Kane heard the weird whistle-pop of a whip deploying. It was not a gunshot or a shout, but that amount of noise would draw some attention.

Kane couldn't undo this attack, the betrayal of their silent approach by Fargo's whip, and cursing his luck wasn't going to do anything toward regaining their stealth. And if he didn't continue his attack on the other Nagah, then both of them were going to be overwhelmed by all manner of guards at Durga's beck and call.

Kane finally struck bone, either the guard's skull or neck bones, but, even so, the point glided inside, deflecting and causing even more trauma as muscle, blood vessels, nerves and tendons scissored against the razor-keen edge of his combat knife. Kane twisted his hand with the Sin Eater and brought the butt up hard against the Nagah's face, feeling nasal bones crunching underneath the weight of his gun.

With his windpipe speared, and now his nose crushed, this sentry was not going to release another sound for the rest of his truncated life. That same life spurted over Kane's forearm, a hot, sticky rain of blood that was as human as anything else. Kane had been a man trained to kill, but the sensation of driving steel into a living creature was not something he relished. It was an ugly, brutal affair, and only his undying concern and loyalty to his friends had forced his hand against Durga's cloned drones. There had been some grim satisfaction, over twenty-four hours earlier, when he'd killed men who tortured and enslaved innocent people, but this was pure butcher's work.

And even when he'd engaged in that bloodbath, Kane had still felt an edge of queasiness as he'd eviscerated his opponents.

This is a necessity, Kane told himself as he lowered the corpse of his foe to the stone floor.

He glanced over to Fargo and immediately saw the reason why he distrusted the man so much. The whip was wrapped around the neck of the third Nagah guard, wound so tightly that it tore and collapsed the hood that marked him as a cobra man. The poor thing's eyes had gone wide, glinting like gems in Kane's night-vision optics, bulging and pouring tears and blood as they popped in their sockets. Scaled fingers clawed at the leather braid strangling him, and the guard, clone or not, suffered a slow, brutal end as Fargo pressed the sole of his boot against the sentry's head.

There was a low, ugly crunch, and finally that guard was no more.

Kane saw the smirk, the self-congratulatory twisting of Fargo's lips, and now more than ever he contemplated simply plunging his knife through the bastard's heart. The trouble was, Kane needed the man's backup for now.

However, there would be time for the killer to meet his justice. Once Brigid, Grant, Nathan and Thurpa were free.

"Nearly gave us away," Kane murmured low enough that his voice wouldn't carry more than a few feet.

Fargo regarded his temporary ally as he wound up the whip. His voice was conversational but not especially loud. "No. I calculated exactly how much noise to make. This was well within my parameters. The others suspect nothing."

"Others," Kane repeated, his words remaining low and soft. "You see them?"

"There are eleven. Nine more clones such as these, Durga and the creature that Neekra inhabits," Fargo responded.

Kane grimaced.

"Your distaste for her speaks of how you know what she did to get that body," Fargo mentioned.

"Enough said about that," Kane murmured. The less said about the images that Nehushtan brought to his mind's eye, the better. "You've got the enemy mapped out. Where?"

Fargo touched Kane's faceplate and suddenly images flared, projected into his eyes through the machine interface. Now, Kane could make out the locations of the guards, and he could also see the signatures of the four prisoners. He frowned, stepping away from Fargo, an odd tingling buzzing at the base of his neck. Kane was fully aware of the origin of Fargo's technological control, but this seeming effortless input of information was nothing short of the kind of witchcraft that inspired less educated and civilized men than him to burn people at the stake. It was a frightening bit of nonchalance that only fanned Kane's paranoia against Fargo.

"That bit of information didn't please you?" Fargo asked.

Kane glared at the man. "Warn me next time."

Fargo snorted.

"All right, since we know where my friends are, we should just go get them out of their cells. Then we have the opportunity to fight our way out of here," Kane muttered.

"That is a more passive mode than I would have taken you for," Fargo responded. "Though, I can now see, you're more concerned about a hostage situation."

Kane turned and looked back up the ramp. He activated his Commtact.

"…got movement up at the surface…"

"Read you," Kane responded.

"'Bout time you activated your Commtact," came a familiar growl. Grant was on the line, too. One sentence, and Kane was heartened by the situation.

"They're moving toward us," Fargo mentioned. "Approaching the ramp and cutting us off from the cells."

"And vamps up topside," Kane added.

"Are we aborting?" Fargo asked.

"No. But find a spot," Kane ordered Fargo. He held up a couple of objects. "Get them both to Brigid."

Fargo took them. One was a spare Commtact plate.

The other was a small pocket multitool. If Brigid got hold of something to undo the lock on her door, then she could get the others out to escape.

"Now disappear," Kane snapped.

With that, the archaeologist took off into the dead underground city. Kane returned his attention to the sound and heat signatures of the Nagah troops approaching. With the spare hood, he had the means to deal with them while they were in the dark.

"Lyta, stay put," Kane said in a quick burst over his Commtact. "I'm going to draw some hell down here."

There was no reply except a single click, the press of a transmit button that signaled the girl had received the message. With that, Kane returned to radio silence.

Stealth had gone out the window. Nine Nagah soldiers were aware that he was on the move down here. There were also vampires returning. Already he could see the movements of the living humanoids, and there was also motion far above. The hijacked corpses had split up, some going down each of the spiraling ramps. There were two who made amazing leaps and bounds from ledge to ledge.

Kane grit his teeth, knowing that if he was to stand a chance in hell, he was going to have to keep the vampires and the cobra men busy, distracting them so Fargo could accomplish the task of supplying Brigid with the necessary tools.

With that thought, he turned and moved into the darkened hallways of the subterranean city. He trod heavily, footsteps echoing now that he wanted attention.

And, as if in answer, he heard the footfalls of his pursuers.

Chapter 17

Grant decided to take a risk and affixed the Commtact plate to his jaw; the implanted pintels sealed the communicator in place. He turned it on and left it in passive reception mode, not needing to give away the fact that he had an operating transceiver by sending out a signal. He listened, allowing his muscles to relax from the effort of picking his manacles' locks with the one tool he'd been able to manage—bones from a long desiccated rodent. He wasn't having much luck, and his hands were cramping from the effort. He could feel the rawness of his wrists where the steel cuffs dug into his flesh.

Maybe, just maybe, Kane had had the foresight to get his Commtact operating, and maybe he also had access to radios so that he could key in the encrypted frequency of the cybernetic devices.

For a while, he let the soft static buzz through his skull. It allowed him to retreat into a meditative state that restored more energy to his tired and battered flesh. He settled into letting the white noise carry his thoughts on divergent streams, calm soaking through his cells, allowing him to bring up thoughts that otherwise would have been lost in the clutter of conscious thought.

Grant lost track of time while in this serene state, but he did figure out a more comfortable position to better get an angle on his keyhole. He'd put the length of bone between his teeth and bent over the manacles. That would keep him from tearing up his arms.

Then he heard the young woman's voice. "Kane. We've got movement up at the surface. Eight of the vampires are returning to the entrance. I repeat, we've got movement up at the surface."

Grant immediately pegged this as Lyta, the girl who'd stayed behind to deal with the men who had employed the Panthers of Mashona. She was a young woman, attractive despite her shaven pate and the bruises all over her when she'd first appeared. After a while, though, all her scrapes and abrasions had faded, possibly because of her proximity to the staff. In a way, Lyta reminded Grant of Domi when they'd first met.

The albino girl Domi had been an outlaw, a robber, a killer and a sex slave forced to claw her way through life as the servant of the Pit boss named Guana Teague. And yet, a simple act of decency on Grant's part had turned Domi from feral enemy to staunch, loyal ally. From there, the young, uneducated woman had grown into a leader and a matchless defender of the weak and helpless.

Lyta was in contact with Kane; he was the only other person who would have had the Commtact and was free. Either the man had picked up a spare or found one of the devices discarded by their gelatinous captors.

"Read you," Kane finally said, even as Grant's mind raced.

"'Bout time you activated your Commtact," he said, letting his friend know that he was aware. He then quickly set about putting his bone lock pick between his teeth and started on his manacle. All the while, he heard Kane speaking to another person, someone who was alongside him. Grant narrowed down the likely suspects to one, just based on tone of voice and their place on the globe.

Austin Fargo. He'd taken a powder, seemingly long before the final assault by the Kongamato and the Panthers of Mashona, which meant that he was being used as someone's ace in the hole. Logic dictated that Fargo was working alongside Durga, but it might have been one of the members of the Millennium Consortium, or another member of the militia's leadership.

Careful, not too fast, he cautioned himself, working the bone pick. Too much pressure and he'd be without a tool to disengage his manacles. Then he'd have to rely on someone else to free him.

While it wasn't much of a matter of ego, it would still sting to have to be rescued when he was in the middle of breaking free on his own. Grant concentrated, working his teeth and lips to maneuver his pick. His neck muscles ached from the stretch and the effort.

Kane's Commtact went silent. He'd already ordered Lyta to go quiet, so he listened for any signs of technology peeking in on their transmissions. Grant wasn't quite certain what would betray the enemy, but if anything was transmitting or receiving, there might be a rupture in the static running through his communicator. Even so, he remained quiet, most of his effort going into breaking loose.

Once he was free, Grant knew that his shoulders and clavicle would hurt like blazes from the long-term sustained effort of picking the lock. But mild aches and stiff tendons were a minor issue when compared to being left to either starve to death or become the flesh suit for one of those blob things who'd taken Brigid, himself and the others captive. He hunkered down, jostling the tumblers within the keyhole with the slender rat bone.

He caught a flicker of movement past the little gap where water would sluice under the door into the depression in the floor, making an extremely low-tech and potentially sickening water dish. It was just the movement of a shadow, no sound accompanying it, and then it was gone.

Kane sent his ally down to the dungeons, probably with something that could help.

Grant conceded that the most likely target of that assistance would be the brilliant Brigid Baptiste. While Grant was a powerful fighter, Brigid showed she had all manner of resourcefulness. Freeing her would hasten the freedom of the other prisoners. Kane probably also figured that Grant would have either broken his bonds or would be in need of actual tools and outside assistance. Either way, the big former Magistrate would be the second one checked on.

And Grant was logical enough to know that it was simple triage. If he couldn't escape a cell of his own devices, then he'd actually need more than his own resourcefulness and brute strength to be freed. These chains were more than enough to entrap a buffalo or an elephant. There was no shame in being unable to break them, and given the tools at hand, or rather at mouth…

Click.

Grant's right wrist was loose in an instant, and he slumped back against the wall, taking a deep breath. With one hand free, he took the pick from his mouth and began working on his other manacle, freeing it from the loop in his restraint belt. He had a good two feet of heavy, dense links, which could be turned into a weapon if not a tool for smashing out the cell door.

Things were not made easier by using his good hand to undo the lock on the other bracelet. The tumblers were different, or maybe it was simply an illusion as he was now using his manual dexterity, rather than the cunning of his teeth, tongue and lips. It was likely an illusion, and Grant forced himself to be gentle, careful just in case he snapped the rat bone. Even so, his confidence was up, and he wanted to at least have his hands free before Brigid appeared at the cell door.

And then he heard the rustle, the rattle of handles and bars on the other side of the cell door.

Sure enough, there stood Brigid, and Grant finally clicked the other manacle off his wrist. He held the chain, the hinged bracelets hanging at either end, and nodded to the woman in the doorway.

"Ah, no wonder you're not the one opening my door," Brigid mused. "That hardware is some serious heavy metal."

Grant nodded again. "Thanks for getting the door for me."

With a groan and grunt, he got off the floor, closing the bracelets around the chains themselves to give him some brutal flails to crash into an enemy skull. Sure enough, though Brigid had her Commtact and a folding multitool in her possession, she didn't have a weapon. Grant's might and martial skill meant that he was the first one she released on her liberation.

"Who gave you the gear?" Grant asked.

"They were just stuffed under the door," Brigid responded. "I was able to unlock my cell, but whoever it was had left."

"Fargo," Grant grumbled.

"Likely. He's the only one out there who'd be helping Kane while Lyta babysits Nehushtan," Brigid concurred.

Grant stretched out. He'd been cramped by his chains, and he was glad to have a moment to limber up before trouble came after them again.

Brigid closed the door gently behind her, and Grant stayed still.

"I heard movement outside in the hallway," Brigid warned.

Grant nodded and stepped to the door lightly, clenching his fists around the chains that had imprisoned him.

They were primed and set to free him now.

Brigid had her Commtact in place, and Grant's own plate did not go unnoticed by her. "Too bad we can't get in touch with either Nathan or Thurpa."

Grant nodded. "But we can connect with Kane, as long as we're certain that Durga is not listening in on the party line."

"I'm going to have to err on the side of expediency with this," Brigid responded. "Durga has not shown the capacity to listen in on us, nor has he done anything which was in anticipation of one of our maneuvers. Even with Thurpa among us, the evidence of surveillance on his part has been utterly negligible"

Grant mused over that for a moment. "You're certain?"

"The only evidence of possible spying upon us accompanies the fact that Fargo may be in collusion with Durga," Brigid replied.

"And he's the one who gave us our radios back," Grant added.

"I know," Brigid returned. "But if Fargo and Durga are allied with each other, then it's likely they won't be operating in concert with Neekra."

"As in, Durga is hoping Fargo is his way out of an alliance with a woman who might eat him," Grant said.

"Just like last time. He's pitting his enemies against each other. It's likely why he took us alive, too," Brigid said.

Grant frowned. "So he convinced Neekra to take us?"

Brigid thought about it for a moment. "She has need of one of us. Either to obtain the artifact or to awaken and liberate her true body. Perhaps a combination of both."

Grant smirked. "This isn't the first time we've been used by someone else to slog through a temple of doom. Though, you'd think by now they'd actually learn that having us open the old Pandora's box tends to blow up in their faces, not ours."

Brigid shrugged. "In their defense, not too many of them survive, let alone talk to each other."

The two fell into silence, listening for the sound of any movement in the hallway. Both had their ears pressed to the door, and while there were footsteps moving between the cells, nothing else seemed to be occurring Grant looked at the monolithic door and how perfectly it was set into the jamb. The only cracks of light and sound came from the trough through which they were to receive their water. He didn't like not being able to see where the opposition was, but at least he could estimate where the sentry in the hall stood by the sound of his feet.

Gunfire rumbled distantly for a brief instant.

Kane was already doing work, battling Durga's Nagah clones no doubt.

Hang in there, Kane, he thought, putting more energy into it than usual. Kane wasn't a doomie, a person with psychic abilities, but he and Grant had been partners for years. Their relationship had gone from professional to friendship to a depth of brotherhood stronger than any random DNA code or accident of birth.

Grant had trusted that Kane would come to their rescue, or set the ball for their release in motion. And his brother had not failed him. Even a positive thought, a jolt of goodwill, was something he had to give. Maybe, somewhere in the subconscious ether that divided dimensions, where quantum mechanics worked to set up a world that the human mind could discern and translate, Grant's thoughts actually became real, tangible, a brief surge of adrenaline or an extra spark of neuro-electric activity that jerked Kane out of the path of a deadly blow.

Lakesh had spoken of the three of them, Kane, Grant and Brigid, as a confluence of personalities whose presence seemed to ensure victory. Grant had enough aches and memories of injuries to realize that luck didn't come without sacrifice or hard work, but maybe it was that bit of unmeasurable quantum influence among them. Maybe their teamwork forged a lattice that could somehow disrupt the probabilities and odds stacked against them.

That was something for Grant to ask one of the Manitius station scientists, probably W. Stephen Waylon, the diminutive genius who had reworked the time scoop when he'd been stranded at the dawn of human history, becoming the source of the myth of Enkidu, the man-bull who'd befriended Gilgamesh. Though Waylon himself wasn't intimately familiar with that kind of science, he'd gleaned a better understanding of the concepts from his friendship with other scientists, many of whom had perished when Cerberus had been turned inside out with the invasion of a renegade Annunaki.

With that thought dog-eared in his mental to-do list, he concentrated on what he *could* do, which was plan out mayhem. He was familiar with the links of chain in his hand, again from when he was displaced temporally, split between a bodiless mind and a memoryless body, both of which were mere shadows of his true form, lost in the folds between dimensions. The weight of steel links in his hands was familiar, and he recalled being bound as a prisoner, though it was not his true body held captive.

On more than one occasion, he'd broken the chains; the tesseract of his temporarily displaced form had far more strength than his normal body, and he'd used the chains against the guards holding him captive, keeping him a living trophy for the dread, leonine scion of Enlil that called himself Humbaba.

His muscles ached with the memory of crushing necks and smashing in skulls with the kind of links he now held. Grant stilled himself, controlling the unconscious urge to build up for fight or flight. If he hit an adrenaline peak too soon, he'd just end up running out of steam when he most needed it. He closed his eyes, concentrating on returning his heartbeat to normal, on calming the butterflies in his stomach, the surge of energy in his limbs.

It was one thing to have great strength and endurance. But to properly control it, to know when *not* to use it, that was what made Grant the success that he was. He'd survived countless battles, and he was fully aware that restraint was as much a part of surviving as brute power.

He would have to bide his time.

Brigid's face was wrought with concern and the gnawing need to chomp at the bit. Kane had put himself in peril for their sakes, and the two of them could only wait for an opportunity to get loose, wait for the best moment in which to act, when their efforts could assist and not hinder their friend's attempt.

The measurement of that time was visible as Grant looked into Brigid's eyes. Her mind was swift, adept, capable of almost magical leaps of intuition. At least it seemed magical, if only because with her photographic memory, the young woman had immense masses of data at her disposal, and she could then put that information back together, drawing from the sum of knowledge that she'd studied to assemble correlations of different, seemingly unrelated instances.

There were times when Grant found himself dumbfounded by what she could remember or anticipate, but, in the end, everything she operated on was based on solid evidence and observable data. To those who didn't appreciate awareness, the power of the human brain, she could have been seen as a witch. Grant, for one, was glad for her witchcraft.

"The hallway is clear," she whispered. "You check up the hall. I'll head down. I don't know which cells the others are in…."

Grant nodded.

The cell door swung open. Thankfully, there was no whine or squeal of metal on metal as the hinges flexed, a small favor, probably due to the impeccable construction of the necropolis. Grant went left and Brigid went right. Both remembered the way they'd come in, and Grant headed toward the entrance to this section of the subterranean dungeon. He paused at an unlocked door and prodded it open, but from the loosed bindings on the floor, he could tell it had been Brigid's compartment.

Grant advanced to the next cell, also unlocked. No person was in there, but he could see that there were empty chains on the floor. The water "dish" was still damp; droplets spattered where his boot landed in the shallow puddle. He knelt and touched the moisture, took a sniff of it.

He grimaced. It didn't smell quite right, but for someone who was thirsty, exhausted from trying to get out of his imprisonment... He wouldn't have noticed the smell or would have attributed it to the old musk of desperation in the cell.

Grant scanned about for signs of tools and saw that there were none. He examined the manacles and noticed that there were scales stuck to them. This had been Thurpa's cell. For some reason, Durga had enough interest in the wayward Nagah to take him out of this row of imprisonment. Grant stood up and looked to the open doorway.

Brigid was there. Nathan was beside her, rubbing his wrists, looking concerned.

"They have our fourth," Grant said, holding up the sticky scales on his fingertip. His nose wrinkled.

"So much for an impromptu card game," Brigid murmured. "Durga's interested in his former minion. Did Thurpa go quietly?"

Grant shook his head. "They poured some water for him. It doesn't smell right. And it looks like he'd already got the cuffs off."

Nathan's brow furrowed. "Almost as if he had his own long, slender tool with which to free himself."

"Fang," Grant and Brigid said in unison.

"Duh," Nathan responded. "So, Thurpa's breaking out—"

"Takes a drink and goes to sleep," Brigid explained. "Durga wanted him."

"You sure?" Grant asked. "Durga rarely does anything in a straight line."

"How snakelike of him," Brigid mused, her frown belying the lightness of her pun. "Neekra? But why would Neekra want him?"

"That's what we've got to figure out, after we hie ourselves henceforth the fuck out of here," Grant concluded.

The three travelers nodded in agreement. They wouldn't do either Thurpa or Kane much good if they sat around solving mysteries and were caught again.

It was time to run and hide.

Chapter 18

Kane's flight through the necropolis was illuminating, to say the very least. As the Nagah clones spread out, watching over the maze of streets winding throughout the plethora of crypt-like houses, he darted and wove. None of the cobra men opened fire, meaning that Kane's suspicion that both Durga and Neekra wanted him alive was correct. Or correct enough for the time being. For a moment, he regretted being so brutal against the pair of men he'd brought down. But he knew that although he'd been lethal, the ends he'd brought to those guards had been swift and relatively merciful.

Even though they were clones, and seemed to have no will of their own, they spread out like professionals. Kane had seen the formation they'd fallen into a dozen times, especially when he and other Magistrates had had to pursue a particularly hostile outlaw into the Tartarus Pits.

Then again, it seemed that the facilities that were being utilized for creating these clone troopers had the means of quickly programming fighting behaviors and tactics into the minds of the newly "hatched." The Kongamato had showed lethal cunning, even when not being directly controlled by either Durga or the warlord Gamal. There had been other electronic equipment around the capsules in which the artificial organisms were grown. Since Kane had only penetrated the facility late in the cycle of producing the clones, he hadn't seen what the extra devices were for, but the awakened creatures had ended up being intensely hostile, if rather uncoordinated.

Of course, Durga had already produced hundreds of the creatures. The ones chasing him throughout the cloning facility were half-baked, but, with their strength and agility, they had still been dangerous.

These cobra-hooded men were likely preprogrammed, as well. The North American continent had been swamped and swarmed by herds of less precisely created entities, creatures that were abominations in the nominal shape of normal humans, some scaled, others with facial tentacles and mouths like lampreys. The wild mutants had been released as a means of keeping people pressured and hunted, to keep their populations low and forced to cower from marauding bands of savage primitives.

By the same token, those laboratories had created the hybrids, the slender, ultra-advanced entities who had taken over the ruling caste of humanity. These genetic elite beings decided who was worthy and who wasn't to live within the gigantic arcologies where they'd reestablished civilization under their iron fists. This weeding of the "unwashed" from their societies was intent on driving humanity further and further into servitude to them. Kane had been one of the willing servants of that regime before he had seen the truth of the situation. Rather than enforcing law and order, they were merely preserving a status quo for a tiny elite whose ties to humanity were thin at best.

Those hybrid barons and their less exalted brethren were eventually awakened, modified by a genetic signal from the ancient biological ship *Tiamat*. The god chromosomes within each of the lab-bred monsters became either one of the overlords or the psychically lobotomized drones called the Nephilim, an ersatz take on the Nagah who were Enki's "brainchildren." Durga's lineage was of an Annunaki who didn't want mindless servants but people who blended the best of multiple worlds, able to create and grow; however, the clones here were no more than the blank-slate Nephilim that Durga had reprogrammed and reconfigured to blend in with Nagah society.

Those creatures, so altered by the fallen prince, had been responsible for acts of terror and murder in the cobra-folk's city of Garuda. They had continued a reign of fear that Kane had thought he'd ended by detonating a fuel-air explosion beneath Durga.

And now he was facing them. He'd had only a small skirmish with them before, a couple of agents, but here was a coordinated hunting force, stalking through the maze behind him. They had the tactics, apparently.

Kane narrowed his eyes, almost in defiance.

You've got a plan, he thought. But can you handle it when you run into enemy action?

As he retreated through the underground graveyard, Kane saw that the cavern spread out farther. Indeed, he could see a dip in the ground beneath his feet. Was there more up ahead? The vaulted ceiling was at least twenty feet above the top of his head, meaning that he had to keep an eye out for foes running along the tops of the low structures about him.

Kane took a running start and dug his feet into a wall, letting momentum carry him upward. He wrapped his fingers over the top lip of a crypt-like structure and dragged himself to the roof. With another kick, he was on top of the building, scanning into the distance.

From his new vantage point, he could spot the Nagah guards. There were actually six of them. Three had stayed back, obviously to protect Durga and Neekra. The guards were armed with typical Zambian militia firearms: AK-47 rifles of old design but likely more modern build. Centuries after the fall of twentieth-century civilization, the simpler, more rugged weapons were easier to assemble.

Africa had plenty of raw resources and still had the technology to make classic pre-skydark weapons, as well as vehicles, electronics and power production, from drilling for petroleum to maintaining electrical plants able to run major cities.

Of course, if Neekra rose, or Durga took the opportunity to conquer the continent, then a mostly harmless region would become the starting point of a world-threatening army. Stage one of handling this was dealing with Durga's clone troopers and Neekra's vampiric emissaries. Granted, the gunmen would be far easier to deal with. Each of the Nagah replicants was scanning, searching for Kane at ground level, using weapon-mounted flashlights to look for him. Kane knew that if he was to have a chance, he needed to keep them from thinking on more than just a two-dimensional plane.

Luckily, Kane had an advantage over them with his shadow suit hood's night-vision optics. He could pinpoint all six of the gunmen advancing through the necropolis. Stealth and tactics were going to be his advantages.

There was a flash of movement up ahead. Kane kept low to the roof, scanning, and he spotted a figure atop one of the crypts. Kane wasn't certain of what kind of senses the entity had, but its human shape but insectlike movements told him that it was one of Neekra's vampires. He clenched his foot-long combat knife, keeping in mind the Sin Eater with its suppressor attached. If he made too much noise, he'd draw the attention of the patrolling cobra troops. That included firing the so-called silenced machine pistol. Even a softened gunshot was still unmistakable. The silencer just made the location of the firing harder to narrow down.

Kane also realized that every time he'd tried to take one of the reanimated horrors down with gunfire, it'd proven tough to slow them down, let alone keep them down. Any interaction with the vampiric things would need to take place at bad-breath distances, with his knife in conflict with their strength and inhuman durability.

Even then, fighting a vampire with only a knife would draw attention.

Which meant that he had to get the drop on it before it could even fight back.

Kane's mind was running through angles of attack and blind spots for the cloned soldiers and the shadowy form in the distance. He took a glance toward the ceiling overhead. Just because he saw one of the things wearing a corpse as if it were a suit didn't mean there weren't others that had shed their flesh shells and returned to their semiliquid forms to defy gravity and physics, slithering along the ceiling.

He was glad that he did, because there were two of the blob-like horrors, stretching themselves from spot to spot, advancing toward Kane's rooftop swiftly.

Kane cursed himself for thinking exactly like he'd wanted the Nagah clones to and for thinking of every problem as a nail because he had a hammer. He, Fargo and Lyta had spent more than enough time discussing the potential vulnerabilities to wood of the gelatinous creatures that he'd thought immediately of his knife instead of the sharpened wooden stakes he'd prepared to deal with these things.

One of the elastic monster's pseudopods whipped toward Kane's face, and he jerked his head out of the way and clasped the butt of one of the stakes. He drew it from his combat belt. With a reflexive snap of his wrist, he plunged it into the gooey, stretching limb and elicited the keening that Kane had identified as pain in Neekra's children.

In an instant, the blob withdrew its tentacle and shrugged back in retreat from the human who knew how to hurt it. Even as that one pulled away from battle, Kane caught the other creature in the periphery of his vision, splashing atop a nearby crypt's rooftop. The flowering spatter of the creature's form suddenly sucked back together, forming into a fountain arc of the blob pushing itself across the distance between the two of them. Kane whirled and faced this new attacker. Even in the dark, the advanced optics of his shadow suit hood allowed him to make out the two major organs floating within its fluid mass.

Brigid had told Lyta that those two shapes were akin to nucleoli in a standard cell. The nucleoli were structures within a cell's nucleus that produced the ribosomes that allowed the unicellular organism to process protein. And Kane figured that the liquid proteins in blood were much easier for these things to absorb through their membranes than actual ingestion of solid food. Kane didn't know what pinioning one of those organs did for stopping them cold, but then, he didn't want to know about cellular biology. He just knew that putting a sharpened wooden stake through one of those masses caused the creatures to lose cohesion and fall apart.

And it was time to get stabby.

The trouble with that was that his current opponent was now forewarned about Kane's deadly wooden weapon. It lunged out one pod, seeking to grasp at Kane's wrist. However, with a deft spin, the Cerberus warrior brought up his combat knife and sliced at the extended appendage. Carving through membrane and cytoplasm was ridiculously easy, and now there was a lifeless splatter of goo sailing off into the shadows as the creature backed off from Kane's attack.

Unfortunately, with all the scuffle now going on, and the wailing cry of the first injured blob, the cobra gunmen had raised their attention toward the dark shadows. The blue-white glare of gun-mounted flashlights caught Kane out in the open, delineating him as an easy target.

So much for a quiet one-on-one fight, Kane thought. He jumped from one roof to another only moments before the air was suddenly filled with the snap and crack of rifle rounds.

As Kane landed, bled off his forward momentum with a somersault, then regained his footing, he cursed whatever training had been placed into the warrior clones. They were firing single shots, not fully automatic. And they were seeking him out with the cones of their torches before triggering the next shots in their volleys against him.

They were trained and disciplined on the trigger. He hopped to another roof and landed just in time to crash into another figure on the top of the small concrete structure. As Kane struck the other in the chest with his shoulder, he could feel the tattered, crusty uniform of a dead militiaman. That was all the identification that he required to bring up the knife and spear the walking corpse through the mouth with the nine-inch-long blade. Steel punched through the skull and up into the vampire's brain pan with brutal efficiency.

Hands rose swiftly, fingers digging like steely claws into Kane's shoulders, trying to push the man back. Before those deadly talons could draw blood or break bone, Kane brought up the sharpened stake in his other hand. He stabbed into the thing's belly, driving upward toward whatever heart might still exist within the reanimated body. Even as the fire-hardened point reached the tough muscle of what used to be its heart, the unliving body opened its mouth and belted out a death screech that threatened to shake the molars from Kane's skull.

Still, the creature's dying cry was the last of its offensive actions against Kane, and when the blaze of a rifle light burned in his peripheral vision, the Cerberus explorer swung the once again lifeless corpse around to form a living shield. Bullets smashed into the dead soldier, giving Kane a brief moment's respite, which allowed him to drop from the roof of the crypt and land behind solid stone. A human body was something of a shield, but when dealing with high-powered rifles, Kane didn't trust it for much more than a shot or two. He'd rather have granite between himself and a bullet.

One vampire was dead, another had received an agonizing injury from one of Kane's wooden stakes and the last one was still out there in somewhat good condition. Kane was glad that his knife didn't have a sawtooth back, as he had been able to wrench it from the skull of the reanimated corpse. The stake was smooth and still in his hands.

Unfortunately, Kane didn't think that the fire-hardened point of his vampire-slaying weapon would do much good against the armored scales that guarded the torsos of the Nagah clones. Luckily, Kane's combat blade would do the job with aplomb. Unfortunately, even in close quarters and sharp corners, that meant Kane would need to get within arm's length of one of those cobra-hooded guards. He sheathed his combat knife and flexed, launching the Sin Eater into his grasp.

The Nagah already knew he was present, but they only had a slight hint of his location, so the silenced weapon was going to have to work. Again, with the suppressor in place, he could hide his muzzle-flashes and avoid giving away his position with the sound of his gun going off.

Sure enough, a Nagah lurched into view, but fortune favored Kane and the soldier glanced to the left while Kane was to his right. He lifted the Sin Eater and pulled the trigger, putting a single suppressed 9 mm slug into the side of the clone's skull. The snap of the bullet striking flesh and shattering skull wasn't quite as loud as the pop of Kane's gun, but it did bring the blaze of three lights spraying toward the falling Nagah. As Kane was out of sight to the side, and about fifteen feet away from the now dead trooper, the other guards held their fire but advanced toward their fallen friend. Kane kept to the shadows, staying put as beams of light burned past corners, casting him into darkness. As long as he was not in the direct shine of the light, they wouldn't notice him immediately.

Even now, the scuffle of feet covered the sound of his own steps, and the Nagah hunters betrayed their presence with their weapon-mounted lights.

Better for Kane, those swiveling beams elicited

hisses of dismay and annoyance from the gelatinous entities.

They don't like bright light, Kane mused. Of course it wasn't far-fetched, since they retreated back underground with the rising of the sun.

That meant that the creatures had some form of visual input, even though he couldn't see a sign of even an eyestalk on the blobs. He'd worry about the specifics of that later, if he managed a later. Right now, he took advantage of their momentary discomfort and skirted down a causeway between several of the small, blocky houses.

Every so often, he'd stop and fire a single shot at a wall to draw them closer, but as he fired, he altered his course, keeping them from anticipating his progress or his path.

Keep them on the go. Keep them confused. Give the others time to regroup, arm up, join him in the fight.

And maybe, just maybe, he could even the odds some more against the forces assembled.

AUSTIN FARGO DIDN'T waste much time around the cells after delivering "the goods" to Brigid Baptiste. He had little desire in showing himself more than necessary, even if Brigid and Grant did figure out that he was present. Dealing with either Durga or Neekra would blow any chances he had of staying out of the embroiled madness of their scheming.

The cobra prince and the vampiric goddess were plotters to the point of fetishism, involving as many different forces and contacts as they could, seemingly for the sheer joy of duping others into doing their busywork. The more arcane their plotting, the better for their personal egos, and Fargo was no longer a fan of such

JAMES AXLER

machinations. The complications added were hardly worth the headaches and threat of failure.

He'd survived a prior encounter with Durga, first meeting as antagonists and then becoming distant allies, ultimately falling apart on opposite sides of the plot when Fargo saw that Durga had become drunk with newfound power.

Still, Durga had made arrangements, and Fargo was supposed to back Durga up just in case Neekra turned out to be the untrustworthy ally that they both knew she'd eventually become. Fargo didn't like the fact that someone imprisoned by Enlil and his compatriots—at great effort and requiring an item as powerful as Nehushtan to seal that deal—was working toward freeing herself.

The knowledge of Annunaki history that was available to Fargo was incomplete, but what he was aware of informed him that they were, at worst, jealous gods and, at best, the lesser of two evils, at least where Enlil and his earthbound compatriots were concerned. Neekra, the figure who was working alongside Durga, was a mere fragment of a far deadlier, far worse entity that Enlil and the overlords had seen as a bold threat to their control of earth.

Fargo knew better than to underestimate anything that Enlil and kin considered a threat. He'd been on the receiving end of what Kane and the other Cerberus "threats" had been capable of, either through brute force and combat skill or the resourcefulness and courage to adapt to threats, which included weathering grenade explosions and high-powered automatic weapons as if they were mere droplets of rain on a spring day.

Neekra's tomb had not been able to contain her, at least her psyche. And that mind was more than powerful enough to mold a human male into an egg-producing horror. The legends of other vampires were spawned from the scions of others Neekra had touched in the past, and the only reason humanity had lasted as long as it had was that there were those who somehow remembered the lessons of the Archons, an intermediary race whom the Annunaki and their Tuatha de Danaan counterparts had created to watch over the planet Earth and humanity. Those who recalled the teachings of the Archons knew the weapons and strategies necessary to drive these body-jacking horrors away or slay them.

Along the way, observers developed their own vampiric myths. The remnants of technology brought to humanity by the alien races became holy items that the night terrors shunned.

Fargo went over what lore he could recall from human legends, knowing that there was merit to some of it, seeking a way to defeat these creatures if Kane and his allies failed. Sometimes it involved a wooden stake through the heart or even the severing of the head.

Fargo knew he'd given Brigid and Grant the tools necessary to escape from their cells, then perhaps to even battle this incarnation of Neekra and Durga and their assorted minions. But they were without guns and other tools. All they could do was talk to each other via the Commtacts. The closest thing to a weapon that he'd supplied to Brigid was a folding pliers multitool that had a three-inch-long utility knife.

Would that be enough of an edge—Fargo allowed himself the pun—to fight their way to freedom?

That was why he needed to regather himself, see what odds he had.

Fargo delivered Durga's ace in the hole to a spot where the fallen prince would be able to locate it readily.

His obligation complete, Fargo turned and left the necropolis.

Whatever the outcome of this conflict between Cerberus and Neekra, it was best observed from afar.

Chapter 19

Thurpa's awakening was not one of comfort. His breathing was ragged and his arms were held out to either side of him, in the position of crucifixion, though it was more appropriately being pinioned, manacled to a wall, chains once more about his wrists. Even as his eyes fluttered open, he saw movement, a pair of leather boots padding away into the shadows on the floor. The thing that struck him as most unusual about those boots was the spurs, the Y-shaped bars of metal each supporting a multipointed, starlike wheel. Only the most remote of societies had never seen a cowboy and his riding spurs, and the underground city of Garuda, with its store of stolen memories of the surface world, even after two centuries, had a treasure trove of cowboy movies within its records, as well as every other kind of cinema on record.

Thurpa had a faint recollection of someone else who had cowboy spurs on his boots, and then he realized that he'd just seen Austin Fargo exiting whatever dungeon he was stuck within. And the damnedest thing was that this was not the one where he'd gone under.

All the effort he'd expended, tinkering with his manacles with his unhurt tooth, was now erased. Something was in his pocket, as well, and Thurpa didn't like that one bit.

He didn't like being a mailbox. He was sure whatever

was in his pocket would be for his teammates or for his captors. Even now, in the distance, he heard the crack of guns, firing single shots mostly. Thurpa stood straight, and the pressure of his chest muscles against his lungs immediately lessened. He scanned around the dungeon.

"How do I get out of this?" Thurpa murmured.

Thurpa gave his wrists a shake and realized that the manacles had slack in them, different from the ones that had held him in place before.

So now he could get out. Then where would he go?

Freedom first, was his main thought. He tugged on one hand, folding in his thumb as far as it would go. The chains wouldn't give him much slack or leverage, but at least he was getting motion. Scales popped from his skin. The sensation was similar to having hairs ripped from skin, except these follicles were in small plates, a combination of hair yanked out by the roots and a too-strong swatch of tape.

The grinding sharp edge of the manacle scraped off long stretches of his scales, revealing raw, pinkish flesh beneath, as well as dozens of tiny prickles of blood where the roots of his scales had been torn up.

But Thurpa's hand was freed. He staggered momentarily, slumping from one arm as his legs weren't used to supporting his weight. He briefly wondered how long he had been out. Then he realized there was a new presence in the cell with him.

"Your...majesty," Thurpa managed to say, his throat dry and raw.

Durga stepped closer, into the light. They'd left him a sconce with which he could see by, and the former prince nodded in acknowledgment of his former subject. A skin of water was raised to Thurpa's lips, and the prisoner jerked his head back and away.

"This isn't drugged," Durga told him.

Thurpa's eyes narrowed, but he was so parched, he surrendered to his need to drink. He took two deep draughts before coughing some up; clear water stung in his nostrils before he snorted it out of his nasal cavities. "Thank you."

"Good to know that I'm still worthy of your respect, if not your obedience," Durga commented, stepping back.

Thurpa felt his pocket was now lighter. Fargo's little "gift" had been delivered to the cobra prince. "That's why you moved me."

Durga rested his hand on the side of Thurpa's face. "Listen. Don't try to think about what happened. Please."

Thurpa, once more, was taken aback by the concern, the same kind of leadership that had seduced him from believing in the reign of Matron Hannah, Durga's former bride, to the formerly crippled prince. There was a goodness in him, but the events of the Kongamato plague, and his first encounter with Neekra while in Durga's presence, weighed heavily on his mind.

"Forget for now," Durga intoned. "Until *she* is gone."

Thurpa's whole body tingled as chills raced from his cheek to the rest of his body. Blind terror stormed past the doors of his mind, threatening to grind him under the hooves of nightmares. Durga's grasp on his wrist, the one that should have still been manacled, brought him back to consciousness. He looked into Durga's amber eyes and realized he was sitting.

"That was Neekra," Durga whispered. "But you held your will against her."

"H-how…" Thurpa asked, sputtering. "How did you know?"

"I'm sensitive to her. I could feel her presence here," Durga responded. He touched Thurpa's forehead. "In there. We resisted her together."

Horrific flashes whipped across Thurpa's mind's eye. He had to fight to keep what little he had in his belly from spewing over his lips.

"I hate this place," Thurpa murmured as Durga pulled him to his feet.

"Then get out now. Chances are that your new friends are free," Durga told him.

Thurpa looked shocked at Durga's betrayal of this knowledge.

"You need to move before I can act on this information," Durga pressed. "I can't hold off much longer, and the four of you need to escape now."

"What about Fargo?" Thurpa asked, woozy.

Durga helped the dazed young man to both feet. "Just move it."

The first step was wobbly, Thurpa's head swimming. The next step caught him, and he reached out, touching wall, fingers clawing at the crease between two blocks to gain purchase and hold himself up. There was a gun lying on the ground ahead of him, and, as Thurpa looked around, he noticed Durga was long gone. It all would have seemed a dream except for the damage caused by the manacles and the undeniable weight of horror from having Neekra inside his skull.

Thurpa knelt and picked up the pistol. It felt real enough, and as his mind cleared even more, he noticed that it was in a holster, a belt dangling from it. It was the setup that he had worn. It had been stripped off when the blob-like vampire creatures attacked him. Spare magazines were in side pouches. He drunkenly fastened the belt about his hips, then looked up to see

Grant and Brigid watching him don his gear. Brigid had a rifle tucked to her hip, but she lowered the muzzle as she looked the scene over. Wariness disappeared within a moment of her observation.

"Are you all right?" Brigid asked, approaching him.

Thurpa nodded. "I woke up, and things just got more weird from there."

"You saw Fargo and likely Durga," Brigid pointed out.

Thurpa blinked, but then he remembered that he was dealing with Brigid Baptiste, a woman who epitomized the same kind of observation and logic as Sherlock Holmes. "Durga would have had access to my gun belt And Durga came by…"

"Because of Fargo?" Grant asked.

Thurpa squeezed his eyes shut. "Brain's not working right. Drugged…things hitting me weird. Nightmare flashes…"

"The same thing that Kane suffered, except over a shorter span," Brigid said. She lifted Thurpa's chin, then looked into his eyes, studying his pupils.

God, your eyes are emerald gems, Brigid, Thurpa caught himself thinking. His cheeks warmed, and he felt ashamed that she might have read that thought.

"You're definitely suffering from shock," Brigid said. Again, Thurpa fought against the stirring feelings deep within him. He remembered Durga's statement that Neekra had been inside his skull, and she must have left him susceptible to the slightest pull of sexual interest.

"Neekra?" Brigid asked.

Thurpa looked at her, confused. She could read minds?

"I'm not reading your mind, but you are oddly interested in me at this point," Brigid pointed out. "Probably trying to get information out of your head."

"That's what Durga said," Thurpa responded. "Though…why would—"

"Whatever happened was to help Durga against her," Brigid stated. He realized that she was bandaging his stripped forearms to give them a chance to heal. "And Durga needs someone to help him against a menace like Neekra. Hence, we're part of his backup plan."

Thurpa glanced toward Grant. He was still half-naked, except for his gloved hands and the length of blood-spattered chain he wielded.

"We ran into one of the cloned guards that Durga made," Grant explained when he noticed Thurpa's gaze fall on the crimson, dripping links.

Realizing that he wasn't operating on all cylinders, Thurpa reached down and pulled the gun from its holster, reversed it and handed it to Grant. "You'll be a steadier shot than I am."

Grant shook his head. "You'll be able to pull your own weight, and, for now, we'll make do with what we've got."

Thurpa nodded. He holstered the pistol, though, not wanting to inadvertently set it off. Sooner or later, he'd wake back up, get his head together. And until then, he'd keep his hands off the grips and fingers away from any triggers until the absolute last possible moment. Better to keep from shooting his allies by accident than suddenly have to learn how well he was trained as a medic.

Even that decision helped to clear his mind a little bit more. He looked around. "Where's Nathan?"

"He's covering our egress," Brigid responded.

Grant patted Thurpa on the shoulder, signaling for him to go back and join the other young man who'd joined the Cerberus explorers on this journey. Thurpa didn't want to think about what the two of them had been saying about him, and he wondered if they still trusted him. In their shoes, Thurpa wouldn't trust himself, either. Durga had separated him from the group for a reason, and it might have been for more than just being a human mailbox between himself and his silent partner, Austin Fargo.

Thurpa also didn't have anything he considered to be a psychic ability, or any meditative training, which made him wonder why he'd been so capable of resisting the dark influence of the blood goddess Neekra.

That wondering didn't go much further than that: he had been hypnotized to resist the witch's influence, and that hypnotism had to have come from Durga. With that programming bouncing around between his ears, there might also be other thoughts and orders that would make him turn against the others.

Thurpa wondered if he would have the will and strength to resist those commands.

Or if, deep down, he really wanted to resist.

Uncertain of who he was anymore, Thurpa just put one foot after the other, praying to Enki for the strength and serenity to cleanse his mind of all doubts. But the young Nagah wasn't going to hold his breath for results. He'd need faith in himself and his allies to make it out of this pit.

KANE DUCKED BEHIND a toppled column, bullets screaming as they ricocheted off stone. The underground necropolis had opened up into a terrain of old packed dirt, with flagstone markers for whoever had been buried down there. The gravestones stood, relatively undisturbed by weather and wind, shielded in the cavernous vault. Around him the markers stuck up like the snarled teeth of a dozen giants who'd fallen asleep with their mouths open.

Once out of the city of crypts, Kane now had far less cover and concealment against the cobra gunmen, but the shadows were deep and long. Beams from their weapons' torches stabbed into inky black and seemed to shine on forever without illuminating any objects or walls.

The cloned Nagah were making at least most of them seem visible. But Kane found himself being steered in one direction, toward one of the walls of the great tunnel. He paused and returned to the toppled column, keeping his profile low. The flashlights on the rifles were doing as much to guide him toward a trap as the actual gunfire.

He switched from the light amplification mode on his shadow suit's faceplate to infrared detection. As soon as he did so, he saw only three bulbs burning next to the still warm barrels of rifles. Kane grimaced and scanned the graveyard for signs of the other two cobra men. As he did, a cold mass moved swiftly in his peripheral vision.

Kane hurled himself away from the fallen column just as a pair of gooey entities splashed against it. There was a third being falling, and it snapped the aged stone; cracks appeared on its landing. This was another of the vampires, the corpses with the blood-blob horrors reanimating them.

That last landing informed Kane that he was going to be in for a hell of a battle. Just as the thing took a step, its leg folded beneath it. The same force that had shattered the column had also turned the bones of the corpse's leg to splinters floating in the meat sleeve that used to be a human limb.

But even with that, the thing recovered its balance and hopped along on one foot.

He'd switched to light amplification, his instincts informing him that the snap of the column was louder than any gunshot. Kane knew that those weapon flashlights would swing toward his back, but he was between the Nagah and the light-sensitive children of Neekra. He stood his ground just long enough to give the nocturnal horrors a face full of LED spotlight, then dived to the ground. Rifle bullets sliced the air that he'd stood in only moments ago. The crack of their passage made his skin crawl with the knowledge that he had no body armor protecting him.

Still, the gambit succeeded as he watched the hobbled, reanimated corpse tumble backward under the impact of multiple bullets. As well, he spotted more movement to his right.

It was the two missing Nagah gunners, and they were holding back, scanning for any sign of Kane before taking action. Kane almost felt as if he were at an unfair advantage over the two cloned soldiers, but, then again, they were hunting him to his death, and they had three of their fellow guards flushing him toward them. Kane brought up the Sin Eater and fired at the one who was closest to looking directly at him, punching a burst of slugs into the reptilian humanoid's chest. The snarl of the rounds cutting through the suppressor at the end of the forearm gun was loud enough to jerk the other gunmen to awareness, but the Nagah that he hit dropped to the gun, the life smashed from it.

The other soldier had good reflexes and discipline but wasn't fast enough to catch Kane, even with the dull flicker that managed to escape his Sin Eater's silencer. His wolflike physique sliced through the darkness, lunging for the cover of a grave marker even as bullets missed their first mark. The reptilian gunman turned on his weapon light, probing for where the human had disappeared to, but that only reinforced Kane's triangulation of where the shooting came from. Kane swung his gun on target and put three rounds into the rifleman as another round splashed against the stone he used as cover.

That would-be killer toppled as Kane's bullets smashed through the cobra-hooded gunner's skull. Unfortunately, the dying Nagah's rifle still stayed lit, its beam spilling across the dirt, casting a blaze of light on the ground. The moment Kane moved, he was illuminated, still within the range of the flashlight, the ever-growing cone keeping him visible to the other three killers who directed rounds his way.

Kane hit the dirt. The supersonic crack of air parting in the wake of their bullets buffeted his eardrums as the Nagah guards missed him by inches. At least on the ground, he was no longer betrayed by the spill of LED beams, but the remaining gunmen in Durga's group were no doubt splitting up, looking to get a better angle on him. He needed either a distraction or some help soon.

"Kane. Free and armed."

Four terse words broke over his Commtact, and Kane had never felt so glad to hear the voice of Brigid Baptiste before.

"Need help," Kane answered with equal brevity.

"On the way," were the only words spoken. Again, Kane couldn't be certain that their enemies were not listening in on the encrypted conversations, so the three of them were stingy with their speech. The less they chattered, the less Durga's group would have to home in on them.

He had friends on the way.

"Vampires here," Kane added.

"We know," Brigid said.

Kane sincerely hoped that the tension in his voice and the increase in gunfire were enough to tell her that he needed their aid quickly.

Then again, this was Brigid Baptiste he was thinking about. The woman's observational and extrapolation abilities were second to none. Hers was a brilliant intellect able to direct them to a spot in a featureless desert without benefit of the global positioning satellites in the employ of Cerberus redoubt and Lakesh.

The sound of distant gunfire and the levels of stress in Kane's voice might as well have been distress flares in the sky for her.

The only trouble with that was the Nagah were not the only enemies coming after him. As soon as he got off the Commtact with her, Kane felt the almost steely grasp of a tentacle wrap around his throat. The pseudopod was trying to strangle him, and the force of the pull was hard on his spine as the creature lifted him off the ground.

The braced amoeboid had more than sufficient strength to haul Kane off the ground like a rag doll, and he kicked at the air, struggling to get traction or to throw off his opponent's balance. Neither happened as he was hurled against the other vampire blob. It was like slapping against mud, and the frame of the gelatinous horror indented, wrapping about him.

This is not good at all, Kane thought instantly. He punched and pushed. The rubbery outer membrane resisted his fists and the skin tried to stick to him, but the force of his punches pushed it off of him. He could feel the stickiness of the vampire's outer layer trying to latch on, to slurp the blood from his epidermis, but Kane had his knees up now, shadow suit trousers protecting him even as he kicked away its balloon-like mass.

As the sticky flesh peeled off his, he could see tiny threads, strings ripped from either his body or from the blob's, and he felt needles stabbing his flesh where the strings let go. Kane jerked back harder, ripping the remainder of those strange cilia away from his body, his boot stamping a deep footprint into the bulk of the jellied beast.

The second of the things reached out with a pseudo-pod, but by this time Kane had his knife tight in fist. He slashed out with the razor-keen edge, lopping the thing in half in an instant. The severed tentacle wormed its way, end over end, through the air. The keening wail from the blob must not have been a cry of pain as he'd originally thought. It withdrew the stump and lashed out with a second of the polyp-like limbs that sprouted from a stretch of flattened skin.

These things were pissed off with him and the discomfort he inflicted on their gelatinous forms. Kane lanced forward, punching the point into the rubbery arm. Its pod speared, the monster suddenly lurched and twisted its wounded limb, wrenching the knife from Kane's grasp. The Cerberus explorer retreated backward, avoiding the trap of slurping membrane closing around his blade in an effort to suck down his arm.

In response to that, he fired the Sin Eater into the dark mass he presumed was either the heart or brain of the vampire. A burst of slugs stitched through its wobbling mass, and the creature retreated. At least a spray of powerful slugs would slow it down.

And then more bullets snapped through the air, one burning across the skin of his back. Kane whirled and threw himself flat, seeing the three Nagah gunmen had swung around and had gotten a good line of sight on him. With that line of sight, they could fire at him with a great chance of hitting. Only his wild battle with the vampire blobs had made him enough of a moving target that he'd survived the first salvo of bullets.

Kane fired a burst back toward the blaze of their lights, then rolled, looking for the boneless things. All was darkness behind him. The creatures had retreated from the blue-white glare of the LED lamps attached to the gunmen's rifles.

But the enemy rifles continued to blaze their beams, remaining silent.

The sudden, odd silence made Kane turn just in time to face a cobra man, hood flared, fangs bared and dripping venom, lunging at him. One hand batted the Sin Eater away, and its gunshot echoed in the darkness of the necropolis.

Chapter 20

You plan for an assault on a vampire queen's underground city, and the first fangs you see ready to tear out your throat belong to a snake-man, Kane's brain managed to flash. He lifted his forearm up, smashing the attacking Nagah clone under his chin, catching him full in the throat. The humanoid cobra's forward momentum ended with those curved, venom-glistening canines inches from his face. Had the raised forearm struck a throat without the dense chest scales of a male Nagah, the impact of Kane's elbow would have left the assailant gurgling, windpipe and larynx bruised if not crushed entirely.

Instead, a cough of fetid breath splashed against Kane's hood and faceplate, the stream of burning poison jetting from the hollow notches in each fang immediately following. The Cerberus warrior was glad for the full head covering that he wore, not only for the advanced night vision that had brought him some advantage against both cloned soldiers and inhuman vampire spawn in the pitch-black caverns, but also because the hood was environmentally sealed, protecting his eyes and sinus cavities from the brutal effects of the spit venom. Kane had seen men dropped and left clawing at their faces in response to a Nagah's spit attack.

Kane had also caught a peripheral spray of that, as well as having been exposed to the same venom injected into him, directly from a bite applied by Durga. The toxins of the Nagah were deadly, and only a quick shot of antivenom had kept Kane from dying. No such provisions were on hand now, and while Kane hoped he'd developed some resistance to the killer bite, he didn't want to test that, not when the attacker looming over him had fangs that were also two inches long and able to stab and rip his throat, as well.

Kane twisted his wrist with the Sin Eater up, but Durga's soldier still had a death grip on Kane's forearm, keeping the muzzle of the Magistrate sidearm away from him. The strength of the cloned cobra man was great, enough to remind Kane that Durga had made use of Nephilim in previous instances, remolding them to resemble either native Indian humans or Nagah soldiers themselves, both of whom were ubiquitous and unnoticed among the citizens of the Nagah city of Garuda. This might have been an "overwritten" Nephilim, a gift from Durga's Annunaki sponsor, Enlil, but Kane didn't care how this thing had been born. He just needed to make it die before it killed him.

Twisting his powerful upper body, the lean, angular musculature of a grown wolf giving him the leverage and might to unsettle, then topple his fanged opponent, Kane managed to free himself and get some distance from the slavering cobra fangs. With that distance, he was now able to bring his leg up, first spearing his knee into the ribs of his opponent and driving the breath from his lungs again. A second jab with the knee made the Nagah convulse, eyes squinting shut from the pain. Kane rolled back a few feet, then swung his boot up in a slashing arc, catching the cobra man under the chin.

An unintelligible garble erupted from snaggletoothed lips. One fang protruded almost comically over the lower lip, and blood glistened from the opposite corner of his mouth. Kane got his hands and feet beneath him and shot himself up to a standing position, looking for the other Nagah fighters.

Instead of Durga's shock troopers, he instead spotted a shambling, bloody man hopping toward him with angry abandon, fingers hooked like talons.

It was the vampire who had broken his leg trying to kick Kane. Even with its chest ripped asunder by sprays of AK fire, the thing didn't know when to quit or give up. Somewhere in the back of Kane's mind, he was reminded of a story of "hopping vampires" from ancient Chinese mythology. As quickly as that thought arose, with the image of those Asian corpses moving on the only good leg that remained to them, Kane pushed it aside and reached for the handle of his fighting knife.

Almost immediately he recalled that his battle blade had been sucked into a corpse-deficient blob, lost.

Kane dropped one shoulder and lunged at the off-balance corpse, slamming the fiend off its remaining foot, as the grasping hands clawed at empty air. Kane's shoulder block hurled the reanimated militiaman's form into the dirt with a thud. He swung the muzzle of his Sin Eater up and fired two shots into the thing's face, blasting it into a pulpy mess of ragged flesh and splintered bone.

Once most of the head was gone, a rubbery stalk shot out of the remnants of the thing's face—the blob that had been operating it like a puppeteer from within decided to take the combat to Kane in a more direct manner.

It was then that Kane pulled the second of his sharpened wooden stakes from his belt. The amorphous horror was in full lunge, unable to stop its forward momentum, even as Kane thrust the sharpened length of wood right through its rubbery membrane. The blob wailed out its cry of pain as oozy cytoplasm and tacky skin rushed across Kane's arm in an effort to escape from the wood that was poisonous to its very existence.

Kane must have missed its nucleus or whatever organs the creature had within its translucent form, because the shapeless thing continued to bound and bounce away from him, seeking escape from the weapons that burned it so.

"Suck it, boneless!" Kane bellowed after the fleeing vampire, feeling the need to add insult to injury.

The challenge was not accepted, but the man from Cerberus redoubt felt a surge of adrenaline in him as he returned to seeking out any other armed killers hunting for him within the underground graveyard he'd found himself in.

Gunshots ripped in the distance, sounding like the tearing of canvas. Kane turned to look in the direction of the sound, and he noticed that a wounded Nagah staggered along, fleeing whoever had opened fire.

Since it was Nagah clones falling and running away, then it was fairly certain that Brigid and Grant were the ones coming to the rescue. He turned and activated the zoom on his hood's optics. He focused on Brigid Baptiste, who lowered her weapon. She didn't seem to have the heart to shoot a wounded man in the back, no matter how hard he'd been trying to kill one of her own. Kane was glad for that. There'd been necessary ruthlessness, but outright cruelty was nothing that he wanted to get comfortable with.

"I'm coming," Kane said before jogging toward them. He kept looking over his shoulder for signs of any of the vampiric creatures.

"Covering you," Grant responded.

Kane scanned his group of allies, but he could only make out Brigid and Grant, and their weapons were "lights off."

Of course, it made sense. Neither of them would want to make blatant targets of themselves. Kane continued along, eventually turning on his own flashlight, illuminating his face, thankful for the polarization on his faceplate's optics.

"You didn't happen to bring night vision for the rest of the class, did you?" Brigid asked.

Kane shook his head. "I'm lucky I was able to scrape this much back together."

The archivist shrugged. "You have any news on how to deal with the vampires?"

"They don't like the LEDs on these rifles," Kane mentioned. "That sent them into retreat. Also, they hate wood."

"We got that," Grant answered. "Well, Brigid learned that from experience, but she's shared."

"Where are Nathan and Thurpa?" Kane asked.

"We sent them up the corkscrew to the surface," Grant explained. "I figured you were keeping most of the gathered gear in reserve up there."

Kane nodded. "That's good thinking. Any other reason why they're not hanging around?"

"Thurpa's having issues of self-doubt after he was removed from one cell by Durga," Brigid told him. "He wanted to make certain he was under guard by someone we all trusted."

"Nathan," Kane surmised.

Brigid nodded. Her green eyes flashed as she swept the empty cavern, the highlights of her irises picking up a flicker of glow from the distant, still burning flashlights on the abandoned rifles. Kane focused in closer on the setup and saw that the cobra men had wedged themselves against gravestones, so as to spray as open an area as they could.

"How long will those lights last?" Kane asked.

"Depends on the batteries and the lights. Since they're LED, it's a low power drain for that much candlepower," Brigid stated, looking back. The three of them retreated from the edge of the graveyard, weaving among the crypt houses. "They'll be burning for maybe a full day, minimum. Maybe even more given their brightness."

"Then the blobs won't want to cross too close," Kane said. "It'll keep them from following us."

"Not by much," Grant said. "There's plenty of dark for them to crawl around."

Kane wrinkled his nose beneath the full cowl. "Great."

"Either way, they won't be back soon," Brigid said. "It seems that they didn't want to mess more than once with a foe who could harm them."

"So they're smart or cowardly," Kane mused.

"Probably smart," Grant said. "I wouldn't go at the same foe twice with the same tactics."

"And you're no coward," Kane agreed. He paused. "Thurpa thinks he's not quite trustworthy? You mean he's worried that Durga might still be somewhere in his head?"

"My feeling is that if he's worried about it, he's not bad," Grant said.

"But then he's programmed Nephilim to work as his operatives back in Garuda," Brigid added. "Durga's damned devious. He even used Thurpa as a mail drop for Fargo."

"So that's why Fargo popped out from the woodwork when he did," Kane said. "It wasn't to help me out or to deal with Neekra before she blossomed into a full-blown horror."

"It could be that," Brigid said. "He didn't stick around much longer than to get us your supplies and to either deliver or pick up an object."

"What kind of object?" Kane asked. "Unless it could fit into a pocket, I didn't see him carrying much aside from his archeologist's shtick."

Brigid frowned as they continued along. Kane was glad that both Grant and she were armed with rifles, obviously taken from the same stockpile of militia arms that Durga had outfitted his cloned Nagah with. Even so, he was certain that those rifles weren't going to be everything necessary to deal with the rest of Neekra's inhuman children, let alone her. If the spawn were as resistant to bullets and knives as they had already experienced, then their sire would have equal, if not superior, resilience.

Kane knew full well from his encounters with Enlil and his Nephilim soldiers that the Annunaki and their drone slaves were tough to kill, and in general, the Nephilim were merely armored and stronger than the average man. The overlords themselves, by dint of genetic manipulation or by their specie's royal genetics, had near immortality and could awaken in reincarnation, spreading their existence across multiple centuries and dimensions.

Something that the Annunaki worried about enough to slam into a prison in the heart of the African continent was a concern for Kane. Neekra was working with a puppet body and still able to birth children from what had formerly been a man.

The three people stopped cold as they heard the slap and squish of the amorphous children of the dark goddess.

"Lights," Kane ordered, drawing his wooden stake. Kane didn't know exactly why they were so susceptible to light and wood, but he wasn't going to look a gift horse in the mouth.

Brigid shook her head, and Grant took his cue from her.

Kane looked up, grimacing as he realized that four of the blobs were on the ceiling above them, and that those spawn no longer showed a lick of interest in the intruders from Cerberus. They were heading back to the corkscrew shaft leading to the surface.

"Oh, that's not good," Kane murmured.

"No," Brigid agreed.

Grant touched his Commtact. "Nate, Thurpa? Come in."

"I read you," Nate answered, audible over the implanted communicators for all three of the Cerberus team. "But I can't talk much. We've got company. Lots of it."

Though Kane could already presume who had just joined the little party at the mouth of hell, he spoke up. "Lyta?"

"Here," she answered tersely. "It's the Panthers of Mashona."

"And it's still night up there," Kane mused, checking his wrist-chron.

The news clicked quickly for Brigid Baptiste, though she tried to hide her concern behind a snarky quip. "Neekra's kids are getting all new clothes for Christmas."

"Stay low, all of you," Kane ordered. "Don't try to

even the odds. Don't try to ambush anyone who seems hurt. Stay out of the way."

"We hear you," Thurpa answered. "What about you three?"

"We'll handle things down here," Grant answered. "Don't worry about us."

With that, they shut down their Commtacts. They didn't want to give away any more information about themselves or their allies than necessary, but they were at least glad to know the situation above.

"Don't worry about us," Brigid muttered. "That doesn't apply to the us who should be worried, does it?"

"No, it doesn't," Grant returned. "But the three of us worrying leads to us solving problems as fast as humans can. So, yeah, I'm sweating, but, hey, we've been in worse positions."

"Vampires and militiamen, with a side order of Durga," Kane added. "Brigid…have we been worse off?"

"Each crisis we've been in has had its own unique issues of peril," Brigid responded.

"You're nervous, too," Kane translated.

Brigid rolled her eyes. "Because I have a pulse."

Kane smirked. "No worries. If I'd eaten more than a tiny snack in the past day, I'd be shitting a brick myself."

"Kane, Grant, Brigid, are any of you there?" a voice came over their Commtacts. It was familiar, Indian accented and sibilant, and the last person they ever expected to call them on the Cerberus party line.

Even though he and the others suspected that the Nagah prince might have been listening in on their communications, Kane still had to force himself to speak the man's name.

"Durga?"

LYTA WAS STUCK ONCE MORE in the role of babysitting an ancient artifact. This was to keep it from falling into the wrong hands and to give her something to deal with any of the vampiric monstrosities stalking the forest. As well, she had a treasure horde of equipment left behind by Kane. Spare guns, electronics, ammunition, grenades, much recovered from their parked truck, the rest cobbled together from the remnants of the Mashonan militia's base. Enough to equip a company of troops and an arsenal that could hold off nearly any threat she could imagine.

The trouble was, she was alone under the camouflage tarp, a ghillie blanket with which she'd hidden from Neekra's amorphous children as they'd spread out, either in their blob forms or wearing the corpses of dead militiamen. There were two others up here, Nathan and Thurpa, who'd come to the surface, escaping the underground necropolis, but they'd had to take cover, hiding themselves only twenty yards distant from her yet a continent away for all intents and purposes.

The Panthers of Mashona had arrived, in force. A full column of trucks and jeeps pulled up, each vehicle bristling with armed dark men. Headlights blazed, at once giving Lyta an idea of the extent of the force arriving while forcing her to squint at the glare. Voices barked orders, and soldiers disembarked from their vehicles.

She'd warned Kane and the others below, using a hand radio that he'd left her, keyed into their Commtact frequencies, along with a secondary channel with which she'd be able to converse with the other two tagalongs, if they had the equipment handy, which she heard that they did. She grimaced, wishing that they'd been able to get farther from the underground entrance before the militia showed up. At the very least, they could have hidden together, and there'd be extra hands to wield weapons if and when this pirate band of marauders discovered them.

Watching from her hiding spot, she could tell that the militiamen were furious as they looked over their looted brethren's corpses. These men had lost contact with this unit at least a day and a half before, but now their search had ended with the loss of comrades and equipment. She could see the frustration writhing on their faces like possessive demons, flickering rage flashing in eyes that reflected the headlamps on their vehicles.

"There has to be someone left," one of the officers called out. "Spread out and find him!"

"Unless we were called by a ghost," remarked one of a pair of troops stalking by. "We showed up as big as day. How could anyone miss our approach?"

"Maybe he's hurt somewhere," the other soldier answered him before they faded out of earshot.

There was more than sufficient racket among the assembled group that she risked turning frequencies. "Nathan? Thurpa?"

"We read," the exotic accents of Thurpa answered. "Are you all right?"

"Safe and sound," Lyta said. "I have you in my line of sight. I want you to come to me."

"Why not come over here?" Nathan butted in.

"Because I don't want to drag a ton of guns and ammunition around where the militia can see me," Lyta hissed.

"Makes sense," Thurpa chimed in.

She could almost hear the young man roll his eyes.

"I might be able to walk around unnoticed, but Thurpa's another matter," Nathan countered. "It's dark, but his cobra hood and scales are going to still stand out."

"So would a woman among this bunch," Thurpa said. "I can be sneaky."

"Kane told us to stay put," Nathan grumbled. "And things are coming topside that—"

The keening of the gelatinous horrors broke through even the racket of the assembled militia, and it made the gunmen pause, wondering what was making the sound.

"Screw that," Nathan snapped. "Come on—we're not taking those things on again."

Lyta rose to a kneeling position. Neekra's spawn were present, and they unleashed their battle cry for all to hear. Even though she'd already been to battle with them once before, even though she'd heard the terrible song of their rage, a chilling jolt ran icicles up and down her spine. Lyta didn't want to see what these things did to feed or to occupy human bodies, and she wasn't going to sit idly by when they went after two of the people who had come to her rescue.

She snatched up the rifle at her side and held it, finger off the trigger to prevent sending an errant round into the ground and giving away her position. The two young men moved from their hiding spot. Lyta saw that Nathan had put himself between Thurpa and the rest of the group, the two of them jogging along, with purpose, looking as if they belonged. Thurpa moved as naturally as he could, staying out of the spill of headlights, sidestepping toward the nearest shadows as soon as it was safe to.

Good boy, Lyta thought. Even so, she was on edge. She knew not to shoulder the weapon, because the temptation to open fire at the slightest trouble would be unbearable. The two of them had navigated halfway across the column of men, keeping to the outskirts of the group and behind the bulk of vehicles.

Of course, when they were out of her direct line of sight, she was at her most nervous. They could be discovered, and with a truck between her and her young allies, there'd be no way she could cover them, protect them.

They could be gunned down, and if they got captured...

Stripped of weapons, tied up, Neekra's spawn would eat them alive.

Come on, you two, Lyta thought. The tendons in her neck were drawn taut, as if their tension could somehow trigger a force field or a cloak of invisibility to fall across Nathan and Thurpa. Each second was either a footstep toward her or a moment in captivity.

Officers barked orders to the militiamen, and the Mashonan marauders set up a defensive perimeter, awaiting whatever enemies had made the cries she knew all too well. Of course, now that the riflemen were organized, that meant there was less slack, less wiggle room for Nathan and Thurpa to appear as normal.

Lyta could tell that the things were in a circle around the column of men, each of them screeching, a hellish cry that was getting to her just as much as it was unsettling the dozens of armed soldiers. These men, who were normally the feared predators in this part of Africa, now knew what it was like to be prey.

She saw a militiaman shout toward Thurpa and Nathan. Even as the rifleman spoke, Thurpa turned, pistol in hand. Lyta saw the look of horror on the man's face, the moment of hesitation.

That might have been more than enough for her to act, but that instant of vulnerability exploded into horror.

One of Neekra's amorphous children lunged from the shadows, its tentacles lashing around the Panther of Mashona's head. His scream was muffled, but a blaze of gunfire erupted from his rifle. Nathan let out a shout as his legs buckled beneath him.

Automatic weapons roared and shimmering, rubbery figures leaped through the night.

Chapter 21

Neekra, residing in the ever-withering skin of Gamal, former warlord of the Panthers of Mashona, felt the world around her through her spawn. Of course, these creatures were no more children than she was puny enough to be confined in the mere flesh of a human being. The "children" were actually tumors she'd produced, semiaware drones that could act and think enough to protect themselves or hunt but were always just a thought from her complete dominion. They would not act on hunger unless she willed it, despite the fact that she kept that thirst for human blood still hard coded into their existence.

The blob-like entities were mostly cytoplasm, with superstrings of proteins acting as the motors that shaped the organism into some form of gigantic amoeba or a hunting octopus. There were two clumps within the creature. One of them acted as a brain, storing data and targeting victims as necessary, processing the devoured biomass of their victims' brains to add to Neekra's own psychic strength. The other was a clump of protein cells that had configured themselves into a natural, organic transmitter, a telepathic organ that kept them in contact with their mistress.

The useless sacs that Neekra had molded into female-looking breasts were themselves copies of that same telepathic organ—one that formed the link between

Gamal's carcass, the other as the central hub from which she commanded her "vampire army." More than once, she recalled the old visual pun of a human male playing with the breasts of his woman, "tuning in Tokyo." Little did the fleshy monkeys realize that their joke carried more truth than they could ever hope to realize.

That was the one weakness in the structure of the otherwise invulnerable beings. The proper force could rupture those bio-organic computer complexes, destroying the amorphous horrors' sole form of sentience. Normally they could escape harm, even if a bullet passed through the redundant "circuitry." But a shank transfixing one of those constructs, either metal or the cellulose to which her imperfect spawn were allergic, shorted out their brains.

Neekra's own true children weren't as sensitive to intense light or to wood. That was why she hated being so crippled and hindered by being stuck in this carcass. That was why she *needed* Kane so badly. Without him, and without Durga, there was no way she could break through the tomb where Enlil had cast her eons ago.

So far, the spawn had been feeding Gamal back the biomass he'd lost in birthing them, feasting on the fresh corpses above and hunting down the remnants of the militia for fresh blood. That influx of vital, still warm juices kept Neekra from totally depleting Gamal's body, though the production of polyp children and the birthing process were agony to the submerged, imprisoned psyche. Neekra didn't know if she wanted the former warlord to live after she abandoned him, but she could easily assume, listening to his sensations of pain and the terror burning through overtaxed neurons, that he'd welcome the black void of eternal death.

Even hell would be a respite after this existence.

Such was the fate of those who let the ancient goddess down.

"I've made you my bitch, Gamal," she said aloud, chuckling as her sensations of his suffering filtered into her, tickling her. His discomfort was better than the nothingness she'd normally feel. She was used to a greater cacophony of sensory input, and only the extreme torture she put Gamal's cells through gave her any semblance of contact with the world as she was used to it.

The trouble was, she was quickly running down the span and utility of this body.

Fresh bodies arriving would give her meat puppet some relief, some extension of its life span.

She turned to Durga. "Thank you, my prince."

The cobra man nodded. "I shall need to withdraw from this city. I have to replenish my forces."

Neekra narrowed her eyes. "They are dead?"

"All but two have been slain by the escaping prisoners and by Kane's assault on the necropolis, and one of those two is wounded," Durga explained.

"I could have—" Neekra began. She stepped closer, brushing her fingers across his chest scales.

"You're already spread thin enough…at least Gamal is," Durga replied. He grasped her fingers gently, full of concern. "And I want my own people with me. Not your puppets."

Neekra nodded. "So willful."

"So lonely," Durga returned. "Besides, would you trust my minions under your command? We've been tense, distrusting of late. And I've delivered proof of my concern for you, my queen."

"You have," she told him. She rewarded him with a

smile. "Once the militia has been reaped, and my army filled out, I shall meet you anon?"

Durga bowed to her in deference. "At your prison? Nothing can keep me from your awakening."

Neekra probed, but his thoughts were slick, agile, as elusive to her as quicksilver. She couldn't quite trust him, but deep in his convictions, he was being honest about finding her immortal prison. Whether that was to forever seal her in—or destroy her—or to release her and somehow take advantage of her bid to conquer the world…that was the question.

Neekra would keep her guard up, but, for now, she'd let Durga leave and roam freely. One saving grace was that he had to stay put while her spawn took on the marauding militia known as the Panthers of Mashona. She could trust her minions, but the humans were likely to shoot at anything that didn't look human. Durga might not have been a rubbery blob man, but he also was notably alien.

Not a single one of those raiders would have thought twice about emptying magazines into his flesh. Durga might have been resurrected by the power of the ancient artifact Nehushtan; he was not immortal. Indeed, while he was as fit as he'd ever been, his chest and stomach scales were no match for automatic weapons blazing away.

"Sir, they're coming!" a voice spoke from aside. Neekra turned and saw it was one of Durga's cloned soldiers. He clutched an injured side, blood seeping over his scaled fingers. "They're coming."

Durga frowned.

"I thought that they would have lasted longer against Kane and his allies," he muttered. She could feel the disappointment flowing off of him. The other of Durga's scaled sentinels glanced to him with more than a bit of concern.

"Help him," Durga grumbled finally, answering the unspoken question.

Neekra was surprised at his concern for what was nothing more than a blank slate of biomass given humanoid form. And yet these creatures had displayed a modicum of skill and cleverness in their protection of the necropolis, driving Kane out into the vast grave plain. They'd proven their worth, failing only in the face of a flanking force with equal strength and firepower.

Durga turned to her. "I'm going to need to get moving. How are things going topside?"

"The militia is putting up a good fight," Neekra said. She could feel bodies squirming against her spawn, inputting the sensations of fresh blood flowing in through capillary hooks that slurped vital juices from humans. The amorphous minions feasted, but not all of them were in good condition. Some had been stunned by bursts of automatic rifle fire, and others had suffered pain and distress as bayonets and machetes were pressed into action. Here and there, one of her bloodthirsty issues blanked out, a lucky stab or slash destroying one of its mental organs.

"Too good of a fight," Neekra continued.

Durga's brow furrowed. "What?"

"I said, some of them know how to protect themselves," Neekra replied.

"Pull back!" Durga impelled her.

Neekra's eyes flashed with anger. "And what if they bring their knowledge down here? They'll destroy everything!"

"Not necessarily," Durga said. "We're caught between two armies."

Neekra frowned. "There are just three of them."

"Armed with the same equipment which I supplied to my guards," Durga responded. "The guards who they wiped out with much less preparation and firepower."

Neekra regarded her ally. "Then…where would I go?"

"Do you need to be here?" Durga asked.

Neekra wrinkled her nose. She didn't want to betray her purpose for being in the necropolis; all she needed was just a little more time. Time she could buy for herself simply by stepping aside and letting two enemies slug it out.

She could feel the ones who'd seized bodies above. They were on the run, avoiding direct combat or playing dead while allowing their brethren to attack. She decided to let the ones converted to her puppets play wounded, falling back and joining with the militia that stayed behind. The amorphous entities were to retreat, drawing them down into the necropolis. Down into the cross fire with Kane and his allies.

She'd seen what the man could do, she'd seen what his allies could do, as well.

Durga had the right plan.

And with that, Durga took her hand, leading toward a back door that she had forgotten about. One that he'd planned to use all along.

DURGA WISHED HE COULD have picked up the surprise on Kane's face when he cut in on their Commtact frequency. The small communicator that had been slipped into Thurpa's pocket was three by five by two inches and composed of some of the very best electronics that the Nagah people had access to. The device itself had miles of monomolecular antenna coil, which allowed it to pierce through even the depth of stone that this necropolis had been built beneath. The hand unit, however, was in direct connection with an even larger computer system, set up in the remnants of the Republic of South Africa, where Durga's ship had come into port.

The system was another of the many Continuity of Government underground redoubts that had been put together in anticipation of a global catastrophe. The communications and computer equipment installed in the facility were able to figure out the frequency and encryption of the Commtacts with some small assistance from Austin Fargo and his brain-dwelling interface. It was an ace in the hole that Durga wanted to keep just in case things went south.

"So why are you talking to us now?" Brigid asked over her comm.

"Because I need to warn you of what she is up to," Durga answered.

"She's looking for something down here," Brigid stated. "Obviously it's some form of key that she requires to escape her imprisonment."

"I'm not certain of the details, but that's the gist of what seems to be going on," Durga responded.

"Since we're aware of what she's up to, why are you telling us?" Kane asked. "It's not as if you want to do us any good."

"I want power. And that power is not going to be worth shit if there's an alien god rampaging across the planet," Durga explained. "I'm still trying to figure out what she needs."

"Where is she now?" Brigid asked.

"She's currently in a trance, with a couple of her spawn standing guard," Durga stated. "I think she's running the assault on the militia. It's hard not to hear what's going on."

Brigid turned off her signal and murmured something.

"Just keep gathering gear," Kane said. "Durga—"

"I don't have much time," the Nagah prince cut off the human warrior. "What I need you to do is arm up and brace for a battle. Neekra is going to want to stall for time until she finds what she's seeking. That means you're going to get very busy and bloody in a few minutes."

"Crap," Kane grumbled. "The soldiers don't really think they can actually fight those things off, do they?"

"They've got an ace up their sleeve," Durga returned.

"You or Fargo," Kane responded.

"Right," Durga said. "I told you—I don't like the idea of having to worry about a goddess, or her vampire minions, running loose."

"Even with a little knowledge, those things are hard as hell to kill," Kane told him.

"Which is why I think you'll be able to handle the militia," Durga said. "They're going through a hell of a beating, despite what they're handing out."

"Great," Kane groaned. "And what will you be doing?"

"Dealing with Neekra and finding out what she wants from this necropolis," Durga answered. "And hopefully killing this body of hers."

Kane frowned. "She didn't need a body to hijack our brains."

"Anything I can do to slow her down," Durga said.

With that, the Nagah prince turned off the radio handset, still hidden within his pocket. He plucked his earplug with built-in microphone and pocketed that swiftly. He saw the avatar of the goddess stir.

Her lips formed into a smile. "I've made you my bitch, Gamal."

Durga knew that she was closing in on her goals if she was in this good of a mood. Her initial emotions and euphoria over the ambush were still high. But sooner or later, she'd realize that things wouldn't be that easy. He'd already used radio equipment from the militia's slave caravan to summon the rest of the forces in the area, alerting them to a dangerous ambush force.

Durga, at least, wouldn't feel much concern for the group of power-hungry thugs when they met their fates. He just hoped that his plots would keep him going. He knew he'd earned a lot of bad karma for his actions, and his chumming with one of the world's deadliest enemies was dancing dangerously close to extinction.

KANE COULD TELL that Brigid didn't enjoy having to scavenge spare weapons and ammunition off the dead, but time was of the essence. Somewhere between them and the surface were Durga and Neekra. Durga had kept at least one of his bodyguards in reserve, and Neekra would not have been foolish enough to leave herself completely defenseless.

Grant was stuffing magazines and grenades into an improvised duffel bag he'd made. He'd also created a harness from which he hung a shotgun, a handgun, a fighting knife and a combat-style machete. The scene reminded Kane of something from a pre-skydark vid about their vision of a postapocalyptic warrior, guns and gear bristling over the man's shoulders. So far, Grant kept his machete in hand as his main weapon, though a confiscated assault rifle was gripped around its forearm, looking small and puny in his powerful hand.

"If I had my bow and arrows, I'd go toe to toe with Marduk himself," Grant muttered.

"Feeling that confident?" Kane asked.

Grant's eyes narrowed. "Feeling that pissed and tired of being chased around Africa. First hiding in the Victoria Falls redoubt, now getting stuck in a dungeon."

"We'll get ours back," Kane told him. His discussion with Durga had him on edge. He'd quickly explained that Neekra was going to throw her other set of enemies at them, especially since the militia had knowledge of how to battle her amorphous spawn and the corpses they reanimated. Or maybe they just knew about the rubbery blobs. Durga was a duplicitous son of a bitch, so his warnings might not go far in giving them an ability to totally dominate a foe he was using as a buffer.

Brigid rose, touching her Commtact, concern in her features. "Good news and bad news."

"How bad for our friends?" Kane asked.

"Nathan took a bullet in the leg," Brigid explained. "It was a cross fire, but no one's paying close attention to them for now."

Kane adjusted his Commtact and picked up Lyta.

"The militia looks like it's driving the things off," she said into the radio. "Thurpa and Nathan are with me now. Nate's leg has already stopped bleeding."

"What about 'low profile' did you not understand?" Kane asked.

"The staff would keep us invisible. In fact, once Thurpa and Nathan got to me, the attention was off of them," Lyta snarled. "If they'd stayed where they were, they would have been sliced to ribbons."

Already, over by the corkscrew shaft, flares popped,

illuminating the base of the two ramps. Kane grimaced as he saw amorphous beings bouncing and dropping to the ground. Gunfire crackled in the air.

"Durga called Neekra's plan. She's making her things withdraw, pulling the militia with them," Kane grumbled.

Grenades dropped, exploding in a sequence of thundering blasts that shook the air violently. Kane could feel the buffeting breeze, but he saw that the rubbery horrors had achieved cover and weathered the explosive storm with ease.

"He probably planted that strategy in her ear," Grant said. "All the better to mess with us."

"And she's drawn them between us and the other side of this necropolis," Brigid added. "We're cut off from where the dungeons lie. Who knows what else is in the catacombs on that side of the underground complex?"

"Another way out?" Kane asked.

"Undoubtedly. Otherwise she'd be as trapped as we are," Brigid responded.

Kane frowned. "Durga said he'd destroy her current body, or at least try to."

"If he can keep that promise," Brigid said before she was cut off by the rattle of automatic weapons and bullets chipping the stones near her. "It's not going to do much for us here…."

Grant scanned the scene. He and Brigid were both adorned with the flat-folding shadow suit hoods, complete with flexible faceplates and advanced optics. He gave a quick assessment. "There's only about a dozen of the blob things."

"That's about what we faced on the first night," Kane mused.

"Yeah. After only a few hours waiting down here," Grant said.

"Grant's correct. Neekra could have birthed many more, given the time we were indisposed," Brigid agreed. "She should have at least three times as many."

"That is going to suck," Kane murmured. "No matter how many soldiers come down here, the leftovers will be able to cork them up in the bottlenecks at the surface."

Bullets began zipping into the ground yards short of the Cerberus trio's position.

"Of course, that's not going to do us much good if they shoot us in the cross fire," Brigid pointed out. "We need to protect ourselves."

"She's aimed them right at us," Grant said. "Take a look."

Brigid and Kane swept the blocks of crypts. Their amoeboid "friends" had disappeared, slipping into cracks and crevices, leaving a clear channel into the shadows that would lead right up to them. Brigid dropped to the dirt, letting a gravestone shield her from the coming storm of bullets.

"I thought that you said she wanted your assistance in freeing her," Brigid mentioned to Kane.

Kane nodded. "That's right. She must have some high expectations of the kind of punishment we can take."

Grant grimaced. "It's not what we can take. It's what we can dish out. And right now, we can make life very tough for that group."

Kane peered around his flagstone shield. "Yeah. A few grens down their throats when they least expect it… Right now they're in fighting-alien-monster mode.

A salvo of modern firepower will take that group totally off balance."

Grant nodded, smiling as his friend saw the vulnerability of their enemy. "Of course, we'll still have to deal with Neekra's kids."

"One army at a time," Kane whispered.

With that, the two men looked to Brigid Baptiste, who knelt, ready to add her fury to the coming firestorm.

Chapter 22

Nathan's knee buckled as soon as the bullet sliced through the muscle around his thigh. Only the lack of jarring shock, the vibration of his femur shattering, made certain that he wasn't completely screwed by circumstance. He watched as an elastic body lashed out toward the source of gunfire, and Nathan tried not to smirk in satisfaction as the chatter of an automatic weapon dissolved into a shriek of agony accompanied by wet slaps and sticky tearing.

Thurpa lunged under Nathan's arm, supporting him on his injured leg. "Let's go!"

Soft pops of gunfire issued from the copse of woods beyond the tree line, their ultimate destination. Lyta fired a suppressed weapon of some sort, spitting bullets out at a much lower profile than the rest of the militia's weaponry. To Nathan's right, he could see a reanimated figure rise jerkily, then get knocked back down by the sputter of full-auto bullets.

Nathan didn't hold out much hope for that burst of gunfire keeping down the skinsuit for the rubbery vampire thing. He pulled the .45 from Thurpa's hip holster, then swung it up to cover the two of them as his sudden injury made him drop his rifle on its sling. Rather than struggle with the bouncing weapon on its strap, he went for an easier to manipulate piece of kit.

None of the militia seemed to give a damn about

the two figures scuttling across the open ground. They were too busy shooting into amorphous shadows. Nathan could hear shouted orders to fix bayonets and to use machetes. To aim for the dark masses within their translucent blob membranes. These were the same tactics he, Thurpa and Brigid had figured out in their first encounter with the killer snot-balls.

Of course, Brigid had been discussing the basis for vampiric myth with Nathan based on the attacker who'd slain his father. Their speculation had proven fruitful, but Nathan, for all the gunfire and screams of man and amorphous beast, couldn't figure out why these cruel marauders had a lick of information about what their foes could be. It couldn't have been the reanimated bodies, because only one had risen so far, at least within observational range of him and Thurpa. And the amoeba-like figures, all tentacles and shimmering, rubbery skin, were scarcely reminiscent of the kind of creatures they'd been thinking about.

The leadership and elite troops, at least, weren't concerning themselves with gunfire to either of the two vital organs floating in their cytoplasm. One Mashonan Panther bounded into their path, angling his rifle like a spear and plunging it through the tough skin of an attacking blob. The point of his bayonet dived deep within. Nathan followed its penetration through translucent hide and inner mucus. The bayonet connected with one of the creature's nerve centers, and the beast unleashed its inhuman howl. The shriek pulsed within Nathan's sinuses as if it were hot pepper spray.

The skilled Panther ripped his rifle free from the bulk of the dead creature, but before he could turn and notice Nathan and Thurpa, tentacles whipped out, one lashing around his face, others about his waist and knees. The militiaman's muffled cry became audible as the skin on his cheek tore, sloughing loose under the grabbing adhesive force of the deadly spawn's barbed cilia.

"Enki preserve me," Thurpa prayed, watching the gleam of cheekbone poke through the tear in the doomed African thug's face. An instant later, his body was snatched up and drawn into the darkness outside the spill of a pair of headlights. Nathan aimed his .45 at the spot where the body had disappeared, hammering out two big fat slugs. If he didn't harm one of Neekra's children, at least he'd grant their human prey a reprieve from a slow, terrible death by skinning and bloodsucking.

Now Nathan *knew* what was meant by a fate one wouldn't wish on their worst enemy. That the poor bastard had torn the flesh from his own face in an effort to escape was sign enough that he and the others had been lucky not to have been subjected to the full power of the tentacled monstrosities. Nathan fought off a horrible chill that poured down into his gut like lumpy, cold mud. Each scream of a dying militiaman was in reaction to the horror of being torn apart or exsanguinated through their skin.

And that was just the men who were *able* to scream. Others could have been muffled, smothered by the elastic bulk of Neekra's spawn. The vampire blobs were on the attack, and now a jeep exploded, flashing brightly in a column of flame. Keening wails from the giant amoebas informed Nathan that this was a resistance tactic by the Panthers of Mashona. The militia sacrificed at least one vehicle, letting its burning demise buy them time.

The paramilitary group prized working vehicles. They engaged in bloodthirsty raids on settlements merely to acquire more jeeps and trucks, risking their lives in exchange for working machinery that was worth its weight in gold. The Panthers were *desperate*. How many lives had been ended just for them to use that set of wheels?

And now, its gasoline—another precious and rare resource among the jungle pirates—flared and blazed. One of the rubbery assailants writhed, twisting as flames licked along its surface. As individual tongues of flame winked out on its shimmering membrane, that skin blackened and puckered before bursting and vomiting out its cytoplasmic guts in a thick, cloying ooze. One tendril reached out, groping in the dirt. The thing's pain was a whistling screech that struck nerves up and down Nathan's spine.

Thurpa threw Nathan to the ground, hurling him roughly to Lyta's feet without ceremony. He glanced up, jarred by the impact, but by then Thurpa had a weapon in hand and he ripped off short bursts into the ground around them.

"Get in here!" Lyta shouted.

The young Nagah turned at her plea. Almost immediately, Nathan felt warm, golden energy pouring through his veins, shimmering all along his bloodstream before focusing on his bullet-ravaged thigh muscles. The sunny, nurturing heat was an intoxicating rush, making his heart skip a beat before he rose to one knee and held out his hand to Thurpa.

"Take my hand!" Nathan shouted.

It was as if someone else was guiding him as his leg supported his weight; words left his lips before he knew what he was saying.

"But—" Thurpa began.

"Take it!" Nathan bellowed.

Thurpa reached out and clasped hands with the young man from Harare.

Suddenly, that warming, giddy glow inside his bloodstream stretched out even farther. Lyta, Thurpa and Nathan formed a human circuit, each of them sharing the protection and care of the ancient Atlantean artifact. And as that circuit was completed, the three of them gathered in the rut that Lyta and Kane had dug to watch over the entrances to the necropolis. Thurpa was the only one with a free hand, and he swept their camouflage blanket over the top of them. Guns and screams still clawed through the night, headlights bursting as reanimated fighters smashed them with rifle stocks. The column of Panthers was growing increasingly dark even as another vehicle erupted into flames, burning from the detonation of a grenade beneath its chassis.

With that, the walking dead pulled back into the tree line as their bodiless brethren retreated back to the subterranean entrance to the necropolis. Nathan looked around as one of the rubbery monsters bounded over them, ignoring their presence altogether. He turned to Lyta.

"The staff can hide us from their senses," she answered in a quick whisper to his unspoken question. He didn't know whether she'd read the confusion on his face or Nehushtan had actually allowed her to access his thoughts. Either way, he felt a sudden wave of relief, and his heartbeat slowed.

The staff calmed him; he could feel the sleepy serenity washing through him, mind to toes. He breathed, watching as the militia pursued the amorphous creatures that had attacked them. They kept out of reach of the bayonets and machetes, shrugging off rifle fire.

Grenades landed in their midst, but that merely stunned the creatures as they ran.

An officer shouted, "You'll bring down the whole tunnel! We'll kill them with stakes. Just keep them on the run for now!"

Nathan looked down at himself and realized that the soldiers were passing within a few feet of them, and they took no notice of them. Sure, they were tucked underneath a blanket loaded with twigs, leaves and branches as a layer of convincing camouflage, but surely there should have been at least one glance through the trees as the soldiers were on the alert for an ambush from creatures who lagged behind. Instead, their gaze was locked either dead ahead or scanned in the opposite direction.

It had to be the staff. The same way it had guided him to Victoria Falls, to uncover the mat trans installation in the redoubt beneath the high-tech hydroelectric dam, Nehushtan had put a subliminal order into the soldiers' minds. There would be no peek, nothing in their peripheral vision that would draw them to any imperfection in their concealment.

Another rescue, old stick. Thank you, Nathan thought.

Rest now, son, a familiar voice echoed in his mind. It was his father.

And with that, the injured young man fell to slumber.

KANE PULLED THE PIN on an implode grenade at the same time Grant charged his. The two men threw in unison, Grant's toss going farther in its arc toward the army of African plunderers. Kane's landed toward the nearest of the group. The distance between the two throws was about forty feet, but Kane hurled his with all his might. The two longtime partners knew the ranges at which they could hurl grens at targets, and their simultaneous launch meant that the bulk of the Panthers of Mashona would be caught between the twin detonations.

Sure enough, both grens erupted in unison with a good span between them. The implode grenades had a twenty-foot kill radius, at least in flat, open ground. With the multiple buildings of the stone crypts around, that perfect circle of devastation was interrupted. However, since the implode grenade operated on overpressure produced by a thermobaric explosion, the spaces between buildings would only provide actual protection several feet from each corner.

The duel blast rocked the air in the cavern, producing a tumultuous rumble that further dazed and stunned men in its area, even making Kane's head hurt before the sound filters kicked in to protect his hearing.

That opening salvo took down eight members of the rogue African militia. Screams and gunshots filled the air as staggered soldiers fired at shadowy figures produced by the sudden shift in light as the torches on their weapons wavered, either tossed about by reflex or by reaction to sudden gunfire. Even as the militia were regathering their wits, Brigid popped up with a borrowed rifle and opened fire on two of the men who had rushed into her field of view. The weapon bucked against her shoulder, but she managed the recoil, focusing a stream of slugs into one of the marauders.

The man screamed as bullets sliced through him at a diagonal, smashing one shoulder and cutting down through his rib cage. The gunman collapsed, body ravaged by Brigid's precision marksmanship, but his companion hurled himself behind cover, just a fraction of a second too swift for her to catch him, which impressed Kane. He would have almost felt respect for the man had it not been that he was part of a group that took other human beings as slaves and thought nothing of dragging them to where they would be tortured.

Any consideration of leniency went out the window, and as soon as the Panther popped up again to return fire against Brigid, Kane punched out a burst of automatic fire into his skull. The heavy slugs mashed the man's head, deflating it with multiple hammer blow impacts.

Kane scanned around and looked for more enemy soldiers. He got the location of a group of them as Grant opened fire with his confiscated shotgun, plowing clouds of pellets down a walkway. Militiamen shouted as the big 12-gauge thundered, filling the air with a dozen .36-caliber balls per pull of the trigger. The land pirates shrieked, bodies torn and slashed by the sizzling clouds of lead. The huge, powerful Magistrate fired from the shoulder, aiming down the sights of the shotgun. Proper form, good trigger control and riding the recoil of the big gun helped Grant drop six more of the militiamen before he cleared that particular alley.

Kane took notice of another of the Panthers who was pulling the pin on a grenade in his kit. With seasoned reflexes and an intuitive knowledge of where his bullets would land, Kane put three bullets through the man's chest. One of them took a short trip through his grenade-hand wrist to reach the grenadier's internal organs. Already rapidly dying, the African let the miniature bomb tumble from lifeless fingers. There was a gurgle of others noticing the hand grenade landing at their feet, and they broke, seeking refuge elsewhere, scattering as quickly as their feet could carry them,

The trouble for the roving bandits was that the original grenade user had been cooking his grenade for a couple of seconds, usually a good strategy that kept other people from scooping up the fallen explosive and hurling it back toward them. However, his allies only had a second to notice that the bomb had dropped in their midst and another to run for cover. And there'd been only a second and a half remaining on the fuse. The detonation of the gren hurled out a wave of high-velocity shrapnel and intense pressure that crushed two militiamen immediately. Fragments whipped into other men, killing one more and injuring the remaining pair who were near the thrower. The blast would easily have killed Grant and Brigid if it had landed where the Panther had intended to drop it. Instead, it did most of the work for the three Cerberus explorers, taking more human predators and scavengers off the face of the earth.

With that group of murderers downed, Kane took a quick inventory of their opposition.

Twenty had come down, seeking to exterminate Neekra's amorphous spawn. Their number was now only a quarter of that after only nearly a minute of contact. Even so, the gunmen had unknowingly come close to killing the three of them multiple times. All of this was mere prologue to what they would have to deal with when they got past the human murderers and had to deal with the post-human creatures.

"Movement coming down the corkscrew," Brigid announced. Kane glanced up and saw that there were figures, more militiamen, coming down. But they moved with jerky gaits, as if they were becoming reacquainted with their limbs once more.

"Vampires," Kane realized. "In the flesh, so to speak."

"That much I presumed but didn't want to state without confirmation," Brigid returned. "How are they in human bodies?"

"They get quicker the more they get used to their skin," Kane mentioned. "And sometimes they end up breaking their bodies trying too hard."

"Trying too hard?" Grant asked.

"One kicked a marble column in half but shattered his leg," Kane explained. "He was aiming for me, and I ducked out of the way avoiding incoming gunfire."

"Shit," Grant murmured. "So they'll mistake the effort necessary to bludgeon us."

"If they're coming for us," Brigid said. "Neekra seemed determined that Kane is one of her keys to freedom."

"Kane is safe. What about the two of us?" Grant asked. He rapidly fed fresh shells into his spent shotgun in the dead time between scattered militiamen and the arrival of the vampires.

"If anything will guarantee me chasing down Neekra, it'll be harm to either of you," Kane grumbled. "We can destroy these things. But it'll take a lot of power."

"I dissipated one with a grenade blast and forced others to retreat in pain, but that was while they were without human bodies to manipulate," Brigid mentioned. "The second blast also splintered a tree, however, and the flying wood may have done most of the work."

"A knife or wooden stake through the chest or head will do the work necessary," Kane told them. He reached into his pouch and produced a couple of stakes, tossing them to Brigid. "Decapitation with normal bullets also makes them leave their bodies. Who knows what a machete slice will do, but it can't hurt."

Grant nodded. The swordlike length of steel hanging in his improvised belt sheath would be called on to do its deadly work. But for now…"We'll see how a blast of buckshot does to those interior organs for the time being. Their bodies are still human and will still fall to pieces, right?"

Kane nodded.

The reanimated corpses reached the bottom of the corkscrew. Even as they gathered, standing shoulder to shoulder with each other, their rubbery brethren began to appear from cracks and holes blasted in the crypts where they'd hidden.

"Here they come," Brigid announced.

Kane handed her a gren. "We soften them up."

She nodded, watching the others from the corner of her eye as she steeled herself to make her own throw.

But the vampire army didn't advance toward the explorers from Cerberus. They were also armed, each with rifle in hand, standing as silent, grim sentinels.

"Why aren't they making any move?" Grant asked.

Brigid narrowed her eyes behind her hood's faceplate. "They're keeping us penned up. Away from Neekra and Durga."

Kane sneered, then activated his Commtact. "Durga, come in."

"If he's pulling something sneaky, why—" Grant began before it clicked with the big man. "Damn it, Durga thought he was putting something over on Neekra, but she outthought him."

"Come on," Kane murmured. There was nothing on the other end of the line, so whatever was going on, Durga hadn't left his communicator on. Where once he was irate over the fact that an enemy could listen in, now he was frustrated that Durga had killed the signal, preventing Kane from warning the fallen prince of the trap he'd stumbled into.

"He has been our enemy, tried to kill us," Brigid noted. "Should we risk it for his sake?"

"His sake doesn't matter to me," Kane growled. "But his scheme was to try to bring down Neekra, or at least slow her down. And if that plan goes to hell, we might not get another chance to take her down, at least not before she's truly awakened."

"So we have to determine what she would be looking for that she could only find with Dur…"

Kane didn't need to know why Brigid Baptiste's speech trailed off. The woman's brain worked at lightning speed, and she must have come up with a correlation that explained why Neekra had allowed herself to be trapped with the devious Nagah prince who plotted to destroy her.

"She wants his threshold," Brigid spoke up. "That's why she came down here, to look for a means to get to her tomb immediately…"

Kane's eyes widened. "Blow them up."

Grant didn't have to be told twice. He started the volley of grenades, and Kane and Brigid swiftly followed suit.

Chapter 23

Durga walked briskly. He kept his thoughts hidden, but he was fully aware that Neekra's psychic powers were vast and insidious. Any secret he held within would eventually come to light, either through his own weakness or through penetrating the minds of others he was conspiring with.

He concentrated, though. Neekra walked apace with him as they traveled deeper, down an offshoot of the ancient necropolis. This underground city of the dead had been built by others she'd conquered, much as she'd overtaken Gamal's body, constructing a base from which to spread out, strike at outposts of the Archons and those whom the caretakers of humanity organized to protect her prison.

A prison that, frustrating to her, she couldn't find on earth. She knew that there was some place in Africa where her psyche could be generated, but her body was separate. She couldn't locate it with any more precision than in the continent of Africa.

When she'd found a mind she could piggyback on, she'd searched high and low, seeking out some key, some clue that would bring her back together with her body. The trouble was finding someone who had the ambition to seek out Neekra herself as a bride and the ruthlessness to seek her power. There had been those who had tried, who had the strength of will to be with her, like Gamal, but then there were minds that simply shredded, unraveling the moment she moved in, stranding her in nothing more than a decayed form until some other human stumbled on her.

Durga knew that he was on exceedingly thin ice working next to Neekra. She'd sired horrors whose exploits traversed the planet. Not a single mythology, not even the Vedas of ancient India, was without tales of vampires. Indeed, even the worst of the demons in the Brahmic pantheon, Kali herself, the darkness within Siva the Destroyer, was also that pantheon's greatest enemy of vampires, destroying them as a service to the world, even the universe. That his home nation's concept of the devil and the angel of death rolled up in one package was that which Neekra created told Durga that she needed to be stopped.

And she could be.

At least for another century, maybe even more.

This was why he led her deeper into the underground caverns.

He could hear the battle above and behind him. Sure enough, Kane, Grant and Brigid Baptiste were engaging the Panthers of Mashona, doing what they did best—fighting those who would do harm to mankind for the sake of personal profit. Durga had ended up on the wrong side of that battle once, and even gifted with the power to absorb matter and bolster his flesh with it, even with the strength of a god, he had been brought low and left a cripple by their efforts.

Durga knew he hadn't really changed. He still wanted to carve out a kingdom for himself in this world. What was the use of having a kingdom when there was a menace like Neekra that was more than capable of ending all life on earth, or reducing the dominant species—

mankind, Nagah included, Durga added reluctantly—to mere cattle? Neekra gave promises to her human paramours, but those were lies whispered on a pillow, seduction and enticements that would bring her to the thing *she* wanted. Once achieved, Durga would be food for her.

"We're not far now from the back way," Durga said, looking back over his shoulder to her. As he turned to speak to her, there was a sudden rush of wind, and the ground disappeared from beneath his feet.

Neekra hefted Durga up by his throat, slamming his back against the wall. "I was born in the eternal night of deep space, fool. Do not act as if I was born *last* night!"

The Nagah prince gasped, held in a grip of steel that pinned him to the wall, all his weight resting on his lower jaw. Even without his air being cut off by her iron fingers, Durga's eyes felt like free-rolling marbles skittering in their orbits inside his skull.

"What…?" he managed to croak.

Neekra let him go, and Durga willed his feet to catch him, his legs to hold him up. Instead, he was prone on the ground, face and chest skidding on the hard-packed dirt.

"What do I mean, lover?" Neekra asked.

Durga winced. He could count the moments of his life dwindling away, falling through cracks and disappearing into the void. The goddess had figured him out. Now she gripped him by his right shoulder, nails stabbing through his scales as if they were soft pudding, blood oozing over her fingers and down his skin. Agonizing fire erupted in his shoulder as she hauled him up to his feet, his eyes level with hers, her aim hefting him as if he were nothing more than a child's doll.

"Surely you would think that I already knew every inch of this necropolis, wouldn't you?" Neekra asked.

Durga clenched his eyes shut. "Who said the back door out of here had to be literal?"

His throat was raw, raspy. Her fingers were meat hooks, and muscle fibers stretched as she hung him on them. Durga's 180 pounds, focused on four talons lanced through his flesh, felt quadrupled. Searing signals from agonized nerves flushed through his consciousness.

"Oh, you intended to take us down here so you would access your threshold, which is notably absent," Neekra said.

"It wouldn't be an emergency getaway if I didn't leave it somewhere with the motor running," Durga said.

Neekra flicked her wrist, and Durga bounced on the balls of his feet. Tears seeped from behind his clenched eyelids, rivulets of salty pain racing in the patterns between his cheek scales.

"Someone teleports in, grabs us and takes us where?" Neekra asked. "Or would he just take you? Perhaps drop off a package that would collapse this tunnel atop me, stranding my consciousness in a withering form until someone was fool enough to burrow all the way down here, down to this distant chamber?"

She reached into his pocket, plucking out the radio he'd hidden there.

"Your 'getaway driver' on the threshold, he'd locate you using this piece of electronic flotsam?" Neekra asked. She flicked her wrist again.

Muscle fibers tore, skin split, scales popped loose. Durga crashed to the ground, landing on his back. He watched Neekra look over his communicator.

"It's a handsome little device," she noted. "And would actually be impressive if I didn't know that it was connected to supercomputers in the belly of a redoubt by a string of satellites. Amazing communications, for someone who doesn't have telepathy, who doesn't have strings of proteins that can do the same thing without need for outside power, not even a cell battery."

She popped the battery case cover off the communicator, plucked them out and inspected them. It looked like a preview of what she wanted to do to him. She tossed aside each battery, letting them plop in the dirt.

Neekra stepped closer, looming over him.

"You've been acting out all manner of violent fantasies with this body," Neekra said. She traced one toe across Durga's chest.

The naked goddess's sex was over him. Durga tried to remember that this was the gelded, mutilated body of a man whom she'd taken over and resculpted in her own image, but there it was, soft, smooth, inviting, atop full, sleek thighs that he knew tasted wonderful, brushed lightly over his tongue, warm and inviting. She played her toe along his chest scales, brushing along his collarbone, tracing it up his throat and lower jaw, gently balancing it on the point of his chin.

"You would cause harm to a work of art as I have created?" Neekra asked.

"No," Durga murmured, mesmerized, even with his shoulder torn open, pumping his lifeblood onto the ground. Its burning was now miles away from him; his mind was locked on her. This wasn't his sexual desire. This wasn't his need for her as a lover. This was Neekra, finally flexing her psychic muscles, finally reaching down his throat and grabbing thoughts and memories from deep within the core of his soul.

He was simply a worm compared to her; he was her plaything, something to use up and toss aside at a whim. The best he could ever hope to do was inconvenience her minimally, play on her good graces long enough for him to die at old age, rather than be flung across a room and dashed against a wall, bursting open like a tomato.

Durga tried to fight her, tried to summon up the will to push out from under her, to at least spit in her face. She pressed her toe down, and once more Durga was racked with pain. This wasn't the mere weight of a normal woman resting on the point of his chin; this was superhuman strength forcing his jaw back into his throat. Neekra was just short of crushing his lower mandible, collapsing his windpipe, but instead she smiled, eased off, edged away from killing him with a step.

She bent, hooking her hand under his uninjured shoulder, lifting him gently and easily. She lowered her head, crimson ringlets hiding her face, and he felt her wet, sensual tongue lapping at his scales. Hot sparks of sensual energy zapped through his wound as her lips slurped at the torn meat. He tried to pull away, fear stabbing through his mind as she kissed and suckled at the rent muscle tissue, the ruptured skin, but the agony he expected did not come. Instead, warmth flooded down into his chest, tingling through his loins.

Durga became aroused as her tongue glided more and more under his skin.

Get out of my body. Get out of my head, bitch!

Neekra lifted her bloodred lips from his shoulder, and he could see that it was as if her claws had never torn him open.

"Don't be so cruel, my dear," Neekra said. With a caress of her fingers, Durga was hurled back down to the ground. Once more, his head swam under the impact.

"Your limitations are so sad," she said with an allur-ing pout. "You wish you had the kind of power even a female of your pathetic monkey species has—the abil-ity to create life. And deep in that bent brain of yours, you hate yourself for feeling so much joy at inducing pain and destruction, because you're just a pale shadow of the real gods. Look upon your shoulder and weep."

Durga tried to fight the urge, but he gazed down at the perfect scales, the tight, ready musculature. His fin-gertips brushed it.

"You came to me, thinking I could be your weapon, an unstoppable engine of destruction," Neekra whis-pered. "But I'm so much more, even in this crippled little shell. I've *birthed* entities that make the dead walk, and I've stitched the damaged cells of your body back together with ease, even sexual pleasure, far more than even that artifact can do."

Durga grimaced.

"And so, you think that I will need your threshold? No, those are the thoughts of others, the humans from Cerberus," Neekra said. "They are coming, running. They are full of worry, for you, a man who they once swore bloody vengeance upon."

Her ruby glinting lips turned up into a smile. "I have made your worst enemies care for you. Worry for you. Earlier they swore that they would bring you down, slay you. And now they come to your rescue."

Durga winced.

Neekra stepped back. "I shall have to teach these children their lesson, just as you have learned yours."

Durga reached out. "No…"

Neekra turned back to look at him. "What, sweet child?"

Durga murmured, uttering gibberish, looking down at his chest, eyes squinted.

"Speak up, boy," Neekra ordered.

Durga repeated the nonsense syllables.

Finally, the avatar of the blood goddess crouched before him, her eyes level with his as he sat there.

"Use your words, Durga," Neekra taunted. Her fingertips tapped against his cheek, and it was all Durga could do to keep his head from flopping to one shoulder. He was already feeling the bruising beneath his scales, the sensation of a fractured cheekbone burrowing in deep and burning in there.

Durga lifted his head and opened his mouth in one swift movement. His venom sacs tightened, and twin streams of venom, the gift of Enki to his serpentine children, shot out and struck Neekra's puppet in the eyes.

The effect was immediate, as if she'd taken a mace to the center of her face. Her head snapped back as if the squirts of poison had the force of high-pressure hoses. Her glimmering red complexion paled around her eyes and across her cheeks; the skin turned white. The eerie keening that her gelatinous spawn often released now reverberated inside Durga's skull, and his eardrums flexed under the torturous sonic pressure slamming into them.

When a flailing hand reached out and backhanded him across the jaw, Durga's brain was already numbed by her wails of pain. Instead of suffering even more under her assault, the Nagah prince succumbed to unconsciousness, toppling from his seated position.

His last thoughts were that Kane and the others better have some way of keeping this hell witch trapped down here.

THE SHRIEK OF THE QUEEN of the living dead cut through even the salvo of grenade blasts and gunfire that Kane and his allies hurled at the reanimated corpses.

Grant had been correct in his assessment that the huge 12-gauge he'd confiscated worked well against the blob-animated walking dead. Blasts of shotgun pellets smashed apart limbs and joints, crippling them as they attempted to stop the three warriors from Cerberus, while shots to the head not only decapitated the carcasses, but destroyed the "brain organ" that Brigid theorized was present in their skulls. So far, twenty of the things had been put back to eternal rest with shattered skulls and crippled limbs.

Brigid and Kane batted cleanup, while Grant rampaged through the grenade-stunned and scattered vampires. Their rifles barked as the two people cut loose with well-aimed but full automatic bursts of fire that induced enormous trauma on the meat puppets that the gelatinous entities contained within them. Some of the creatures decided that mobility was much better than the insane strength they possessed while riding inside a shell of rotting flesh, and as soon as their chests were burst by Kane or Brigid, they ejected themselves, blowing through the horrendous wounds cut into them or simply gushing out of mouths.

Brigid grimaced at the brutal work, but she knew that these men had already been killed brutally by the banshee-voiced blobs leaving their ruptured corpses. Desecrating the dead was nothing when those dead were being used as weapons and armor for inhuman creatures. She fired again and again, her rifle bucking hard against her shoulder, bullets shredding through unliving flesh and rubbery membrane alike, viscous, clotted blood and cytoplasm spraying under each savage impact.

Kane rolled a grenade toward the creatures she left stunned and scattered, and Brigid whirled back out of the path of any shrapnel. It wasn't an implode gren, it was just one of the regular fragmentation munitions that the Cerberus explorers had taken from the Panthers of Mashona militia. The six ounces of high-density explosive inside the core still produced a supernova of overpressure that crushed limbs. Bodies flopped on the ground from the first blast. A few walkways over, a second miniature bomb burst, tossing more severed parts around.

And then Grant was back, his shotgun recharged with the big red plastic-hulled shells that were thicker than three of Brigid's fingers were wide. Grant worked the big, booming weapon. Roars of thunder shook the air, while, downrange of that fat pipe that belched fire and metal, monsters shrieked and broke apart, fist-size chunks of reanimated corpse and stretchy membrane vaporizing. The big former Magistrate continued his advance against the spawn of Neekra, his 12-gauge now empty, but at this point, he was too much on a roll. He drew the four-foot machete from the sheath he'd strapped across his back. It was a two-handed device, meant for lopping through branches and cutting sugarcane. In Grant's hands, it was a sword.

A *no-dachi.* Brigid remembered the name for the oversize, dual-handed sword from Japan. The *no-dachi,* however, was five feet long and meant to be used against horsemen. In Grant's hands, it was balanced more like a regular three-foot *katana,* perfectly scaled for the six-foot-four warrior, who wielded it as if it were feathery light. While a *katana* would have had a much keener cutting edge, this didn't slow Grant down any. The machete was backed by his melon-size arm muscles, indeed, his full weight and trained strength.

The walking dead moved in to try to stop him, but Grant swept among them, the blade whisking left and right, bodies bisected with one clean slice, carving in two the reanimating gelatinous horrors hiding within. The separation of their internal brains proved lethal. Halved corpses flopped to the ground with cytoplasm bleeding and pumping into the dirt.

Just to be certain, Kane moved up quickly behind his friend and punched bullets into the heads and hearts of each of the fallen. The last thing he needed was to be swarmed by the terrors. Even so, as he looked down at some of the bodies, he noted that Grant had struck the heart as often as not, and the darker, destroyed protein strings in the cytoplasm were as obvious in his shadow suit hood's advanced optics as if they were glowing green blood.

Brigid brought up the rear, scanning for signs of movement among the dead. However, this time the second end was sufficient to keep them down. She made certain, not because she didn't trust Grant's warrior prowess or Kane's observational abilities, but simply because they were dealing with an alien life-form, one that had shown remarkable resilience to harm. Along the way, she stooped and picked up a standard two-foot machete from one of the fallen militiamen; his torso had been cleaved apart by the raw power of Grant.

"Sometimes, there's just no substitute for a big-ass knife," she said.

"That's the truth," Kane agreed.

Grant looked back toward his companions, his smirk hidden behind his hood's faceplate. Considering the path of destruction he'd wrought through the heart of the vampires, the smirk was readily apparent in his stance, if only for a moment. Then he turned back, looking for any more of the revenants, ready to strike out again with his mighty sword.

Then, back toward the very dungeons from where they'd just escaped, came a keening that drowned out the wails of wounded and terrified spawn. It was the banshee shriek of something huge and primal. A wall of sound struck the three people, and even the automatic sonic dampers built into their shadow suit hoods couldn't keep out the spiking pain in their ears.

"Neekra," Brigid shouted over the unholy cry.

Kane found a machete, grabbing a bandolier of grenades. "Durga's hurt her. But that's not enough."

"Kids," Grant spoke into his Commtact. "We need the artifact. Now."

"We're on our way," Lyta responded. Only the transmission of vibration through his mandible to his inner ear gave him any chance of hearing the sound of her voice.

"Do we have a plan?" Brigid asked Kane.

"Pepper the bitch with grenades until we get Nehushtan," Kane answered. "Then stab her with it."

Even as the three people gathered themselves for their assault, the surviving spawn of the deadly goddess advanced through the necropolis, hurtling themselves toward the source of the agonized siren of Neekra.

The subterranean battle was far from over.

Chapter 24

Thurpa swooned as he felt, deep within his bones, the sudden rush of horror and pain that struck Durga. The whole thing made his knees go rubbery, but he held his footing, shaking it off. Nathan had Nehushtan, the ancient pre-Atlantean artifact that had passed through the hands of men such as Moses and Solomon, of adventurers and juju men, aliens and humans. Just by holding it, the wound in his thigh was gone. Lyta clenched an assault rifle in her hands, fear on her face from the urgency with which Grant had called them, but not giving in to her urge to run.

With the demon-stopping staff of Suleiman in hand, Nathan could sense his new friend's sudden swoon, feel a sudden presence of another among the trio.

"Are you all right?" Nathan asked.

"No," Thurpa answered, opting for truth over his concerns that they might think he was a traitor. "I feel like I've been beaten up by a Kongamato mob."

Nathan looked around. "It could be a psychic attack by Neekra...."

"Then why aren't the two of you showing anything?" Thurpa asked.

"Lyta was never close enough to her to be influenced by her, and I've got this," Nathan responded. "It's logical, right?"

Thurpa reached out and touched the staff, but the

sensations of a broken jaw, of a slashed-open shoulder, of eardrums rocked by the ground zero bellow of an agonized god, went nowhere. These came to him through some other source. They weren't inflicted by Neekra, but rather they were echoes, aftershocks of what someone else felt.

"Nathan—" Thurpa started to say.

"We have to move now," Nathan cut him off. "Our friends need us. We need to fight through this pain. Feel the power of the staff, let it flow into you, cleanse you."

Even as the young African spoke, Thurpa's nerves tingled, his muscles trembled, his whole body warmed under the power within the ancient artifact. It had healed him before, bringing him back from near death under the assault of a winged, hulking mutant. This was similar, but as his neurons fired off on all cylinders, there was something different surging inside of him.

And then the echoing sensation once more. He was transmitting.

The knowledge of who he was transmitting to was obvious, and it turned his blood to ice water. He had a direct link to Durga.

Thurpa didn't want to know why, but then he looked at Lyta and the courage she displayed, descending into the damned underground entrance to Neekra's necropolis. When the future revealed how he was truly tied to the damned Nagah prince, Thurpa would go to face it, no matter what hell he'd be dragged down into.

DURGA'S VENOM STUNG, burned with the heat of a sun, even through the dull filter of Gamal's flesh and central nervous system. Neekra had never known that kind of sensation could strike her so deeply, so completely, especially when it was from a mere human, albeit one that had had its genetic structure "enhanced" by an Annunaki by the name of Enki. And yet, here it was, a blinding, mind-numbing surrender to the flames of a dying star.

She tried to think beyond it, to clear the vision of her humanoid avatar, but there was no response from Gamal's body. Neekra could feel the bumps of her shoulders against corridor walls, the feel of the ground beneath her bare feet, the cold damp of the forever dark cavern she crawled through.

But Durga's venom was still slicing, still attacking her.

It has to be affecting the protein strings, she managed to think. The "brains" she'd grown, the telepathic biocomputer constructs by which she could reach out and control others, they had to be vulnerable to Enki's venom design. Enzymes implanted in his children, the Nagah, had the power to attack her kind's very core.

And it felt like hell.

It *was* hell.

We were meant to be the guardians of the earth, of humanity, Neekra. Durga's thoughts raced past her blurred vision and screaming nerves. Did you really think that Enki would not know about the monsters that his brethren battled?

Neekra gritted her teeth and turned, looking through the shadows. Different spectrums were still obfuscated by her tears, by the venom attacking her system. She could only make out fuzzy blurs, creatures racing toward her in the ebony night of the unlit underground.

Panic overtook her, and she dug her fingers into the wall, ripping a sheet of stone off and collapsing it into the corridor before her. Bleats and squeals of sympathetic pain reached her ringing ears, and she realized what had rushed her.

"My children," she murmured.

She pressed against the slab of stone blocking the hallway, pushing with all the strength she could draw from the human flesh she inhabited. She could feel the stone crack, start to shift. Rubbery limbs whipped around the sides, oozed through the splits she made in it. As each membrane touched her skin, blood from the murdered militia, only stale by minutes, seeped through her russet skin.

Neekra drank, and the pain of the venom started to subside; it was akin to drinking milk to smother the inflammation of pepper heat. Even so, she still struggled to stay on her feet, to retain her concentration. What salve the blood brought to her besieged senses was minimal.

Gamal's chest churned, sizzling heat pressing over the former man's heart and lungs. Her breasts, actually the sheaths for the protein structures granting her psychic power, were overheating as the venom's enzymes sped through Gamal's bloodstream. Neekra bit down, lower lip bursting and spilling hot crimson down an already glittering red chin. She drew back one fist and slammed it against the slab of stone. Another crack, another heave and shift of hard rock.

More tendrils reached through, caressing her skin, lending their strength to hers.

"Thank you, my children," she whispered.

As she said that, hard objects clunked against the other side of the slab she'd intended to protect her.

The odd impacts were metallic, clinking as they bounced off the granite.

Grenades, she recognized an instant before the stone

slab shifted violently and beams of searing heat burst through the cracks she'd made to reach her spawn. Jets of pressure buffeted her and threw her back into the dirt.

Kane and his allies had arrived, and they'd declared war with their thrown explosives.

Neekra's vision cleared even more, and she watched as tendrils severed by the grenade blasts burned, sizzled, blackened into curled wisps of charred tar.

"Kane!" she shrieked, lifting both fists together and hurling them against her granite barrier. Stone burst, disintegrated into clouds of white dust, and when she stepped through the hole she made, she could make out, numbly, fuzzily, the silhouettes of three people.

"Kane, you will learn your lesson," she growled.

KANE THOUGHT THAT HE WAS seeing things when the amorphous blobs were suddenly cut off in the tunnel ahead by a swinging slab of granite, blocking their forward process so thoroughly that even their semiliquid bodies couldn't seek a way past.

He skidded to a halt, not wanting to draw the attention of the dozen or so rubbery amoebas as they pressed and pawed at the improvised door barring their path.

"Is that something Durga set up?" Grant asked softly, crouching beside his friend.

"No, I don't think so," Kane said. "There's nothing else down here that looks like it could be a trap like that."

"The material of that barrier is identical to the walls of this particular cavern," Brigid spoke up. "I'm examining them both through the shadow suit's optics. Someone broke a piece of the tunnel off and swung it shut like a door."

"Neekra," Kane and Grant said in unison.

"Apparently the bodies her spawn take over don't have the same durability that she does," Brigid stated. "Otherwise, she'd have never moved that rock."

"Hit that thing," Kane growled.

"Not yet. These grens won't scratch that slab," Grant told him.

Kane nodded, acknowledging his friend's knowledge. He'd temporarily forgotten that they didn't have implode grenades, and even those might not have the punch to cut through her slammed door.

"Got to say, when Neekra slams a door, she slams a door," Brigid muttered.

The tunnel around them shook violently. Faint cracks emanated from the barrier that the goddess had put up, dust drizzling down on them.

"This is going to be another Remus situation, isn't it?" Grant asked.

"No. We don't have to worry about harming her. That's our whole point down here," Kane answered.

"We're really going to hurt something that is shaking a tunnel cut through bedrock?" Brigid asked. Even as she said that, she reloaded her rifle, making sure she was armed and ready to put up the fight of her life.

"We're going to try," Kane answered, growing calm. The concept of battling a god was ridiculous, but he'd fought those who had claimed such omnipotence.

He'd won those other times, but those were usually instances where he'd edged out a victory by the skin of his teeth. Durga had a plan, but whatever it was, it had disappeared the moment the earth quaked around them.

The Nagah prince was either dead or dying. And with Nehushtan behind them and Neekra in front of them, Durga was not getting a third chance at life. Not unless he found some means of cheating death.

Again the slab cracked, and the amorphous beasts squirmed.

"They're pushing through the cracks," Brigid said. "And they were likely full of nutrients. They're trying to strengthen her."

"Strengthen her? Why?" Grant asked.

"She closed off the tunnel to protect herself. She must be vulnerable," Kane replied. "Otherwise she wouldn't start breaking her own shield."

"What could have made her vulnerable?" Brigid mused. "It can't be anything to do with the threshold—if Durga had attempted to use it, Neekra would be long gone."

"No," Kane murmured. He glanced toward Grant. "Any ideas?"

"I'm drawing a blank," the big Magistrate replied. "She's strong, she can access human minds. She can create those snot-balls, even bragged about birthing them…"

Brigid narrowed her eyes. "Wait. She's operating within the confines of Gamal. Gamal didn't show telepathic proficiency. Rather he utilized technology to control the Kongamato. She reconfigured him to be her current base."

"Those cracks are starting to get bigger for her," Kane mentioned.

"There has to be some biological analog for our communicators built into Gamal's current body, and a similar structure which Gamal and Durga had encountered beforehand," Brigid stated.

"Similar structure?" Grant asked. "Like that navigation chair back in Louisiana."

Brigid nodded. "She made a new body out of Gamal, despite the fact that Durga and Thurpa had seen her.

However, upon her appearance, something didn't seem right to Thurpa. As if she were not really there, a psychic illusion, perhaps."

Kane looked over toward Brigid. "So when she separated us from our own minds, she was using us as her base."

"A temporary repository, at least until she could acquire a more permanent form," Brigid stated.

"So why not take hold in me? I was unconscious for long enough," Kane asked.

"Because you kept fighting your way out. And Durga, as well. Your wills were just too strong," Grant concluded. He looked to Brigid for confirmation, and the woman nodded.

"But Gamal's wasn't, though he still had enough brainpower to operate the control interface for the Kongamato," Kane added. "Or his willpower dipped after he was badly wounded…."

"Having your foot shorn off really wrecks your concentration," Grant added.

Another hammer blow shook the tunnel, cutting off their brainstorming.

"Hit it!" Brigid shouted.

They threw their grenades, then retreated, seeking cover. The trio of bombs landed and erupted, filling that section of the corridor with a brilliant flash. Polarization on their hoods kept their eyes from being burned out by the sudden flash, and shock waves and heat washed over them.

Kane slapped at his bare chest, feeling his skin redden as the temperature rose. He felt as if he'd gotten an instant sun urn, and he realized that the combined explosions had likely given him minor heat damage, a first-degree burn. Grant and Brigid also grunted at their discomfort.

"Did that hurt her?" Grant asked.

"No," Brigid replied. "But it kept the spawn from giving her nutrients."

"And healing her from whichever injury Durga inflicted on her," Kane added. "But what did Durga do?"

"He did what his people are supposed to do, what Enki designed them to," Brigid answered. "I've been going over the ancient legends that had been scrawled, imprinted, on the walls of Garuda."

"Enki chose them to be his guardians for humanity, to watch over us, at a lower profile than the Archon Initiative," Kane added. "So…"

"What is the one thing that cobras have that humans don't?" Brigid asked.

"Venom," Grant replied. "So, her weakness is cobra venom?"

Brigid nodded. "She must have infected Gamal's body when he discovered one of her old hosts. She's a biological-based force, like Kakusa."

"A sentient protein which claimed Enlil trapped them in octo-slugs," Kane said, catching up. "We've already figured that she and Kakusa were cut from the same cloth…and that cloth, it's a protein string."

"Enzymes metabolize proteins," Grant threw in. "And snake venom has digestive enzymes in them."

"Right," Brigid answered.

"So that's how he hurt her," Kane mused.

"Kane!"

Neekra's voice cut through the darkness. He looked toward the broken slab of stone. It was still blocking his view of the entity on the other side of the slab but not her shout. In front of the granite barrier, her spawn

were nothing more than sticky black webs of inciner-
ated cytoplasm and membrane. The grenades had neu-
tralized them. All that pressure and heat had broken
down their living structures, reducing them to greasy
shadows on the stone.

Another blow shook the ground at their feet, and a
wave of dust, particulate granite dispersed by an impossible impact, washed over them.

Through their hoods' advanced optics, Kane, Grant
and Brigid could see Neekra standing there, her shoulders heaving. She was still a statuesque, naked woman,
her physique belying the power that could smash stone
into powder. But there was a fury in her twisted face.

"Kane, you will learn your lesson."

Kane grimaced and opened fire with his Sin Eater,
pumping a full twenty-round magazine into the lethal
goddess. The bullets peppered her body, and he could
see their impacts making her skin dance and jiggle as
if he were beating on gelatin.

Grant and Brigid opened up just as Kane's weapon
locked empty. Shotgun and rifle slugs slashed into her,
but she walked forward, ignoring the horrific carnage
the flying lead wrought on her borrowed flesh. She was
bulletproof, more so than her "children," who at least
were stunned by the impact of slugs slicing through
them.

"Fall back," Kane ordered. He switched to his rifle,
ripping round after round into Neekra/Gamal's face
on full-auto.

Grant and Brigid took his order, scrambling out into
the necropolis. Nothing good would come from trying
to fight Neekra in an enclosed space. The strength that
she demonstrated meant that she was instantly lethal
to any human within an arm's reach, and the tunnel

had been scarcely wide enough for the three of them to enter abreast.

Kane held his ground. The goddess had said she *needed* him, which meant that she would be loathe to kill him. He could bide his time retreating down the tunnel, but he couldn't risk the lives of his beloved friends on that same need.

Before the assault rifle could empty its magazine at six hundred rounds per minute, Neekra reached out. Her hand crushed the barrel and caused a backfire in the weapon. Kane grimaced as splinters of metal peppered his naked chest; the shadow suit's faceplate kept his eyes safe from the shrapnel of the destroyed rifle.

Neekra grinned at him, standing nose to nose with him.

"So, teacher, what's today's class?" Kane asked her.

She wrapped her fingers around his throat. It was like before, when the blob had tried to grab him. For an instant, Kane felt as if his head were going to come off his neck, blowing off like the cork on a bottle. Then she relaxed her grip, enough to keep his throat from collapsing under stone-smashing force.

"You've been a bad study, my sweet," Neekra told him.

His feet kicked helplessly in the air, inches above the ground. Kane punched at her forearm, but she paid no notice. He might as well have been dropping grains of sand on her limb.

"You…won't…hurt…" Kane sputtered. He could breathe but only barely. She was in control now.

"I won't hurt your brother, your *anam-chara?*" Neekra asked.

Kane grimaced. Any further words were caught beneath her steel grip.

Neekra continued to stride forward, holding Kane as if he were a cupful of water. His feet kicked, bicycling in empty space trying to give himself leverage.

"I will do whatever I damned well please, you overrated little monkey!" Neekra spat. "I need you to open my tomb, to tell me where it can be found."

"Why…me?" Kane rasped.

They were in the open now. Kane cast about, trying to find Grant or Brigid in his peripheral vision. He wished he could talk to them, but he could barely get out two words before the force of her fingers on his throat stopped him. Apparently, somewhere deep inside, he possessed a map to Neekra's tomb, the final resting place of her true body.

If she found that, the world would be damned to her whimsy. If she could manipulate a human body to be this powerful…

"Shoot…me," Kane gurgled. He hoped that they heard him through his Commtact. He wasn't sure if they'd kill him, but if it was a choice between his life and that of the earth, he hoped that they'd make the right choice.

"Go right ahead!" Neekra agreed. "Kill your soul mate, your brother! As if I do not already have what I need to free myself."

Kane tried to say something else, but she had upped the pressure of her fingers around his windpipe. He could breathe, but speech was now out of the question. He fumbled, gripped the wooden stake in his belt and brought it up, spearing it at her.

The point plunged through the palm of her hand. Again she winced, and reflexive impulse made her drop Kane to the ground like a discarded, dirty shirt.

"Wood," she grumbled. "Still allergic to it. It still hurts a little."

And then she closed her hand around the stake. It exploded into a mass of sawdust and splinters. She shook her hand at the inconvenience, the discomfort, and looked down at him.

"That was your final gambit, Kane," she told him.

Kane gulped air. She bent and plucked his knife from its sheath.

His Sin Eater was empty; he hadn't had time to reload it. Almost all his weapons were gone now.

And still, Kane refused to get up, clawing the .45 from its spot on his hip.

"I'm not giving up, bitch," he growled.

Neekra smiled. "I love it when my prey are spunky."

Chapter 25

Grant watched his best friend in the world on his back, aiming a pistol at a being who had shrugged off hundreds of rounds of gunfire already. She loomed over him, a smile on her face as she taunted the downed man.

The pistol erupted, and she didn't flinch as the first round struck her in the cheek. She didn't react to the other impacts, either.

Neekra simply smiled.

He turned back to the corkscrew. He spotted the cones of light put out by the flashlights of their three companions.

They came, just as they had been called for. And he could zoom in on them, seeing all three bristling with weaponry, primary among them the ancient artifact known as Nehushtan. It had altered its head. When they had first seen it, it was a cross with twin serpents wound around it. Now it was a round, blunt club at the top. Even as he looked closer at it, he could see odd waves emanating from where the face would be if the club were a humanoid skull. Bat wings flexed out from where the neck and shoulders would be.

And Grant felt an uneasy surge through his spine. The very image of the staff now was one of blasphemy. He recognized more as it grew closer—it was the snot-ball-like octo-slugs that they had encountered in Florida, the tentacled parasites, except this had no intention of hiding. It was as if the thing had engulfed a person's head.

Where the wings came from, Grant didn't know, didn't want to know. But the arrival of the artifact down here on the floor of the underground cavern drew not only his attention, but Neekra's.

"Ah, and as if on cue, the second part of my delivery is here," she said. "Stay put, little boy."

She stepped around Kane, ignoring him as he fumbled a magazine into his emptied pistol. Neekra ran with the light leaps of an antelope, crossing the distance between her and Nathan Longa in a few bouncing strides. Grant pushed more shells into the magazine of his shotgun, rising from his hiding spot, issuing his stentorian challenge.

"Stay away from those kids!"

Neekra paused, looking back at him.

And within an instant, Grant slammed a shell full of bone-crushing and flesh-pulping buckshot into her chest, spinning her about. Neekra wasn't the only one capable of ground-eating strides, and with each landing, Grant pulled the trigger on the big semiauto 12-gauge, watching her skin splash, liquefying under his assault. The goddess grimaced under each of the first six bursts that hammered into her, and then Grant was within two arm's lengths from her, raising the muzzle toward her face.

Neekra's hand flashed up and crushed the barrel, twisting the metal pipe and wrenching the weapon out of Grant's hands even as he triggered the final shot. In a way, Neekra had saved Grant's hands from enduring the backfire of the self-destructing shotgun. She glowered at him.

"Sit down, Grant," she snarled. She took a step closer and poked him in the chest with her splayed fingertips.

Grant's feet flew out from under him, and the sensation of her push was akin to when someone had hit him in the chest with a particularly powerful firearm while he had been wearing his Magistrate armor. He landed in the dirt, skidding along as skin abraded off his shoulders, his ribs aching from those finger jabs. He rolled on his back, sucking in air, trying to return his breathing to normal after she'd emptied his lungs of oxygen with her strike.

Grant saw movement out of the corner of his eye. He saw Brigid Baptiste take charge of defending their three young friends. Her rifle hammered, and the sheer force of bullets hitting Neekra in the skull at a range of only three feet bent her neck until her cheek touched her shoulder.

Grant knew, however, that the very fact that Neekra still had a head, despite the firepower emptied into it at close range, meant that Brigid was out of her league. For a moment, Grant thought that the brave, brilliant woman had made an incalculably wrong decision, but as Neekra pushed against the stream of automatic fire, cupping her palm over the muzzle to give herself time to think, Brigid let the weapon go and danced backward.

"What's this, Baptiste?" Neekra asked.

"Your shoe's untied," Brigid responded.

Grant was thrown, as was obviously the goddess, who looked down at her bare feet.

As she did so, a flash-bang grenade went off. The sound was a sheet of force that slapped Grant in the face, but he hadn't looked directly at the detonating gren. He could see the glare of its burst reflecting off the stony roof of the necropolis. Neekra, on the other hand, was staring right at it. And since she was seeing the Cerberus exiles and their allies without benefit of torches or flashlights, she'd been caught looking at the flash with her eyes in light amplification mode.

Her children hadn't liked the burning gaze of LED flashlights that produced a fraction of the candlepower put out by the grenade. Neekra threw one arm up to cover her eyes.

"Little ginger bitch!" the goddess bellowed, slashing the air with her free hand.

There was the sound of metal impacting meat, and Grant sat up just in time to see Nathan swing the blasphemously topped artifact against Neekra's side. Bone crunched on impact, lifting Neekra from her feet. The ancient tool strengthened Nathan, giving him an edge against her, the same way it had allowed the young man to battle hulking creatures that were 250 pounds of muscle and rage a week ago. Nathan struck again and again, hammering at her with all his might.

It was a brutal beating, and if the woman on the receiving end of that mystic weapon hadn't just left him gasping for breath with a mere caress, Grant would have thought it unnecessarily cruel. As it was, he was still uneasy rising from his hands and knees to stand. As much as he hated the sight of a woman being pounded on, this same entity was a global-level threat. She shrugged off guns and bombs as if they were minor inconveniences.

"Keep swinging, Nathan," Grant whispered, gathering up his strength.

Kane was on his feet, too, advancing toward Neekra from behind, having paused only to scoop up the two-handed machete that Grant had dropped. Grant then spotted movement to his right and spun. He was relieved to see that it was Lyta, bringing him his bow and quiver of arrows.

"Maybe staking her with some of these might work," the girl said. "She's been shrugging off bullets so far."

Grant slung the quiver over one shoulder with a practiced, fluid movement. "Thanks, Lyta."

And, in an instant, he'd drawn an arrow and nocked it and aimed at the she-beast.

Neekra wasn't going to take her beating for long. Somewhere along the way, she must have recovered from her blindness. Suddenly, she was wrestling with Nathan for control of the artifact. Grant took aim at her head, then thought better of it. They'd been shooting her in the head with bullets, but all that had really done was force her to readjust her facial features in the wake of those attacks.

He aimed for a spot under her arm and fired. The arrow sang as it sliced through the air, rocketing to catch the goddess in the side. Neekra whipped her head around as the feathered end poked from her ribs, glaring at Grant.

"I am growing tired of you stupid little apes," she grumbled.

Kane was almost to her, winging the two-handed machete around to take off her head. Unfortunately, her peripheral vision must have been as healed as her normal sight, because she ducked out of the way of the swinging blade and the point carved a crease across both of her shoulders. Even as the blade slipped free of her skin, the wound sealed, zipping up and healing with uncanny quickness.

Between the arrow and the machete slash, her attention was off Nehushtan, and Nathan retreated from her.

"Give me that!" she snapped, reaching out for the

fleeing young Longa. She put her foot down, and the tremor of her stomp made Grant totter. Kane's knees gave out from under him as the ground flexed under her impact.

Grant quickly recovered his balance and nocked a new arrow. He fired again, catching her through the shoulder blade.

Where the last had penetrated into a human heart and not drawn a single glance from her, this one staggered her. Neekra turned around; the point was visible over her left aureole. Her face twisted in agony.

"I'm getting real tired of your shit, Grant," Neekra rasped.

Grant didn't bother to nock another arrow, knowing that he wouldn't have the time. He did, however, bring up an arrow point-first. He lunged out with it, as if it were a fencer's foil, aiming for the spot between her pendulous breasts. As the arrowhead speared through her solar plexus, she showed no reaction, no pain. And then her hands were clasped on either side of his head, a mind-reeling clap resounding through the inside his skull.

Grant collapsed, eyes blurred, brain reeling from the impact. His hood absorbed most of the concussion, but enough got through to stun him. He peeled off the face mask, just in time to prevent the induced nausea from getting caught in it and choking him.

His shoulders shook as he heaved.

Right now he was helpless. Any hope he had of standing up again was shot by that hammer blow to his head. He wished that he could do more, but he was folded into a fetal position, helpless, hurting.

He hoped Kane and Brigid could do without him.

Neekra stood over Grant, and Kane hurled himself

back into the fray, realizing that she had reacted with much more discomfort when the point of his arrow had pierced the front of her chest. Something was wrong, even as another point burst out just to one side of her spinal column. This one elicited no reaction, so it had to be the shaft that pierced at this angle. He leaped on her back, grabbing on to the arrow's jutting end with both hands.

Neekra whirled to reach back for the human who'd grabbed on to her, but with Kane using the handle stuck to her back, he remained out of her reach. Her fists slashed through the air with such force, they whistled. Kane winced at the force he had to struggle against as he was whipped about like a scarf, the arrow flexing in his grasp.

"Get off of me, Kane!"

"Not until you walk away," he growled. Of course, neither was willing to let the other be free. She needed something from him, and Kane refused to allow such a menace to wander unhindered.

Neekra let out a grunt and jammed her finger into her chest. Suddenly the handle that Kane gripped splintered from within her torso. He slid off her back and landed lightly, leaping aside just as she brought her elbow down where she thought he'd be. The crash against the ground reminded Kane just how deadly she was, even without producing a litter of sentient blobs, blood-drinking amoebas that sought out the dead and took over their bodies to turn them into the thirsty undead.

She turned around again, glaring at Kane, who pressed forward with the muzzle of his .45 automatic. Neekra wrinkled her nose and chuckled, then immediately regretted her overconfidence as Kane touched off the pistol right in front of her eye.

The bullet's impact was not enough to cause her any discomfort. Neekra rebuilt and restructured Gamal's skull and head, keeping herself the same beautiful, seductive demoness that she'd been since Durga had first met her. The only trouble for the goddess was that she also was dealing with the muzzle-flash and heat from the end of the barrel. Once more, her vision blurred under intense light and heat, and she staggered backward, away from the belch of burning powder.

"You…" she gurgled.

Brigid cut her off by lashing out with her machete, swinging the two-foot blade in a lunge. She'd also seen the painful response that Neekra evidenced. And the keen edge of the machete struck Neekra across one breast, cleaving it in half, horizontally.

The goddess let out her wail of pain, reaching out and clutching the steel blade of the machete. Her fingers closed on it and mangled the length of solid metal. With a shrug, she pushed the garbage that used to be a steel weapon to the ground, then embedded the crumpled mess deep into the dirt.

"You're not…the only ones…who can blind people," Neekra growled.

Brigid and Kane struggled to see her outline through the sudden wave of dust filling the air. Light amplification and telescopic vision were one thing, but penetrating the dense cloud of airborne particulate temporarily stymied the two people.

With a sudden shrug, Neekra clapped her hands together, creating a sharp boom akin to a grenade going off. Luckily, their hoods' audio filters protected them from the bulk of the sonic assault, but the pressure wave still shoved them away from her. Unfortunately for the goddess, it also cleared the air of her smoke screen.

Nathan was up again, spearing at her with the semi-sharpened end of the ancient staff. He saw that Brigid's assault on one of the goddess's breasts had given her pause. Yet even as he lunged, her torso reconfigured, and Neekra brought up one of her arms to block the point. Nathan grunted as he was jarred off Nehushtan by the sudden crash.

As Neekra deflected Nathan's assault, Kane watched her torso grow heavy plates around the rib cage, evolving.

"I'm not going to be seducing anyone for the rest of this night," she growled. "So might as well draw those in and armor up."

Kane swung the two-handed machete again, and the blade caught Neekra across her upper arm. Flesh separated and bone snapped under the chop, but when he struck her chest, it felt as if he'd struck a brick wall. Vibrations rolled up the handle and his forearms, sending a wave of numbness through his fingers. Kane toppled back from the assault, cursing himself for losing the weapon. Even though it didn't work on that armor-plated torso of hers, he could still do something about the rest of her limbs.

Brigid waved him off of keeping up the attack.

Kane decided to give her a kick to remember his presence, aiming at the side of Neekra's knee. Though the joint popped like a boiled chicken leg bone, she didn't show any discomfort at that.

Still, she went down into the dirt, and that would buy him time.

Except as she lay on her face, her leg straightened, and a tendril began to grow from the stump of her upper arm.

"Where's Thurpa?" Kane growled. "Maybe he can do something about her."

Kane turned and saw Thurpa standing, blank-eyed, perfectly still and off to one side. No, not perfectly still. He was trembling but not from fear. His back was straight, his legs straight, as well, hands down at his sides. Something held him still, binding him.

"I've been burned once by his kind's spittle," Neekra snarled, rising from the ground. The tiny stalk grew thicker, becoming a branch, complete with twigs generating fingers, muscle and skin flowing down the limb. "You think I'd let you—"

"She's distracted, split in concentration between holding down Thurpa, and maybe Durga, and battling us," Brigid whispered quickly to Kane over her Commtact. "That's why she hasn't simply obliterated us."

Nathan blazed away with his pistol at Neekra, drawing Kane's attention back toward the goddess. He could see the ebony staff lying on the ground, and he rushed at it and scooped it up.

Neekra whirled and lashed out to strike Kane, but he brought up Nehushtan. It was her uninjured fist, and it landed like a falling tree, but strength flowed from the ancient object and into Kane's own arms. He held, blocking her attack.

"This is the weapon of demon slayers," Kane spat. "And apparently, their souls live on in me."

With a mighty surge, he pushed her back. Her newly grown hand wrapped around the staff in an effort to wrest it from him, but Nehushtan kept pumping might into Kane. Even with that strength, he gritted his teeth and sweat trickled down his naked arms, though the environmental effects of his shadow suit hood whisked the sweat from his eyes.

Neekra's lips curled back from her teeth, curved canines that grew even as she strained against him. Her pupils were vertical slits, catlike or reptilian, their red glow capturing his attention. Her thoughts were creeping into his mind, but he held his ground. He focused his thoughts, putting up a barrier against her intrusion. He opened the gates of his lowest emotions, letting hatred flush through his brain and lash against her. Tingles ran along his cheeks, like ants crawling all the way into his ears. She wasn't going to give up, and with each moment, she drew on more psychic energy, increasing the pressure to penetrate Kane's thoughts.

You're not learning shit from me, became the taunt that he spray-painted on the wall he put up in the goddess's path, drawn in ten-foot-high yellow letters.

Thurpa suddenly appeared over her shoulder, and Kane realized that moments had disappeared as he was focused on battling her. His fangs swiveled into place, and he bit down on her neck. Neekra was wracked with spasms as the venom plunged into her system, and her eyes and skin turned from crimson to dull gray.

That didn't do anything to her strength. She shrugged, and Thurpa grunted, one tooth snapping off in her neck. Blood poured from his mouth as he fell.

"You—you can't…" she sputtered. Tar-like froth bubbled over her pallid lips.

She pushed against Kane again, and he backed up. Obviously the power in both of them had died down dramatically, drained by their battle and Neekra's sudden affliction from Thurpa's Nagah venom.

Kane regathered himself and charged forward, point straight out.

Give me one more boost, he prayed, hoping the staff could still acknowledge him.

Her torso shell cracked, and the blunt point crashed through her armor and plunged deep through her torso.

Nehushtan grew hot in his grasp, and Kane let go, his palms seared by the sudden flare of energy. Neekra threw back her head and howled, a blast that reverberated through the underground city, forcing Kane to his knees from the trauma.

Things went black for a moment. At least it felt like a moment.

And then he was aboveground, in the sun. It was midday from the position it hung in the sky, and Lyta and Nathan were attending to him, Grant, Brigid and Thurpa.

"You took a beating," Lyta told him. "We were all knocked out."

Nathan stood, leaning on the artifact. It was back in its original form, a cross with twin serpents wound about it. The healing light.

"Nehushtan helped my eardrums, woke me up. We've been restoring everyone's health all morning," Nathan admitted.

"We were that bad?" Kane asked.

"Your eardrums were ruptured, not to mention all manner of stress fractures up and down your arms," Lyta said.

Kane looked at his arms, taking a deep breath. "The staff told you?"

"It gave us a triage," Nathan answered.

"And Neekra?" Kane inquired.

"She's a greasy smear on the floor of that underground cavern," Grant said. He sat on a blanket, sipping water. Kane could tell that they'd all been through the wringer. And rather than all of them being hospitalized, or permanently deafened, thanks to Nathan's crazy ancient stick, they all felt more like they'd gone a week without sleep.

Kane lay back on his own blanket. The sun felt good on his skin, and he closed his eyes.

"You say that she's a greasy smear," Kane spoke up. "But that was Gamal's body she used. He's finally dead."

"Her avatar is defeated," Brigid said. "But she herself is somewhere. Out there."

Thurpa's voice rose from a trembling whisper. "Durga's looking for her. Still looking for her."

Kane lifted his head and looked toward the young Nagah.

"At first I thought that maybe I was brainwashed, hypnotized," Thurpa continued. "But things haven't been adding up."

"Like why Durga brought only one Nagah with him to Africa?" Brigid asked. "A young, inexperienced but still trained warrior?"

Thurpa nodded.

"And then when Durga tried to stop Neekra...I felt him. I felt the injuries he suffered," the young man continued. "When the staff healed me, I became a transmitter. I helped him recover."

"I knew he was missing," Kane mentioned, sitting up and turning to his Nagah companion.

Brigid nodded, her emerald eyes alight with this new information. "He made a brute squad full of half-Nephilim, half-Nagah warriors, but he wanted something else. He wanted a son...."

Thurpa's eyes were glistening with tears.

"Despite whatever nurture and genetics he put into you, you still fought for us. You still fought to protect us," Kane added. He reached out.

Thurpa took Kane's hand.

"We won't let your father ruin whatever life you choose to make," Kane told him.

Thurpa managed a smile.

Kane lay back again. "Once we rest up a little more, we'll take the rest of the militia's explosives and blow up that cavern."

"Not going to save any for Durga and the real Neekra?" Grant asked.

Kane took a deep breath and closed his eyes. "We'll cross that bridge when we come to it."

TO BE CONCLUDED...

* * * * *

JAMES AXLER

DEATH LANDS®

Desolation Angels

Bad to the bone...

Violent gangs, a corrupt mayor and a heavily armed police force are hallmarks of the former Detroit. When Ryan and his companions show up, the Desolation Angels are waging a war to rule the streets. After saving the companions from being chilled by gangsters, the mayor hires Ryan and his friends to stop the Angels cold. But each hard blow toward victory proves there's no good side to be fighting for. As Motor City erupts into bloody conflagration, the companions are caught in the cross fire. In the Deathlands, hell is called home.

Available July wherever books and ebooks are sold.

ROGUE ANGEL ™

AleX Archer
THE DEVIL'S CHORD

**The canals of Venice hide a centuries-old secret
some would kill to salvage...**

In the midst of a quarrel on a Venetian bridge, the
Cross of Lorraine is lost to the canal's waters. Suspecting a
connection between the cross, Joan of Arc and Da Vinci,
Annja Creed's former mentor,
Roux, sends the archaeologist
to search for the
missing artifact.

After facing many difficult
situations when retrieving the
cross, Annja discovers that
the artifact is fundamental to
unlocking one of Da Vinci's
most fantastical inventions. But
the price Annja must pay to
stop this key from falling into
the wrong hands may be her life.

*Available July wherever
books and ebooks are sold.*

GOLD
EAGLE ®

GRA49

The Don Pendleton's
Executioner®
PACIFIC CREED

A terror campaign leaves a trail of bodies in Hawaii

When female tourists are kidnapped in Hawaii, Mack Bolan is sent in to investigate. While all clues suggest a white slavery ring, he learns there is more going on than simply girls being sold for guns.

With his cover thin and his disguise temporary, Bolan knows the only way to find the Samoan leader behind the terror campaign is to prove his worth to the tribe. The Executioner has only one chance to convince the Samoans of his loyalty— and to stop their deadly plan before they destroy Hawaii.

Available June wherever books and ebooks are sold.

GOLD EAGLE ®

GEX427